David,

It was great meeting you at GenreCon 2014! I hope you enjoy the book!

A Noble's Quest

Published by Ryan Toxopeus at CreateSpace
Cover art and map art by Harvey Bunda

Copyright 2014 Ryan Toxopeus

Dedication

To my friends Anthony, Ian, Stu and Nikki who helped me to flesh out the world of Illuma.

To my wife for stalwartly facing many lonely nights and for her invaluable support while I wrote.

To my editor, Jen Hiuser, without whom this book would have never reached its readers, and my Aunt Mary who went through the story again with a fine-tooth comb.

Map of Tamorran Empire and Surrounding Regions

(Full sized map available at: http://goo.gl/gNDX3i)

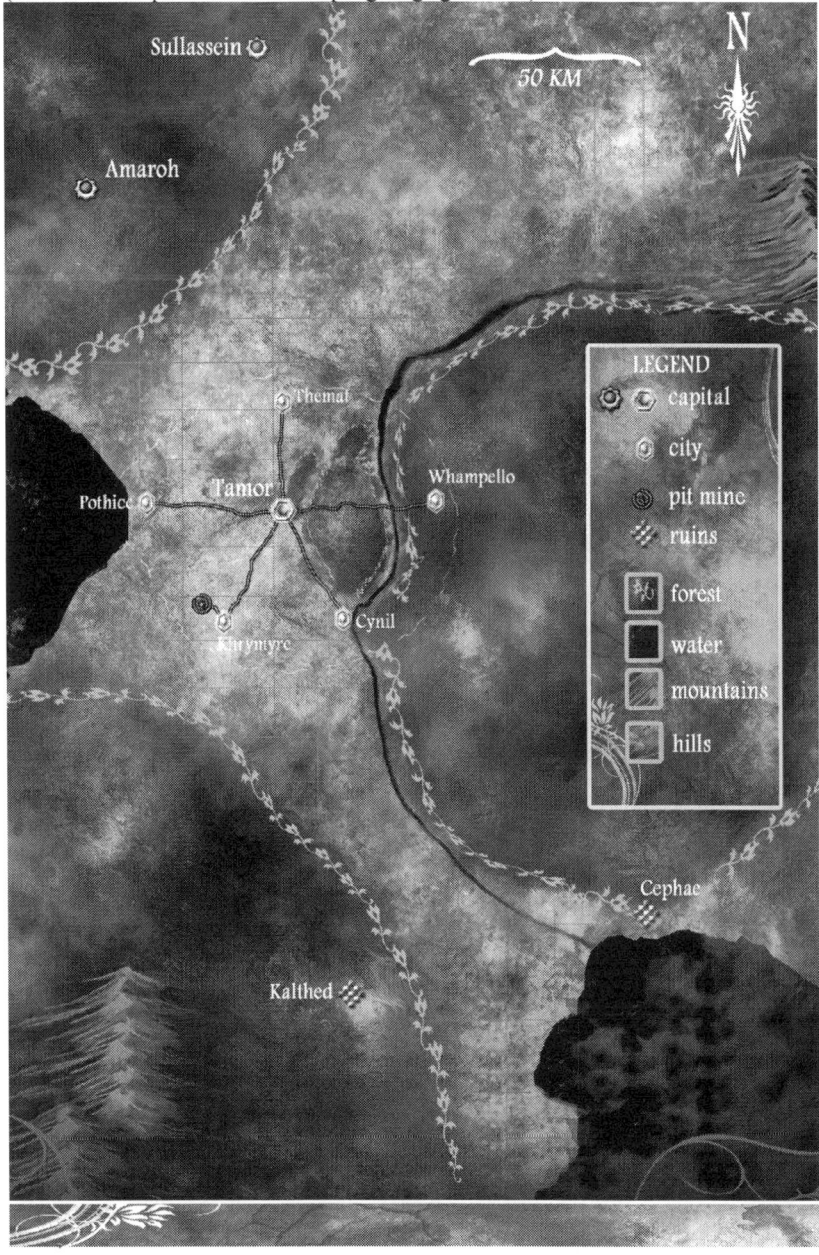

Prologue: 450 years After Gods' War (AGW)

Matthew ran blindly at top speed. The heat of an inferno licked at his back, while smoke stung his eyes. He knew he was reaching the outer edge of the smoky cloud as he saw the faint glow of his sword through his tears.

Unable to hold his breath any longer at a full run, he was forced to inhale and draw the acrid smoke into his lungs. He coughed violently but kept running. His only thought was of escape. He needed to stay alive long enough to warn his allies.

For eight hours, Matthew Strongblade, humanity's greatest champion and hero, had battled in the Two-Towns mountain pass against the invading armies. His troops were dead, including one of his descendants, Vincent Strongblade, who had fought valiantly until the end. Had the past two hundred years of Matthew's life not been magically extended, he would have fallen with them. But he had studied warfare since his youth, when he had been forced to take up his trusty blade against heartless slavers.

Now a new enemy sought to overthrow humanity once more, and Matthew feared he had not the strength left to stop them. He only hoped that his powerful allied wizards, who were at least as old as he was, were faring better. With a combined eight hundred years of magical learning among the four wizened old sages, Matthew had to believe they could withstand the main assault force.

Neither could he discount the aid of elves. In their time of greatest need, their allies from the northwest had come to fight alongside them. Matthew had also anticipated the coming of dwarves, but when he had rushed to defend the pass he was now fleeing, there had been no word.

Brilliant daylight burned his eyes, and when he exploded from the rolling grey wall he gulped in cleaner air. He fell to his knees and looked upon the relieved face of his closest friend. "Hendricus," he gasped. He drew in several more hacking breaths before he could continue. "The pass is lost."

"I thought you were dead," Hendricus Wyrmstriker said, kneeling down and holding Matthew close. "I was riding hard to meet you when I saw the mountain erupt. The others?"

"Dead, long before the fires," Matthew solemnly stated. He turned to watch the smoke slowly dissipate. "I fought alone for what seemed ages. I heard the fire coming, and I ran as fast as I could. Tell me there is better news elsewhere."

Hendricus frowned and shook his head. "The artefact was destroyed before it could be brought to the front lines. The enemy was aware of our game changer, and neutralized it."

Matthew sank to the ground, pounding his fist in the dirt. They had worked tirelessly to craft the artefact in order to wipe out their enemies by the hundreds. Now their losses would be staggering, if they could manage to fend off total destruction. He looked up at Hendricus. "Can the wizards hold them off without it?"

"No," Hendricus said. His voice caught in his throat, and he looked away from Matthew's searching gaze. "That's why I rode here. I must tell you that there is no hope. Sylvain used her magical sight to gaze across the lands. Far to the west, the dwarven town of Kalthed has fallen, and our allies have retreated into their mountain homes. Wizard Borneam fell in the surprise assault on Cephae. Survivors are being ushered further to the west to an area her visions cannot penetrate. We cannot know what doom they face."

"The elves?"

"Lorrie'nar led a defensive force back to secure their forest. Sylvain has been in magical communication with them ever since they were sealed in the forest. Apparently Jordak summoned some mighty powerful creatures to fend off the invaders, and gave his own life in a sacrificial ritual to shield their woodland home. However, that shield works both ways, and Lorrie'nar is unable to return. A few hundred elves remain with us, but they are hard pressed. They may have centuries of experience, but they are few in number."

"Whereas our enemies appear to be limitless," Matthew finished. He knew his friend's mind. One could not share two centuries without being able to finish the other's thoughts.

"Take my sword," Matthew said. He unbuckled the ornate leather sheath decorated with mithril filigree, and slid his glowing blade inside. "It must be preserved."

"Madness," breathed Hendricus. "You'll need it again before the hour has passed! Once those fires burn out, they will come."

"If they wait that long."

Matthew and Hendricus shared a long look before Hendricus unsheathed the Strongblade. The adamantium weapon had been created across the sea by a dozen of the finest dwarven craftsman. Ten wizards had worked for days to imbue the blade with its incredible power. The sword was a legend among humanity, for with it Matthew had freed their race. For two hundred years it had carved a bloody swath through enemy lines. Initially it allowed them to steal a fleet to sail to a new continent, but it had been well used in the coming centuries as they built their country from nothing. Matthew had battled ferocious orcs, fierce giants, fiendish gnomes, and feral halflings to secure their place in these lands. Generations of humans had revered him as a godlike figure, and the unique enchanted blade filled many mythical tales.

But the blade did not glow in Hendricus' hands. He had stood by Matthew's side through many of his exploits, using his own hidden serrated daggers to support Matthew's typical headlong rush into danger. He slid the sword home and looked up at Matthew with misted eyes.

Matthew decided. "Please. I beg you. I can fight with any blade. But when I die this day, I cannot allow my sword to fall into their grasp. It must be preserved. Once, it enabled escape for our people. If this enemy does not kill us all, but takes survivors to the west, perhaps my sword will find its way into worthy hands once more, and help to turn the tide against this new foe."

"You mean for me to take it to the elves, then?"

Matthew nodded. The elves were the only race with lifespans long enough to hold onto his memory, if his country fell. Elves would be ideal keepers of the sword.

He looked around the base of the pass, and noted the enemy and friendly bodies littering the area. This is where their fight had begun, hours ago. They had pushed their adversaries back, and held the pass, and now it appeared the fight would end where it had started. Matthew picked up the steel blade of one of his fallen men.

"I should be fighting beside you. This feels wrong," Hendricus said.

"It's all wrong, Hendricus. We worked for two hundred years to secure our new country, and now it is on the brink of collapse!

No, this is not how it should end, but perhaps this end is but a new beginning. It may take generations before our people sing songs of freedom, but this time will come. The human spirit is too powerful to be crushed forever. But in this moment, when darkness threatens to snuff us out, I need you to keep the Strongblade safe. Take it to the elves, my friend. I am certain your part in this fight is not yet over, and you will avenge me. But I must hold them here as long as possible so the others can regroup, if they are to have any chance to turn the tide of this war."

"Always you think of others before yourself," Hendricus said. He hung his head, his hands slowly closing around Matthew's scabbard. "If I were in your place–"

"Do not think about it," Matthew interrupted. "Go. The searing flames have spent their fuel. They will be marching here soon."

"Be safe," Hendricus offered, as he had hundreds of times before. But Matthew knew this was their final farewell.

"Thank you," he uttered softly, before turning back to the pass, sword in hand. Hendricus remained unmoving for a moment, and Matthew knew his friend was still trying to think of a way to change his mind. But in the end, Hendricus' footsteps moved quickly and quietly off to the east, back in the direction of their people.

Matthew did not have to wait long. The figure of a lone woman soon emerged from the wispy smoke up the pass. She strode forward dressed in gleaming, golden, scale armour. A claymore rested easily on her shoulder. Her brilliant green eyes locked on Matthew and did not waver. Matthew sensed that she was more than she appeared. Having lived as long as he had, he was intuitively aware of the agelessness of others who counted time in centuries, instead of years.

"You lived." Her melodic voice betrayed neither surprise, nor fear.

Matthew adopted a forward facing stance, holding his deceased soldier's long sword in both hands. He marked her smooth gait. Her lithe form held more power than seemed possible, swinging her large sword back and forth before her. He thought of his own sword and how over time it had become a part of him.

"I will give you a warrior's death," she said, coming to a stop several paces away. Her eyes, like his, were cold and calculating. The difference was that he was looking for weakness, and he got the impression she was eyeing up a meal.

In her eyes, victory was assured.

"I am Hallo'mien," she said. "You have killed many of my finest warriors. I had not intended to fight here this day, but you have forced my hand. Many of my kin are impressed and feel you should be spared, but you do not strike me as the type who will come along peaceably."

"I am Matthew Strongblade." He waited a moment to see if she showed any recognition, but her gaze was impassive. Had he said the same among his own people, they would understand that he never backed down in the face of adversity.

"I shall endeavour to remember your name," Hallo'mien said. "Your sons shall die, of course. I pride myself on extinguishing all heroic lineages, in order to reduce future complications."

"I'm sorry to disappoint you, but my sons are already long dead," Matthew said. He saw no point in further banter. Hallo'mien's stance was flawless, and her grace was obvious. The best he could hope for was a battle worthy of stories and song.

He approached with even strides, as did Hallo'mien. Despite her far larger sword, she did not fly into battle in a rage, like so many other warriors who chose a purely offensive weapon. Matthew took the first swing, aiming for her neck, but Hallo'mien's sword easily intercepted his. She smoothly moved aside, angling her blade and swiping diagonally.

Matthew jumped back, narrowly avoiding the weapon, but maintaining his footing. Balance, as any warrior knows, is the single most important element in a fight. Lose it, and you're not likely to be the victor. But whereas he merely managed to keep steady, Hallo'mien danced across the battle field. His thrusts were always expertly parried, leaving her in a strong position to strike back.

The two danced, weapons clashing again and again. Matthew found a rhythm in the whirl of bodies and blades, gaining confidence. Adrenaline replaced weariness, and his swings came harder and faster, forcing Hallo'mien back.

An opening appeared, and his blade stabbed low at her stomach. With inhuman speed, her claymore swept his blade aside, and effortlessly plunged through his solid steel breastplate. He looked down as she slid her blade out of him, and collapsed on the ground.

All around, Hallo'mien's forces appeared, moving forward to congratulate her for besting the human who had kept them at bay. Without her, Matthew would have kept them bottled up indefinitely before succumbing to fatigue.

He fell to the ground. Matthew could not feel his legs. He did not comprehend that his spine had been severed, leaving him paralyzed. It hardly mattered anyway. There was no aid. He would slowly bleed to death in the dirt.

His mind grew foggy. Looking up to the sky, his last thoughts were for his friends, family, and his legacy. He wished Hendricus safe passage as he spirited the Strongblade to the elves. In their care, one day his sword would avenge him, and bring his people the freedom they deserved.

Chapter 1: 980 AGW

Sarentha dropped a copper penny down the town's well. "I wish I had more money."

The wide streets of Whampello's run-down market were teeming with dozens of people enjoying the warm noonday sun. The broad leafy trees surrounding the town cut down the wind, making the early summer day warmer than elsewhere in the Tamorran Empire. Sarentha's linen clothing was the worse for wear, dirty perhaps from days of working out in the surrounding woods chopping down trees, or more likely from hours of avoiding work and napping in a shaded, dirty hole. His dark brown eyes darted around quickly and his fingers raked through greasy black hair; he looked back into the eyes of his lifelong friend.

Thomas frowned and looked down the well, where the penny had disappeared. "I wish we had that coin back. I could use a loaf of stale bread and a mug of ale from the inn more than I could use your silly wish. You know the penny's probably just going to get hauled up in the next bucket anyway, and someone else will wander off with your wish."

Thomas was good looking, as men from the small town of Whampello went. He was just shy of six feet tall, making him a likely candidate for tallest person in town. His body was thick, with well-developed muscles apparent even under his loose-fitting tunic and pants.

Although they had both grown up in Whampello's orphanage,

the two had drawn from this experience very differently. Thomas had enjoyed growing up with so many other children to play games with, while Sarentha had thrived taking lessons from the priests. Books were a rarity in Whampello, and Sarentha had greedily soaked up all the knowledge he could. Children's stories of brave adventurers and cunning rogues had filled his dreams. He often imagined stumbling upon a treasure chest filled with gold and jewels and retiring in a noble's manor.

Sarentha shrugged and slapped Thomas' wide shoulders. "I'm wishing for more than stale bread to fill our stomachs! I'm talking about the riches of kings!"

Thomas' frown deepened. Sarentha had talked about striking it rich as long as they had known each other. He always failed to come to grips with the reality that they were simple working peasants. Those few copper pennies they earned were needed to pay the rent for their one-room apartment, and buy what food and drink they could afford. In Thomas' eyes, tossing hard-earned money down a well on a whim was unwise.

"Gods forgive him for his foolishness," Thomas muttered, pulling his friend away from the well to allow a matronly woman her turn at the water. "Don't worry, I'll buy dinner."

"I knew I could count on you, Thomas," Sarentha said, a mischievous grin on his grubby face. "So, where are we off to tonight?"

Thomas said, "It's noon, Sarentha. We have to get back to work."

The smaller of the two men shrugged. "I mean after, of course. I can't think about work. It's bad for my ... heart."

Thomas grunted what may have been a laugh, or disdain, it was difficult to tell sometimes. "Cutting down trees isn't my idea of a fun time either, friend, but it pays the bills."

Sarentha was about to say something about wanting more money than was needed to pay said bills, but fell silent when he saw *the look* from Thomas. The two walked out of the market and headed back to the worksite. Down a shaded road, covered by an overhead canopy of broad leaves, they entered a wide-open area in the forest with trees in various states of disrepair. Off in the distance another mighty tree fell to the chorus of "Timm-berrr!"

Sarentha pulled an old set of hole-filled work gloves over his hands, sighing as he picked up a small, well-used hand axe. Thomas easily pulled a much larger axe free from the earth, and they headed into the work site. They had not made it more than ten paces before an angry voice called out, giving them pause.

The foreman of the group, Frank Grimbling, pointed to the sun, his face as red as a tomato, cursing their existence in languages Thomas could not understand. Although Thomas was taller than Frank, he still found his boss intimidating, knowing that his pay was directly linked to whether or not the man felt they were worth keeping around. The brawny fellow stood before them and scolded, "You two are lucky I don't wring your useless necks right here! You're late! We've got trees in the east quadrant that need to go down straight away! Where were you two? Never mind! I can guess, you worthless rats! Get back to work, lest I use an axe on something other than a tree!"

Sarentha kept walking, not giving the man a second glance, while Thomas apologized for them both, swearing it would not happen again, just like he did every other day. Trotting up to his friend, heading east, Thomas looked up at the sky, noting the position of the sun. "How can he tell time by that, anyway? I've never understood it. Did we really take too long for lunch?"

"Of course we didn't," Sarentha assured. "Trust me, we're never actually late. He just likes to shout and kick up a fuss. Some people are only happy when they're yelling. I'd explain how to tell time from the position of the sun to you again, but I know you'd just forget anyway. Ugh! Look at this! All the trees to the east are huge!"

"Well, don't strain yourself," Thomas said sarcastically. "I know, I know, your delicate hands get blistered. Think about it; if you didn't toss a copper down the well every week, you could have bought a new set of work gloves ages ago."

"These ones suit me just fine."

"Because they get you out of work," Thomas stated flatly, waving in greeting to some workmates who were lugging a mighty oak away.

"It's not that I dislike work," Sarentha said. "I just dislike *this* work."

"Well, if you can find a better job, take it," Thomas answered. They closed in on a tree, Thomas hefted his axe and tossed it impressively end over end. The heavy axe bit deeply into the trunk, marking it as theirs for the hewing.

"I hear there's lots of opportunity in Tamor," Sarentha said, cautiously watching his friend's face for signs of trouble. He had broached this topic before, and it had not ended well.

Sarentha had told Thomas all about all the other cities in the Tamorran Empire. Sarentha had read about all of them, and chatted with travelling merchants in the marketplace every chance he got. The capital, Tamor, was centrally located in the midst of the other five. Tamor was supposed to be a beacon of prosperity, in which all five races of the Empire worked together in harmony. To the north, Themat was an extremely wealthy city populated mostly by halflings. The halflings may have looked small and endearing, but they had used their innocent appearance to become expert traders who regularly brought in outstanding profits. To the west was the port city of Pothice, the Empire's only city with access to the sea. The elves of Pothice were a proud sea-faring folk, although a plague of dementia had crippled many of the older citizens, leaving a heavy burden for the youth. In the southwest was Khrymyre, a city of stout stone buildings which burrowed down below the earth, instead of above. Khrymyre's dwarves were expert crafters whose fires burned unceasingly in order to produce tools, weapons and armour for the rest of the Empire. Cynil, to the southeast, was a strange place of gnomes and their fantastic wonders, blending ingenuity and machines with magic. Because the results were sometimes catastrophic, gnomish technology was never allowed into the hands of outsiders. The gnomes wished to avoid any lawsuits greedy halflings might bring against them.

Whampello, a small town nestled in the woods on the eastern part of the Tamorran Empire, was different. Largely forgotten by most of the Empire's residents, the halfling traders liked to say, "Nothing good ever comes out of Whampello." The population was entirely made up of humans. The populace was aware that other races existed within the Empire, but except for the few noble land-owning families on Whampello's west, most had not seen them personally. The small open-air markets were located centrally, and sold goods purchased from the halflings at exorbitant prices. The people not fortunate enough to live in a noble's manor or amongst the merchants lived to the east. Other than the handful of nobles, the people of Whampello were poor. Lumber, the town's only export, was still generally undervalued by halfling traders as most of the Empire preferred stone for their homes and buildings. Elven ships were so well-constructed and long-lasting that there was little need for more wood. Some wood was used to keep fires going, but dwarves generally relied on other mysterious fuel sources, unknown to outside races. And gnomes found wood to be simply too flammable for reliable use.

Life was not easy for the peasants of Whampello, living off a few copper pennies a day. Most lived in run-down communal apartment buildings and had little in the way of food to eat. Hungry and destitute, the peasants had little to look forward to. What little extra money they did make was generally spent on alcohol to help them forget their woes for a short time. Most accepted their lot in life, for they had never known anything different. With little money and a constant need to work, there was no time to travel, even for just one single day.

The combination of these factors meant that no one much bothered with the town of Whampello, and the people of Whampello did not bother with the rest of the Empire. No one expected trouble from such a quiet, innocuous place. Perhaps someone should have paid more attention...

Thomas withdrew his axe from the tree, and in one graceful motion swung about and slammed it back into the bark, left to right, chips of bark littering the forest floor. "No."

Sarentha planted the end of his smaller axe into the ground, and leaned on it, looking imploringly at his long-time friend. "Why not? The capital is huge! There's actual variety there! I mean, I hear you can even see elves and dwarves and–"

"No," Thomas reiterated, driving this single word home with another sharp strike of his axe.

"Okay, so you're not interested in the different races,"

Sarentha conceded, "or the busy lifestyle of the people there, or different food and drink. Nor the sites to see, like the wizard's tower. The castle as big as a mountain probably doesn't interest you either. And the *huge variety of not mind-numbingly horrible work* would be pretty dull for you, too."

Thomas frowned, tirelessly slamming the axe in again and again, listening to his friend list off the great things about Tamor. "I have everything I need here," Thomas answered. "My job keeps me fit, it pays the bills."

"*I want more than just paying the bills!*" Sarentha said in an exasperated voice. "This isn't living! It's existing! When was the last time we went out and had *fun*?"

Thomas chipped off a large chunk of wood, leaving his axe there for a moment as he turned to Sarentha. "Playing cards at night isn't fun? Going to the Dented Stein for a few drinks and songs isn't fun? How about those ladies you eye up at the Grizzled Bard? You can't tell me you haven't had fun with them!"

Sarentha grinned a little, "Aye, but I think maybe that's the reason *you* don't want to leave. You can't tell me you don't fancy Jessie, or Belle, or Harriett"

"Enough," Thomas said, his cheeks colouring.

"Well, they fancy you, too, you know! I heard them talking about you when you came in the other night. Big strapping young man with–"

"*Enough.*"

"Fine, fine," Sarentha said, wiping the grin off his face and the dirt from his blade. "You know, you might even get one of them to stay for longer than one night if you had a decent job."

"And didn't live with my best friend in a one-room apartment," Thomas added, taking to the tree again with a steady rhythm.

Sarentha pounced on the idea, "Exactly! Exactly! You see, we're in agreement! If you and I did something more worthwhile than–"

"Standing around doing nothing?"

Sarentha spun around quickly, noting the three broad-shouldered, no-necked thugs approaching. The Grimbling brothers were notorious bullies, who loved picking on Sarentha or anyone small around the camp. Despite the three-to-one odds, they knew better than to pick a fight with Sarentha right now. Thomas made them at least slightly nervous.

"I'm not doing nothing," Sarentha sputtered indignantly, holding himself up straight. "I'm ... supervising. Excellent work, Thomas!"

Hank, the oldest brother, laughed dully. "Huh. Stupidvising is more like it!"

Buck hit Hank in the head, and said, "That ain't a word, dummy!"

Adam hit Buck in return, and said, "Don't hit me bruther!"

The three broke into a tumbling ball of fists and feet, until Hank came out on top, like always. "I was being funny! Anyway, get to work, shrimp! If I don't see you swingin' that axe, I'm tellin' Pa on you!"

Having already had a run-in with their father, the foreman, Sarentha was not keen to have the angry man breathing down his neck again. Hefting the small axe, he began working away on the opposite side of the tree from Thomas.

The brothers wandered off to bother someone else, and Sarentha paused a moment to wipe sweat from his brow and nurse a sore spot on his hand. "I suppose I'd be an angry jerk too if those were my sons," Sarentha murmured, walking around the great girth of the tree to stand on the opposite side, out of sight. "I swear this pain is never going to heal," he said, squeezing his palm, and examining it closely for some unseen injury.

"You could always visit the on-site healer," Thomas said with laughter in his voice, continuing to work methodically, his shirt showing signs of sweat from the steady swinging of the big axe.

Sarentha frowned, "You know she hates me. She'd just lie and say I'm making things up again; she would say the pain is all in my head. I tell you, that tree *did* fall on my hand!"

"I know, I saw it," Thomas said. "Maybe if you had complained less before that incident, she'd believe you now when you're actually hurt." Sarentha had a pained look on his face, but Thomas continued before he could argue. "Let's see, there was a snake bite, very bad burns from a fire, your eyes felt like they were going to explode, you sprained your ankle when you ran from a wolf you thought you saw, and you hit yourself in the back with the flat of your axe blade."

"That one actually happened," Sarentha stated firmly. "Never mind that it was because Hank told me there was a big spider on my back."

"I could've told you it wasn't there," Thomas answered, pulling his axe free of the tree, and circling around it to inspect his work. "You want to tell the rope crew to come over? This one's about ready to come down with a few more swings."

"Your skills amaze me," Sarentha said, looking at the quick work Thomas had made of cutting the tree nearly in half.

Only too happy not to have to swing an axe, Sarentha left to find the crew who would help guide the tree down.

Minutes passed while Thomas rested against the tree,

enjoying a drink of water, when he heard a commotion nearby. Looking up, he noticed the rope crew coming towards him, along with another group led by the three Grimbling brothers. The Grimblings were waving their arms angrily. Thomas spotted Sarentha slinking back slowly, defensively.

One of the brothers threw a heavy clay mug at Sarentha. Thomas' imagination instantly foresaw the fight escalating: with Sarentha too small to defend himself, the three brothers would hurt him badly and leave him flat in bed for a week, or worse. Their income reduced by half, the two friends would have to sacrifice food or shelter. Thomas pictured them homeless, Sarentha lying motionless in the gutter while he struggled to shelter his friend from the elements. He gritted his teeth, a violent rage flaring inside his chest.

The next few moments were a hazy blur to Thomas, but Sarentha was all too happy to retell the story afterwards, over and over again.

Sarentha had been holding his head, writhing in pain on the ground, and the brothers laughed mockingly. Thomas, like a thing possessed, came charging in full fury with his large axe in one hand, howling at the men. They turned, stunned into silence as the axe spun end over end, the way Thomas had manoeuvred it a hundred times before to hit a tree at a distance. This time the axe clove Hank's head easily in two. Buck and Adam looked to each other, looked down at Hank's lifeless body on the ground between them, looked up at Thomas, and howled back, rushing at the larger man. The collision of flesh and bone was the worst Sarentha had ever laid eyes on. Thomas shifted his weight, giving his blows full force against the pair of surviving brothers. Adam and Buck instinctively shied away from the flurry of fists, attempting to defend themselves. Despite witnessing many bar fights, Sarentha had never beheld such a crushing, brutal brawl. Screams of pain and anger filled the air. In the end both of the surviving Grimbling brothers lay beaten and unconscious on the ground. Thomas towered over them, his chest heaving with each deep breath. Buck had a bone protruding painfully from his forearm, and Adam's legs dangled awkwardly.

With the immediate threat dealt with, Thomas kneeled down beside Sarentha and peered at his head. There was definitely a goose-egg forming, but Sarentha's quickness had saved him any real harm from the thrown clay mug.

"You killed Hank," Sarentha whispered, although the truth of the statement was glaringly obvious. After the relief of seeing that Sarentha was not too badly injured, Thomas looked back at the three men lying on the ground. He immediately knew he had overreacted, and that real trouble was sure to follow. Whatever form of harsh justice was to come, he felt that he deserved it.

Sarentha stared in shock, unable to take his eyes off the grisly scene. The trauma to Hank's skull reminded him too clearly of the noble he saw being beheaded when he was a boy. He had expected Thomas to come to his rescue when the mug was thrown his way, but he never could have imagined the deadly force Thomas would retaliate with.

The other men all stood in a half circle, looking down at the carnage with wonder and disgust. It was not long before many stomping footfalls approached. Somehow word had reached the rest of the camp, and the place was in a frenzy.

"My boys!" the foreman yelled, collapsing over Hank's corpse. "No! No! Who could do such a thing?"

His wild gaze fell upon Thomas and Sarentha, then, kneeling

in the dirt not ten paces away. Tears streamed freely from the foreman's eyes, but he blinked them away, choking out "You!" like a guttural curse.

"It was self-defence," Sarentha said quickly, leaping to his feet. "They attacked me!"

The foreman meant to stand, but four big men held him in place. "Get out of here! And never come back, or I'll break your heads open!" Frank looked down at Hank's split skull again, and sobbed, falling over the body.

Sarentha and Thomas ran, glancing backwards from time to time to be sure the foreman was not following them. A healer had arrived to help set the broken bones, but they knew there was nothing to be done for Hank.

"Thank you," gasped Sarentha, when they left the camp. They stopped running and turned to make sure no one was giving chase. "I don't know what would have happened to me if you hadn't been there."

Thomas looked down at his bloodied hands. His jaw and arms felt aching pain where the brothers had landed solid blows on him. With his adrenaline rush fading, he knew he would soon be hurting even more. Yet it all seemed so distant, as he stared numbly at the blood on his hands. He had never killed a man before. True, the blood was not Hank's, having killed him from afar, but the symbolism was what shook him.

"Thomas?"

But if Thomas heard his friend, he did not answer. His feet plodded ahead mechanically and Sarentha guided him back home, waving away any onlookers.

Chapter 2: E.W.

"Hearing horrible news always reminds me that I live in the most pathetic part of the Empire. It ruins my appetite," the Duke of Whampello, Lord Calarin stated. He cut into a rare steak, popping the bloody piece of meat into his delicately shaped mouth, and quickly brought a serviette up to dab at his lips. "My compliments to your chef. My own has difficulty preparing meat the way I prefer it. Honestly, I hate Whampello. Between the abundance of brutes and lack of decent help, it is amazing we manage to survive at all."

The other noble looked across at the Duke, whose hardened, tanned, pointed features made him look like a snake devouring a rodent. His fine silvery coloured clothing hanging lightly on his muscular frame softened this impression, even if his attitude did not.

"And what horrible news did you hear today, Your Grace?" The noble's use of the formal title was both appreciated and unusual, for most people in the backwater town simply referred to him as Duke Calarin.

The Duke spooned some herbed potatoes into his mouth and ingested them before responding. "There was a killing out at one of the logging camps today involving the Grimbling boys – you might remember them; I sold their father the lumber yard just before the demand for wood fell. The brothers picked a fight with another worker named Sarentha. The peasants in this town brawl so regularly you would think they were savage animals, but today was different. One of my healers was present, and later described the scene in far too much detail. Apparently a burly beast of a man named Thomas took it upon himself to protect Sarentha. He killed one of the Grimblings and severely injured the other two." The Duke shuddered visibly, agitating his long copper hair.

The other noble chewed a warm slice of bread thoughtfully. "Really? I have not heard of a murder in Whampello in years."

"Bah," the Duke choked on another piece of juicy steak. "I did not say murder, did I? It was apparently an act of self-defence. If the Empire bothered to station any soldiers around here, there would be an investigation and we would know for certain. As it is, the two men fled the scene." The Duke looked up to see his host abruptly rising from the table. "And where are you going? Certainly you do not mean to leave me dining alone in your home."

"You must excuse me, Your Grace. I must go. I have just remembered that my niece requested my presence today to witness her new-found love of archery," the noble explained quickly as he neared the dining room's large oak double doors.

Too quickly, he feared. But the Duke waved his dinner companion away with a flourish. "Send my affections to her, would you? We will meet tomorrow to further discuss our plans."

"Of course, Your Grace," the noble said, bowing low before he left. With the door closing behind him, he sprinted up to his chamber. An act of self-defence leading to murder was indeed noteworthy. Since the execution of his father, the noble had spent ten years planning against those who had been responsible. He would never be able to scour the image of his father's beheading from his mind, yet in that final moment he had learned a lesson. The late Samuel Winston had acted too brashly. He had not hidden his tracks, and had not made certain his alliances were sound. But Winston's son had learned well, and bided his time. The wheels were finally in motion to get justice for his father's murder. He had spent years cultivating close personal relationships with those in vital positions throughout the Empire. He had surrounded himself with only those he could trust absolutely.

There were, however, a few key steps remaining before justice could be served, and the truth finally revealed. Subtlety and anonymity were required. A doorway of opportunity had just now been opened, and he would not miss this chance.

* * * * *

Not far away, east of the manors, Thomas and Sarentha were locked in their apartment. Thomas could not seem to get clean enough. He stood over the basin of dirty water in their room, scrubbing at his large hands. He had taken a life. It was only Hank, Sarentha had assured him, as though that made it all right. Ridding the world of a Grimbling certainly could not be that bad, his friend had said. They had heard excited voices from down in the streets reporting that the other two brothers had been more or less successfully attended to by the healer. Adam would be lucky to walk again, and Buck might have to learn to work with his left hand instead of his right. Thomas had defeated them, utterly.

As he stared at his hands, a plate was placed in them, with a potato and half a roast duck. He glanced over at Sarentha looking worriedly at him. Sarentha said, "I know we probably can't afford the duck, what with losing our jobs today. I just figured you could use a good meal, by way of a thank you… I owe you. Anyway, I, uh, sort of found some loose change in the brothers' pockets, so I didn't really pay for it."

Thomas nodded grimly, and sat down on the floor. He considered the steaming duck. Half a duck. The image of Hank's cleaved head sprung to mind, and Thomas threw his plate. He stood up and retched in the wash basin.

Sarentha picked up the food from the dirty floor, and set the meal aside for later, when Thomas would regain his appetite. "I was thinking... we could head down to the Grizzled Bard for a drink or two. I think Daphne's working tonight."

Thomas shook his head. He was in no mood for alcohol or women.

"How about a walk?" Sarentha suggested. "We could use some fresh air. Here, I'll dump the basin out, and let the air clear. I'll even take your duck and potatoes with us, in case you get hungry."

Sarentha threw the basin's contents out the window into the street below. He packed a sack of supper. Thomas rose grudgingly to his feet, and moved towards the door. The people they passed in the hallway gave them a wide berth, having already heard of the deadly fight. Whampello was small, and news of death travelled fast. Even the children playing in the fading light of day stopped their games to gawk.

They meandered through the darkening streets while Sarentha prattled on about wealth, women, and anything other than work or Hank. At the city cemetery at the south-western edge of town, Thomas stopped and sat sullenly atop a gravestone. From the north, the temple loomed large above them with its carvings of the various gods Thomas had never bothered to learn much about. Most people in Whampello were atheists or agnostics, despite the clergy's work. In Whampello, where folks struggled just to survive, it was hard to believe in the existence of gods.

Grave markers sat silently in rows. Some had a family name carved into them, but others were simple stones or wooden boards that marked the burial of bodies. A few graves had flowers, but overall the cemetery was a colourless, dark place. It suited Thomas' mood almost perfectly. He looked up at the darkening sky and thought that rain would match his downcast state of mind.

"He'll be buried here, somewhere," Thomas said quietly. "Hank's dead, and he'll be buried in this very cemetery, probably with his grandfather."

Sarentha put an arm around Thomas' wide shoulders and patted his back. "What's done is done. There's no turning back death. Even the nobles' best healers can't perform that miracle."

"I know that," Thomas said. "But it's my fault. I don't know what came over me. I just lost control."

"Well, I would have done the same for you," Sarentha said.

Thomas' brown eyes looked up at him questioningly. Sarentha chuckled softly and said, "Well, okay, maybe not *exactly* the same thing. I mean, for starters you can handle yourself quite well. I might trip someone up if I saw they were going to get the upper hand."

"Right," Thomas said. "But that's still not killing someone."

"Hey, he could fall on my little axe. Take it right in the throat, maybe, yeah? Accidents happen!"

"I don't think others see this as an accident," Thomas replied gloomily. "And neither do I."

"And neither do I," said a soft voice.

Looking up, they saw a cloaked figure standing in the shadow of a large tomb. Startled to find they were not alone, Thomas wondered how the stranger could have heard his words from such a distance.

Thomas asked, "Who are you?"

"You can call me E. W.," the cloaked figure said, and motioned them to come closer. Sarentha started off immediately to meet the newcomer, while Thomas moved more slowly and cautiously. The figure was shorter than he was, but then most people in town were. It was impossible to tell the build, age, or even gender under the heavy cloak, but he knew it was a man from the whispered voice.

As they approached, E. W. moved back, further from the street, and waited. The spot was well-concealed by large mausoleums of Whampello's few rich families. "I heard about your difficulty today, Thomas," the voice said gently, the hood turning from side to side, appearing to watch for any who would intrude on their private conversation. "And I have heard of you also, Sarentha. It is a pity you have lost your jobs."

Thomas hung his head, but Sarentha moved a little closer, trying to glimpse the face within the hood's darkness. "You've heard of me? Have I heard of you?"

"That matters not," the figure replied. "I have a job if you are interested. I require several specific components to help create an item of great importance," he offered cryptically. In the moon's dim light a silver coin's flash enthralled Sarentha. It was the equivalent of a week's work of cutting down trees. He salivated at the thought of the good food and drink they could splurge on with that sort of money.

Thomas looked at the coin more pragmatically. It could stave off hunger long enough to find new jobs.

"There is a mausoleum here, much older than the rest. The royal family it belongs to died out long ago. Find it. The name engraved into the rock will be 'Callipso'. If you desire any small trinkets you see inside, you may take them. No one will likely enter that place again, in any case. There is one object I need. You will see a central stone coffin, with a draconic symbol etched into the lid. Inside is a glowing purple gemstone. At first glance, it may appear to be merely a stone, but this is what I must have." To their surprise, he handed Sarentha the silver coin. "If all goes well, I will employ you further in my quest. You will receive two more coins in exchange for the stone."

Sarentha's head spun around so fast that Thomas wondered how it did not pop right off. In the darkness Sarentha hissed, *"Three pieces of silver!"*

"Why us?" Thomas asked suspiciously of the cloaked figure.

"The circumstances are favourable," E. W. replied smoothly. "You find yourselves out of work. Honestly, half the town likely appreciates what you did out there, and the other half are just afraid to admit it. Nobody needs that type of scum. A good deed such as that deserves a turn in your fortunes. I may have more work for you if you succeed in this simple task."

The hanging promise of such grand money was too much for Sarentha. He blurted out his acceptance before Thomas could even consider the proposal. E. W. nodded his hooded head, and he said, "When you have done as I ask, head to the Grizzled Bard. Order fine elven wine, and tap the silver coin on the counter. We will meet again."

Sarentha silently agreed and pocketed the silver coin, treasuring it. Without another word, the two friends headed into the darker depths of the graveyard.

The Duke of Whampello materialized beside E.W., similarly hooded in the shadows. "Peasants? One of whom is the killer I mentioned over dinner, no less. Why would you enlist the help of lowly simpletons? Too much is at stake."

"I am thinking of the long term," E. W. responded in hushed tones. "I need them to prove their worth. I cannot very well leave the city to search for our other requirements, as those in higher power would take notice of my absence. Secrecy is critical."

The Duke nodded, but asked, "And what if they fail?"

"Then I may have a mess to clean up," E. W. responded.

Meanwhile, Sarentha was nearly crying for joy, shaking Thomas with glee as he skipped past the grave markers. "Did you hear that? Who could he be? He *must* be a lord to be paying us in silver pieces! No commoner in Whampello has that sort of money on hand!"

"We only saw one silver piece," Thomas said soberly, observing the emotion on his friend's face. "It could be a trick. I don't like this sneaking about in dark unfamiliar places for strange stones."

"And I don't like chopping wood," Sarentha replied, the eagerness plain in his voice. "So since one of those job options is out for us, we will try the other! It might grow on you!"

Thomas could not deny his friend's pleasure and hope. "Fine, but let's be cautious. There must be a reason he won't go in there himself."

"A lord in a tomb? Hah!" Sarentha grinned widely, pulling Thomas along, looking up at the names on the mausoleums in the moonlight. They continued walking deeper into the cemetery, passing the familiar names. Eventually they reached a few run-down stone buildings bearing unknown names at the edge of the forest. Sarentha spotted *Callipso, 3 AGW – 791 AGW*. The letters were deeply engraved with a cursive style. Luckily the vines and brush that covered most of the mausoleum had not obscured the name. He did not know what the numbers and "AGW" stood for, but he was not going to worry about that.

Sarentha's eager hands pushed aside vines to expose the heavy door, and brushed away dirt caked into crevices by years of neglect. With a twinkle in his eye, he motioned for Thomas to open the door.

Figuring that they were already involved in this mess, Thomas thought they may as well get it over with quickly. He approached the door but did not see a handle. He put his shoulder to it and heaved. Strong as he was, the door only budged slightly, loosening a little cloud of dust and making him cough. About to protest, he saw the determination on Sarentha's face. Setting his feet firmly, he pushed with all his might, and the door finally gave way with a loud grinding.

Eerie yellow light filled the stone stairway inside. Thomas hurried to close the door to stop anyone outside from noticing the glow. Closed in the tomb, Thomas felt very small, and very trapped. The stagnant air smelled musty, making his stomach turn. Down the stairwell there were brightly lit torches set in sconces.

"Impossible," Thomas breathed quietly. "No one's been in here for ages!"

Sarentha approached the first torch and gingerly waved his hand over the flame. It did not flicker with the movement, and he felt no heat. Upon further examination, Sarentha noted that the torches were well bolted into place and caked with the grime of many years. "Magic," Sarentha said admiringly. "Pity I don't have any tools to pry one free. Can you imagine how useful an ever-burning torch would be?"

"Yes, for whenever we find ourselves in ancient, lightless mausoleums," Thomas whispered sarcastically. "Come on, let's go find this stone and get out of here. This place gives me the creeps!"

"Why are you whispering?" Sarentha asked, as he rushed down the stairs, dust moving about his feet. "There's no one in here."

"It just feels wrong to speak loudly in such a place," Thomas said, continuing to use hushed tones. "Shouldn't you be more careful? There could be bones buried under the dust on the stairs that you could trip on."

Sarentha froze, allowing Thomas to catch up. "You're right! I should be more careful! There could be traps. There are always traps in the old fables."

Thomas shook his head. "Old fables about tomb robbing? I've never heard of those… and where would *you* have heard of them?"

"The Grizzled Bard," Sarentha answered. He continued down the stairs more slowly, examining the surroundings. "Believe it or not, they actually *do* have bards there sometimes. I suppose you would have missed that experience, what with all the distracting serving women."

"While I might believe that, I don't believe you actually know what you're doing." Thomas said. "How do you know what a trap looks like?"

Sarentha shrugged, continuing to peer at the stonework. "I don't know, but I think it would be obvious. The bards talk about stones sinking into the floor, or trip wires set across hallways. You'd think that sort of thing would stand out."

"If traps stood out, why would anyone use them? Everyone would avoid them," Thomas said.

Sarentha did not respond.

Down below, the stonework was damp with moisture from seals broken long ago. The faint rhythmic sound of dripping water could be heard from further down the corridor. With their first steps, they felt slick lichen covering the stone floor. To make matters worse, the magical torches were now fewer and farther between, leaving some sections dimly lit. Along the way Sarentha paused periodically to poke through spider webs and ancient remains in the alcoves. The rattle of bones sounded too loudly to Thomas' ears when Sarentha disturbed the dead.

"Would you stop that?" Thomas begged.

"E. W. said we could have our pick of trinkets," Sarentha said defensively, looking back at the appalled look on Thomas' face. "What? If we're going to rob *one* grave, why not look through them all?"

"I hate this," Thomas breathed, refusing to watch. He was not a religious man, but Thomas could not abide the thought of his own tomb being vandalized. Although he had not heard the stories about trapped tombs, he knew plenty of ghost stories and did not fancy the haunting of angry spirits.

Sarentha had no luck finding anything of worth in the alcoves. Their pace was slowed as they made their way deeper into the crypt. The walls and ceiling narrowed, making the hallway uncomfortably tight. Thomas had to duck to avoid rubbing his scalp on the stone. Their arms grew wet with the moisture that coated everything.

Finally he whispered, "Sarentha, I can't go any further! I'm going to get stuck!"

"Claustrophobic?" Sarentha turned back to his friend. "I can see a chamber ahead. Not much further. If you want to wait here, I'll go the rest of the way on my own."

Thomas nodded his approval.

Ahead, Sarentha found himself in a small circular room. Unlike the hallway, this place was dry. The grey stone appeared firm and strong, untouched by growth. The room was ringed by more alcoves, each covered with stone doors and etched with unfamiliar, gently flowing runes. Turning his attention to the room's centre, Sarentha saw a large stone coffin with the carving of a handsome man on the lid. The man's chest plate bore the inscription of a dragon in flight. Sarentha remembered E. W. mentioning a draconic carving. There was, however, a problem.

"The whole thing's made of solid stone," Sarentha called back through the tunnel. "I don't see a seam for a lid! There's no way I can move this. I bet you couldn't move it, either!"

"I'm not going to go in there to try, then," Thomas replied, his voice echoing through the small chamber. "Look for something to pry it open with, maybe?"

Sarentha scanned the room for some sort of tool – and hoping for treasure – but it was clean and bare. Looking more carefully at the carving, he noticed fine etchings covering the whole sculpture. The detail in the man's features was impressive. He had high cheek bones, and a prominent chin. The eyes were closed peacefully, and his long wavy hair lay like a halo around his head. His hands rested on his chest, clasping a small pendant with a brilliant red gemstone. When Sarentha poked and prodded at the ruby, the jewel suddenly sank. Sarentha started calling back to Thomas with his success, but when a sharp stabbing sensation emanated from his shoulder he yelped in pain. Looking down, he noticed a small protruding dart. Sarentha yelled feverishly for Thomas.

Not knowing what was wrong, only that his friend was in

trouble, Thomas charged in. He fought his claustrophobic reflex, ignored the stone digging at his flesh, and wriggled through the damp, tight space. When he burst into the room, Thomas saw Sarentha squirming wildly on the floor with a small metal dart lying beside him. The top of the coffin was gone, and inside Thomas saw the skeleton with arms crossed over its chest and a faint purple glow emanating from its gripping finger bones.

Leaning down towards Sarentha, he heard his friend gasp, "The stone! Take it! Hurry!" Thomas shook his head and Sarentha yelled, "Take it! If that trap resets, we'll both die in here! Take it, or this is for nothing!"

With a grimace, Thomas again stood over the sarcophagus and looked at the purple gem. The smooth ellipsoid stone, about the same size as two fists put together, was covered in strange symbols. Dark purple circles and swirls intersected each other randomly all over the paler violet surface.

Thomas noticed a fine dust beginning to rise up out of the box and take shape. The lid of the sarcophagus, which had disintegrated at Sarentha's touch, was reforming! Thomas' eyes widened when he heard a faint 'click' from the other side of the room. What if Sarentha was correct and everything was resetting?

Growling to himself, he reached in, pushed the boney fingers aside, and pulled free the eerie purple stone just in time. The top of the sarcophagus reformed into the solid image of a man lying atop the slab. The ruby that had enticed Sarentha was again in place. Thomas' only thought was to get his friend out of that awful place.

Sarentha had fallen unconscious. As Thomas looked from his limp friend to the tight exit, and to the stone glowing in his grip, he wondered if this was worth all the danger. He'd have this E.

W.'s head if Sarentha died. But what choice did he have, now?

Thomas cemented his resolve, gathered up Sarentha's limp form, and squeezed through the painfully tight tunnel. Trying his best to ignore the blocks scraping at his flesh again, he gradually made his way across the wet stones. When they moved to the wider, more comfortable zone, he heard another faint 'clink'. From the dim light of a distant magical torch, Thomas saw their single silver coin lying on the floor. Picking it up, he knew what to do. Sarentha had once told him of the nobles' healers. If this E.W. was a true noble then he would have such healers in his employ. Thomas uttered a curse, followed by a soft prayer that his friend would not die.

Chapter 3: Preparations

Sarentha yawned and stretched, vaguely aware of his comfort. The morning's light shone through a little window, making him warm and cozy. His mattress felt softer, and his clothes felt lighter. The blanket he was under... blanket?

He sat bolt upright, looking quickly around the unfamiliar small stone room. The bed was certainly not his own; he could never have afforded one this luxurious. The bed's frame appeared to be of solid, rich cherry wood with posts rising up at each corner. He touched the down-filled pillow: a far cry from the balled-up shirt that he usually rested his head upon.

Thomas was slumped in the corner; his form was still as he slept on what appeared to be a cushiony chair. Sarentha pulled at the soft, clean garments he wore and whispered Thomas' name to gently rouse him from his slumber. When that did not work, his foot did.

Thomas looked up groggily, and a smile spread over his face. He, too, was wearing new clothes. What were they? Cotton? The material felt light and smooth compared with their usual rough woollens. The pale blue for Thomas and grey for Sarentha seemed to match them well enough. But where were they? What was this room?

"Thank the gods you're all right," Thomas said, the emotion clear in his cracking voice. He was up out of the chair and embracing Sarentha in a heartbeat. "You gave me a scare, friend! The healer said you were lucky that poison was so old. Had it been fresh, you'd have been dead straight away!"

Sarentha paused, trying to think back. He remembered the mausoleum, and the sarcophagus, but anything beyond that was gone.

"I took you to the inn, after," Thomas continued. "I dragged you in, and tapped our silver coin on the counter just like E. W. had instructed. I was taken to a back room. Apparently our lordly employer had sent a middle-man to pick up the stone. Turns out he was a healer, who muttered something about a Winston always being prepared for the worst. He prayed, and crushed up some herbs in a cup of tea. You swallowed a bit while unconscious, but coughed it all up and then some. The healer was pleased and said you'd be fine, but that we had to follow him. I carried you to this manor in the rich part of town. He made me drape a blanket over you and wear a heavy cloak so that no one could identify us. We've spent the night here, in this room."

The heavy oak door swung open, and a man who could only be a noble entered. His long brown hair was gathered at the back, and his brown eyes looked back and forth between Thomas and Sarentha. When he saw they were both awake and well, he smiled. His hands resting on the hips of his purple velvet pantaloons made him appear indignant, but his voice was friendly. "You two gave me quite the scare last night! Luckily for you I sent Peter to the inn. He is quite the accomplished healer and almost makes me wonder if there may actually be gods out there. At any rate, welcome to my home. It is about midday now, so you will not be permitted to leave, but you are welcome to a meal, if you wish."

"What do you mean, not permitted to leave?" Sarentha jumped up, still a little shaky on his feet. "Are we prisoners?"

"No, no, of course not," the noble replied. "I simply cannot have the two of you leaving in broad daylight. Imagine it: two unfamiliar peasants, who had not been seen entering, suddenly walk out of Lord Winston's estate? There would be too many political ramifications for my liking. No, you can stay until dark, and then if you still wish to leave, you may."

Again Sarentha was quicker than Thomas to pick up on their host's subtleties. He asked, "Why wouldn't we want to leave?"

"Let us discuss this over lunch," the man replied, and with a flourish of his showy purple cloak, he left the room. Sarentha observed the cloak's emblazonment: a white arrow, tilted at forty-five degrees and encircled by a white ring. He remembered seeing this symbol ten years earlier as a little boy, from the top of the tree at the orphanage. He stood in silent shock. The door remained open.

Thomas nudged Sarentha, and they followed, down hallways adorned with pedestals holding bronze and silver urns, windows letting in sunlight to feed the occasional green leafy shrub, and tapestries bearing strange symbols hanging on the stone walls. Glancing out a window Sarentha saw they were up on the second storey. Seemingly far away, he thought he could glimpse the shabby little two-storey building he and Thomas called home. He felt that the small, stone room he had slept in was far cosier than the larger, sparsely furnished room they rented.

Their host opened another door, and the trio descended some stairs. Another door opened and they found themselves in a grand entry chamber filled with plush couches and chairs, two fireplaces, thick luxurious rugs of bright fabric, more greenery, and people. To their surprise, the people were not all humans. There was a dwarf clad in thick black armour with ridges of short spikes covering nearly every surface, and dotted with long spikes jutting out randomly. The stout figure paced up and down the room. A group of elegant elves whispered among themselves. The tips of their pointed ears poked through their long hair just enough to reveal their heritage. Across the room, a gnome perched on a chair far too large for him was clinging to an envelope and looking around with small darting eyes. When he spotted the three newcomers, he leaped off the chair towards them. "My Lord Winston, I have news!"

"Excellent," the noble responded, taking the envelope and continuing towards a large set of double doors, intricately carved with the images of trees. "You will join us for lunch, Igatiolus?"

The gnome bowed his head while keeping pace with the much longer legs of the human. "As you wish, Lord Winston. There is much to discuss."

Two armoured men saluted the host and swung the doors open before them. Sarentha and Thomas gasped. The table in the dining hall was a rich cherry wood similar to Sarentha's resplendent bed, with twelve ornate wooden chairs running its length. Gleaming silver platters and table setting were positioned on the table. Again there were multitudes of tapestries hanging, solid in colour with foreign symbols woven into them.

A handful of servants promptly entered the room as soon as Lord Winston was seated, bringing forth apple pies, peach pies, dates, garlic mashed potatoes, and several small loaves of manchet sprinkled with ground clove. They found their places, and Sarentha felt completely out of place at the fine table. Platters laden with savoury roasted ham, pork sausages, and cheeses arrived. Fine silver goblets filled with sparkling water were put before them, and the servants left as quickly as they came. Sarentha looked to their host for a cue. Lord Winston nodded, and waved one free hand as his other picked up a steaming loaf of bread. The gnome Igatiolus waited, not at all interested in the food. In stark contrast, Sarentha and Thomas immediately dug in, hurriedly stuffing their mouths. After months of living on stale bread and dirty water, Sarentha felt like they had won a high-stakes game of dice. The flavour of hot, juicy cinnamon peach pie exploded in his mouth, and the tender ham was succulent. The fresh-baked bread dripping with rich butter was scented faintly with herbs he had never before tasted. No peasant could afford herbs. Cheese was a luxury unknown until now. Even the water was exceptionally refreshing.

"Can we speak privately, my lord?" Igatiolus looked disgusted at the strangers' lack of table manners.

Lord Winston frowned at the gnome before looking at his guests. "These men are associates of mine. They have recovered something very precious to our cause. What you have to say, they may need to hear. Please, go ahead, Iggy."

The gnome's nose wrinkled slightly. Sarentha tried to slow down in an attempt to appear civilized, but his stomach demanded to be filled with more delectable food.

Igatiolus continued after a moment's pause. "My lord, the cartographer in Tamor has the map you requested. The detail is low, but it illustrates the results of Zinzibar Foodle's life-long quest to fly beyond the borders of the Empire and map the terrain. It is, of course, extremely vague in the southern stretches, since there is no recorded history of civilization in the desert. Unfortunately, I could not secure the map for you, because I did not possess the required funds. But then, I doubt it will sell before you can purchase it, since virtually no one else has any use or desire for Foodle's work. Most believe the map is cursed."

Lord Winston nodded, then delicately popped a morsel of cheese into his mouth. He chewed slowly, appearing to contemplate the news. "We will wait. We must avoid drawing attention to our interest in this map. For now, it is sufficient to know that it exists. I will have Wizard Wettias' men watch the shop to make sure that Foodle's map does not leave before we move to acquire it. You say the detail is vague? Did you get a good look at it?"

"The cartographer allowed me a brief glimpse, only to prove that the map was as he said it was," Igatiolus replied. "The object of your curiosity was clearly labelled."

With this, Lord Winston smiled.

At the far end of the room, the large double doors opened. Sarentha tried not to choke when the striking woman purposefully entered the dining hall. Her hair, as dark as night, flowed down in luxurious rings, framing her lovely, pale face. The contrast between dark and pale made her green eyes seem to glow. Her violet dress was low-cut, drawing his gaze from her eyes down to a small crystal pendant, which glimmered radiantly even in the room's dim light. No other jewellery adorned her, but her natural beauty was astounding. Sarentha had always believed that the serving women at the taverns they frequented were comely, but every one of them would have looked homely beside this woman.

She came to a sudden stop opposite Thomas and Sarentha. She stood imperiously, her gaze taking everyone in. "Yes, Uncle? You called for me?"

"My dear Eliza," Lord Winston said, rising to bow to her. "How was your morning?" Sarentha and Thomas both leaped to their feet, Thomas' chair toppling behind him, to bow to the beautiful lady.

She frowned, briefly, ignoring Thomas' and Sarentha's eager ruckus. "Uncle, you did not summon me across the manor to ask about my morning."

"Perceptive as always, niece," Lord Winston said, nodding. "I have a job for you."

Eliza's eyebrows went up in surprise, but she did not speak.

"I need you to get Ben. Tell him to assemble some soldiers. I want you to suit up as well. Take Thomas and Sarentha here to the armoury. Make sure they are given standard issue gear. You are going to pay a visit to the goblins this afternoon, and you should be prepared in case of trouble."

Eliza's stony look transformed into a sly grin. The way her green eyes narrowed and sparkled made Sarentha think of a cat playing with a mouse. "Trouble with the goblins? Ben will be happy to hear it. Who are these two?"

"Friends," Lord Winston answered, winking at Thomas and Sarentha. "Friends I will be paying handsomely to accompany you and see to your safety." Eliza scoffed, but Lord Winston continued, "As you know, we have had recent dealings with a local goblin leader to ensure our merchant caravans are not waylaid. The leader, a witch doctor, has two emeralds I am very interested in acquiring. First, I want you to offer him a sizable amount of money, though I doubt he will accept. Take them by force if necessary, as I simply must have them."

Eliza did not question her uncle's need, and nodded her agreement. With a commanding look at Thomas and Sarentha, she said, "Come," and turned toward the doors.

As though compelled by magic, Thomas and Sarentha followed. While leaving, they passed the armoured dwarf heading into the dining room. His deep voice rumbled through the hall with a string of curses strong enough to make a sailor blush. As the doors closed behind them, Thomas and Sarentha could still hear the dwarf's yelling about the dire need to speed up the plans to–

They entered the armoury before they could hear any more, but Sarentha knew he could never imagine talking in such a way to a lord, or anyone else for that matter.

"I hope you can find a set that fits," Eliza said, motioning towards a large cabinet. "You will find leather breastplates in there. Smaller items such as gloves, bracers, helmets, greaves, and boots you will find in the trunks, just take a look. Weapons and horses will be given to you outside. Suit up, then come out when you are ready."

Eliza left.

A few moments of silence passed as they tried to sort out what was happening. Giving up, Thomas asked, "What in the hells is going on?"

Sarentha shrugged, walking over to the cabinet and opening the plain wooden doors. Inside were leather breastplates of varying sizes. The light brown leather was etched with the symbol of an arrow on the chest, the same one emblazoned on Lord Winston's cloak. Sarentha handed the largest one to Thomas, and found a smaller one for himself.

Thomas looked at the various straps and buckles, appearing perplexed. "So that's it then? We're just going to do as we're told, and not ask questions? I mean, who *is* this guy? We don't owe him anything. We found his weird purple stone, and now he wants us to go on missions with *soldiers*?"

"And he wants to pay us handsomely," Sarentha added. He was smiling as he pulled open a trunk and sorted through various protective pieces of leather gear. His stomach was full of wonderful foods, and his clothes were cleaner than they had ever been. With three silver pieces in their pockets and the promise of more, Sarentha was elated. "Let's face it, Thomas, we don't have a lot of options here. We're out of work, and for some reason this guy has taken a liking to us. I can think of worse fates than working for a lord!"

"Have you ever heard of Lord Winston?" Thomas asked, reaching to catch a pair of leather gloves that Sarentha tossed his way.

"I've seen the arrow symbol before. Remember back in the orphanage when I told you I saw a lord beheaded?" Thomas groaned and rolled his eyes. Sarentha snapped, "I'm telling you, it really happened! I wasn't making it up! Anyway, this guy must be related to him somehow."

Sarentha turned back to the trunks for the rest of their gear. "No, I have not heard of this particular lord before. But that's not really surprising, is it? These lords and ladies don't exactly mingle with us 'common folk,' do they? And you hear how he talks about suspicions and whatnot. He's totally paranoid, so he probably hides out in his manor all the time. It's likely that we've never passed him in our own city streets!"

"But what is he afraid of?" Thomas unbuckled some straps, and worked at putting on his breastplate, as other pieces flew in his general direction from the trunks. "What would these other lords do? What sorts of secret plans does he have? I tell you it was very strange coming here last night all hidden in cloaks. I'd like to know more before we provide our services to this man. What if he's looking to start a war with other lords in the city? Maybe working for him will get us killed!"

A Noble's Quest

"Well, you can go ask him what his plans are, if you're really that worried," Sarentha replied with a snort and a laugh after he closed the last of the trunks. "For my part, I'm delighted with the idea of being paid more than a few copper pieces a day for back-breaking forestry work. This is *fun* Thomas! It's an adventure to get us out of our normal rut."

"And a chance for us to risk our lives," Thomas repeated gloomily. "I've heard goblins can be quite fierce. The bards say that goblins have sharp teeth, and are cunning and manipulative. They might trade for the emeralds and then knife us in the back!"

Sarentha replied, "You're letting your imagination get away with you again. We're travelling with soldiers. If there's trouble, they can handle it. I think the armour is just a precaution."

"Then why do we need weapons?"

Sarentha sighed, noticing that Thomas had still not successfully fastened his leather breastplate. "Listen, after this, if you still don't feel comfortable working for Lord Winston, we'll take our money and be on our way. We'll be paid well enough to live for a while."

Thomas moaned, looking down distractedly at the senseless armour, tracing his finger over the arrow design. "There really isn't any other work here for us, is there?"

Sarentha tightened the straps on his own armour, and moved over to help Thomas put on his breastplate. "Well, you could be a bouncer at a tavern. You're certainly bigger than Jim, and he does alright."

"He fights dirty," Thomas amended, watching Sarentha's fingers work on his buckles and straps. "Besides, as fun as it is to go to the taverns, I'd rather not work at one. Those types of places steal your soul after a while. You can see it in their eyes. Think we'll wind up moving to Tamor?"

Sarentha smiled a little as he finished up with the armour. "Well I can certainly hope, can't I? We'd have enough money to spend some time there looking for well-paid work. Maybe not lordly wages, but better than chopping down trees."

"That sounds like you'd be willing to take a pay cut," Thomas said, sounding surprised.

"Well, you give a little, you take a little," Sarentha chuckled. "I guess I can't have it all. If you'd be willing to move out of this single-minded town, I'd be willing to take a pay cut – just a little one, though! I intend to find a great job in the capital."

"Fair enough," Thomas laughed. "How do I look?"

"Like they should have had a bigger breastplate," Sarentha admitted, seeing Thomas dressed awkwardly in his suit. "It'll do. Like I said, I don't expect we'll be doing any fighting anyway. The way Winston said it, it sounds like we're just bodyguards. And honestly, what kind of trouble is a lady like Eliza going to get into?"

They snickered, and headed out of the room. In the main entry chamber, they passed the whispering elves. Outside, they were surprised to see a platoon of thirty soldiers standing at attention. Two figures stood before them, talking quietly to each other. The man was huge; he was even bigger than Thomas. His head was covered with a shining, open-faced bascinet, and his skin was a rich brown tone. The soldier's arsenal of weapons was equally impressive, with a long sword sheathed at his left hip, a short sword and hand axe at his right, a battle axe across his back, and daggers in each metal boot. Unlike his troops, he wore a shining metal breastplate, polished and etched with the tilted arrow that adorned so many of Lord Winston's belongings.

Sarentha wondered what the significance of the slanted arrow was, but filed this question away for another time.

It took a moment for Thomas and Sarentha to recognize the other soldier was Eliza. She looked completely changed, with her hair hidden away under a metal cap, and her shapely form obscured beneath a dark suit of silver-studded leather. In contrast to her larger companion, she carried only a single, ornate dagger at her belt and a small crossbow slung across her back. Bows were often used by hunters in Whampello, but Sarentha had never seen a crossbow. They were rare weapons of war crafted by dwarves.

"You were saying something about a lady like her staying out of trouble," Thomas muttered under his breath, as the big man and Eliza turned to look at them. Sarentha grunted humourlessly.

The soldiers behind them wore leather armour, from neck to feet. Over their chests, they wore white cloth tabards with black arrows embroidered on the front, shields on their backs and long swords at their sides. There were enough waiting horses held by stable hands for all to ride.

"It's about time," the man called out to them, and Thomas and Sarentha descended the grey stone steps down to the courtyard. Two large oak trees stood to either side of the central path, which was lined with large flat stones. High stone walls surrounded the area, with a black iron bar gate to keep people out.

"Oh shush, Ben," Eliza scolded. "We have only been standing here for a minute or two." She turned to the two newcomers. "We have not been properly introduced. I am Eliza Winston, and this big lout is Ben."

"I'm the commander of Lord Winston's forces," Ben said, offering a hearty handshake to both men. "Any friend of Winston's is... well, you're still under my command, so take that how you will. You two will be assigned to guarding Eliza. Don't let her out of your sight. This is harder than it sounds, trust me. This firecracker has a mind all her own, and half the time she doesn't listen to orders, even from me!"

"And the other half, I am only doing what you say because I happen to agree with your judgement," Eliza stated.

"As I was saying," Ben continued, smiling at Eliza, "You're guarding her because I don't want the headache of doing it myself. Mount up; let's get going. I want to be back for dinner!"

In unison, the soldiers marched to the horses. Thomas and Sarentha followed Eliza and awkwardly climbed into their saddles, with the help of the stable hands. Neither of them had ever ridden a horse before.

Thomas was given a large courser. The horse had a brown head with a splash of white from its forehead to its nose, and a mostly white body, with the exception of some large brown spots on its hind quarter. The horse jolted Thomas as it moved, its trotting motion jarring him. He sat awkwardly in the saddle.

Sarentha had an easier time on his more compact jennet. The small, black horse moved smoothly under Sarentha's unpractised hand. Sarentha had the feeling they had been profiled by Lord Winston the moment they met, and the horses handpicked to suit their personalities and sizes.

Eliza came to meet them on her own chocolate-brown palfrey. Though larger than Sarentha's jennet, Eliza's horse glided effortlessly. Sarentha knew that her horse must be worth quite a bit more than the ones they rode, as palfreys were highly valued for their grace.

Eliza watched them work to keep themselves seated upon their mounts. "Have you never ridden before?" They both gave her incredulous looks. How could poverty-stricken peasants ever afford to keep a horse? She smiled back at them and said, "Hold the reins firmly. Not too tight, Thomas! Try to sit up straight with your shoulders, hips and heels aligned. No, do not arch your back like that, Sarentha! Right, there you go. Straight-backed. Keep your hands low when you hold the reins. Point your heels down. That is a good start. Do you feel how that gives you better balance? Well, let us join the others, and I will teach you more about how to guide your horse where you want to go."

The soldiers rode ahead in two columns. With Eliza's guidance, Thomas and Sarentha caught up and marched out into the city, off to meet the goblins.

Chapter 4: Green-Eyes

The ride down the forest path was peaceful, and once Thomas got the hang of steering his horse he began to enjoy the experience. The sun was filtered by the high leaf canopy, a wisp of a breeze filtered through tall cedars and oaks. There was no conversation among the three dozen men and women; the soldiers kept their eyes open for signs of trouble. It was unlikely that anything truly ominous lurked in the woods, but they all knew stories of pesky woodland faeries, goblins, and even the rare ferocious orc. That was enough to keep them all on their on their guard.

In the city, Eliza had informed Thomas and Sarentha that the goblin camp was not far away. Generally the goblins did not bother the townspeople, who in turn left the goblins alone. But Thomas had heard that times were changing. Orcs had been sighted coming in from the deeper east woods, and goblins were more afraid of orcs than of people. If orcs were influencing or even dominating the nearby goblin tribe, it meant trouble for travellers moving west to Tamor, and for those coming from Tamor to Whampello. Merchant caravans did not hire guards, and even so market prices were high. If a few caravans wound up disappearing, things would get ugly quickly for the underpaid, overworked peasantry.

Thomas learned that this was Eliza's first mission with the soldiers, which made him feel a little better about his own lack of combat experience. Although she had been training with the troops for several weeks, she had not expected her uncle to put her in the field so quickly. Upon learning that Thomas and Sarentha were in the same position – with no training and no military experience at all – she laughed and said she was glad she was not alone.

Before long Thomas was wishing for a larger breastplate. With the constant up and down on horseback, the suit was chafing him badly. That, added to his bruised ribs from the tomb's tight squeeze, left him wondering if eventually he would have no skin left. Apart from this constant irritation, his ride was fairly good. The horses were well trained, and with Eliza's guidance he felt more confident on his mount.

There was a call from the front of the line, and Thomas reigned up as he saw others do, and his horse came to a stop. A call came out for Eliza to approach the column's front, and Thomas and Sarentha followed suit. When they trotted up, Thomas saw one of their soldiers holding onto a small green-skinned humanoid. Orange dots speckled its face like freckles, and a dirty rag hung over its shoulders in a semblance of garb. The little creature bared sharp teeth, yellowed and chipped, and tried to bite its captor.

"We've attempted to communicate with it," Ben said. "But I don't think it speaks our language."

"Of course not," Eliza replied. "Goblins have their own language, and they are not smart enough to learn anything else." To their surprise, Eliza grunted and whined, and the goblin stopped resisting. With a wave of her hand, Eliza signalled for the goblin's release. The soldier stood back while keeping a hand close to his sword's handle.

Eliza removed her metal cap, shaking out her long dark curls, before grunting and gesturing in the guttural language. The goblin responded in kind, calmly pointing this way and that. Eliza, it seemed, was perfectly fluent in the goblin tongue.

As the conversation progressed, the goblin sniggered and shook its head vehemently. Eliza was obviously put off by the refusal, and her tone grew unmistakably angry. Shaking its head again, the goblin turned and bolted in a flat-out run off the path and into the woods.

With a single fluid motion, Eliza's crossbow found its way into her hands. It was already loaded with a crossbow bolt: smaller, yet several times heavier than a hunter's arrow and without the fletching. She lifted the stock to her shoulder, and stared through the iron sight. Aiming carefully at the fleeing creature, she said, "One for the heart." The bolt launched, but her aim was off, and instead of the heart, the projectile pierced the soft area where the back of the skull meets the neck. The goblin was down without a sound.

"You missed," Ben chided, smiling down from atop his horse.

Eliza shrugged, reloaded her crossbow, pulled it back over her shoulder and retorted, "It worked."

Sarentha asked, "So what happened? Why did you kill it?"

"It insulted my beauty," Eliza said in hurt tones. Ignoring the incredulous looks of her protectors, she pointed further down the path. "The goblin camp is that way, and not far. The one we are looking for is called Green-Eyes. He is their spiritual leader, and has the gemstones my uncle wants."

The group continued their march, with Eliza, Thomas, and Sarentha again falling back to the rear of the column. It took a while, but eventually Thomas could contain himself no longer. "You didn't *really* kill that goblin because he insulted your beauty, did you?"

"Goblins are disgusting creatures," Eliza said without remorse. "If one of those barbaric little maggots said you had the look of a flea-bitten, moss-topped, mangy orc wench, you would probably have done the same!"

"Well, I doubt it," Thomas said. "I've been called worse."

Eliza looked askance at him, raising a fine eyebrow. "Really? Well, no one talks to me that way. Especially not a goblin! It is more a case of needing a reason *not* to kill them, as goblins go. Anyway, its tribe might not even notice. Scouts are expendable to goblins, and often go missing for various reasons."

Sarentha asked, "How do you know so much about goblins? And where did you learn to speak their language?"

Eliza smiled brilliantly at him. "I have studied! I am fluent in goblin, orcish, elven, and dwarven. Well, their common languages, anyway. There are specific dialects I have not yet mastered. My mother insisted that I learn as many languages as possible, from a young age. When she passed away, Uncle Erwin also wanted me to study hard, so I would not wind up being some empty-headed trophy wife to another noble. I am not sure how learning monstrous languages will help me achieve that, but he insisted I learn goblin and orcish."

Thomas asked, "Uncle Erwin? You mean Lord Winston?"

"Of course," Eliza said. "He has taken care of me since my mother died several years ago. He has been like the father I never had. He protects me, but at the same time encourages me to be strong and independent. As far as I am concerned, he is the greatest man alive."

Thomas and Sarentha exchanged looks, before Sarentha continued. "He's offered us more work, you know. Not just this job, but to keep performing tasks for him as needed. How does he treat people like us?"

Eliza looked them both up and down, "Well, I cannot honestly say. I have never seen people like *you* in the manor before. No offense, of course. I just mean my uncle deals exclusively with other nobles and military types, and I have never known him to employ peasants. He must see something in the two of you that is not readily apparent to the rest of us. I mean..." Eliza blushed and looked away.

Thomas frowned, but Sarentha chuckled. The ride continued in silence.

As promised by the goblin, before long the column came to a halt. The wider route had shrunk down to a winding deer path. Pieces of crudely-worked stone, leather, scraps of meat and bone littered the area, indicating that they were nearing their destination. Again Eliza was called to the front.

Ben turned when they approached and said, "I'll go in with you three. The soldiers will follow at the rear. We don't want to spook the little green devils, so we won't show them all our troops outright. If we need help, they won't be far away. Ready?"

Eliza nodded her head. Thomas and Sarentha concurred, and the four dismounted and started in on foot.

Thomas was certain they would have been able to find the camp from the smell, even without that first goblin's help. The stench of rotting refuse led them easily to the 'camp,' which was little more than a bonfire surrounded by piles of debris and one small tent of ragged animal skins. Despite the lack of structures, there were at least three dozen goblins milling about the area, picking through their own garbage or fighting over scraps. Eventually one of them paused long enough to notice the newcomers. It let out a howl and ran straight for the tent.

An uneasy moment passed, while the other goblins stopped their activities to eye the strangers. Some bared their teeth to remind the visitors that they were on goblin ground now, under goblin rule. Finally, a small grey-green goblin shambled out of the tent, covered in a half dozen layers of matted fur and ragged leather. It held a gnarled old stick in both hands and hobbled forward, peering up at them through two enormous green emeralds fastened to its head with a wire frame.

The goblin grunted and whined softly, and Eliza responded. After a few words in the crude language, she pulled a bag off her belt and opened it up. The goblin leaned over the bag to see shining golden coins and precious gemstones glittering in the afternoon sun. Sarentha nearly fainted at the sight, and Thomas wondered what could be so special about the emeralds that Lord Winston would offer such a huge sum to procure them.

The goblin looked in the sack for a moment, then shook its head, grunting and wheezing its denial. Eliza's voice became more forceful, but the goblin was unwilling to trade. Before it could turn and leave, one of Ben's big hands clenched down on the shoulder of the little creature to hold it in place. The goblin squealed and grunted, and Ben suddenly jumped back in shock, stunned by the tiny bolts of electricity radiating from the creature's fingertips.

Thomas had no idea how to respond, never having seen magic before. But Ben, recovering quickly, unhooked the battle axe from his back, and with one smooth motion brought the blade up over his head and down, chopping the little shaman in two. The other goblins, outraged, came lunging at the group.

"For Winston!" Ben cried out, abandoning his axe, and

unsheathing his long and short swords. Thomas fumbled with his axe, and Sarentha slid out both of his daggers, looking around to assess the situation. Eliza, always ready, loosed a bolt from her crossbow into the chest of an oncoming goblin. The creature screeched pitifully and coughed blood as it fell, grasping weakly at the shaft that pierced its lung.

Ben's call echoed throughout the woods; in answer, the soldiers ran through the trees to close on the goblin camp. A dozen goblins came in that first wave, Ben taking the brunt of the assault, slicing his blades back and forth. With one swing his long sword cut off three heads, and the bodies crumpled down on each other. Thomas brought his axe up too late; he fell to the ground, wrestling two goblins intent on tearing him apart. After a moment, they jerked upright, their eyes wide in shock; falling aside, they revealed Sarentha, his blades running with black blood. "I told you I'd save your life."

Nodding thanks to his friend, Thomas wasted no time in swinging at the next charging goblin. His axe found the creature's soft belly, sending it spinning to the ground, howling in pain. Thomas peered over and saw Ben had now lost his swords and was crouched down, daggers in hand, stabbing at the goblins piling on top of him. Eliza launched another bolt into the face of a clambering goblin, before taking her dagger and stabbing at the creatures on top of Ben.

And then help arrived. The soldiers charged into the fray, blasting the heap of goblins off Ben and forcing them back. Thomas watched Ben rise up and charge forth with his troops, obliterating the remaining goblins, and forcing those not brave enough to stand and die to flee. In moments, the sounds of battle faded, and the soldiers regrouped.

Sheathing his blades and reclaiming his axe, Ben appeared to have suffered only superficial cuts and bruises from the battering of the goblins. He reflected, "Well, this group won't be causing anyone any problems any time soon." Reaching down, he removed the wire-rimmed emeralds from the head of the goblin witchdoctor, and frowned. "Strange that he would not trade these for the riches your uncle offered, Eliza."

"He said he had no need for gold," Eliza answered, wiping her dagger off on a patch of grass.

Sarentha followed suit and wiped his blades, but Thomas paused. He stared at the black ichor on his axe and looked at the surrounding carnage. "Did we really have to kill them? Couldn't we have just taken the gems and left?"

Eliza looked curiously at Thomas. Ben answered, "Lord Winston said by any means necessary. Honestly, with the rumours of orcs in the area, it was likely only a matter of time before this tribe was turned against us, anyway. Better to thin their numbers now, while we can. Had that little devil been involved in an army, his magic would have been far more devastating than the little shock he gave me. The first rule of fighting a caster is to strike quickly, and strike hard. You rarely get a second chance when battling someone who has mastery of the arcane."

"I've never seen magic before," Sarentha said, looking down at the dead goblin who had summoned electricity from nowhere.

"I was raised in Tamor," Ben said, handing the emeralds over to Eliza, who added them to her bag of coins and precious stones. "Wizards can be a scary bunch, but then so can priests. You might think they have healing powers, but they can kill people, too, if they have their mind set on it. Take my word for it, if you're not in range to kill an angry spell-weaver, you're best to get out of their line of sight and hide. Make them come to you. Sometimes that doesn't work, and they'll level a building you're in, but the less powerful ones can't do that sort of thing. I don't know what sort of level of magic this shamanistic goblin had; that might have been the extent of his power. But I didn't want to find out by being hit with a blast of lightning."

Despite Ben's words, Thomas still somehow felt responsible for the little corpse on the ground. The goblin had appeared old, and had certainly been sentient. Had they the right to take his life just to procure the emeralds? Had they the right to take the lives of almost every goblin in the camp? Was there a greater purpose, or were they only mindlessly following instructions regardless of the consequences? How could this violence ever bring peace? What did they really know of Lord Winston's motives? These questions swam through his mind as the troops travelled back to Whampello.

* * * * *

Lord Winston entered the main hall just as his dwarven guest stomped out to the courtyard. The patiently-waiting elves stood and bowed to him, and Lord Winston returned the honour. Earlier in the day, there had been three, but now only two remained. They had come a great distance to meet with him. Beyond the bounds of the Tamorran Empire, far to the north, a secluded group of elves lived in the jungle. These two hailed from that region, and had come as quickly as possible when Lord Winston summoned them.

Lord Winston bowed low. "I am sorry to have kept you waiting so long. My friend Thurzin had a few grievances to bring to my attention. Did you know that dwarven horses should not be stabled with regular horses? I had no idea."

The elves both shook their heads. "There is nothing to

apologize for. What feels like a long time for you is but a moment for an elf," the first elf, Kel'shorie, stated. He was shorter than most human men, and very slender, but despite his stature Erwin knew that he was a great warrior among the Kashtriya caste. Two long slim blades hung from his belt. His eyes remained focused and alert at all times, as though he expected the stones themselves to come alive and attack. The other elf, Pau'sien, was smaller still, and her pale blue eyes had a more playful look about them. She had no visible weapons, but Erwin knew she kept a wand under her plain white cloak. The magic of the elves was legendary, and he was grateful to have them as allies.

Pau'sien said, "Even so, we regret that our companion, Shah'lao, had to take his leave so soon; he asked us to send his greetings. He had a time-sensitive meeting in Khrymyre he could not miss. I performed the spell you requested." A wizard of the Brahmin caste, she was extremely powerful. She spoke softly, though they were alone in the entry chamber. Even with the manor's runed tapestries that prevented magical listening, Pau'sien was careful. This caution pleased Lord Winston.

"And there was nothing interesting, I assume," he said. If there had been anything of note, he would have expected her face to be bright with the news.

"On the contrary," she said, her expression unchanging, "I believe you will find the results quite noteworthy. The genealogy of your two new guests is nearly as interesting as your own. The little man, Sarentha, is in fact the descendant of the hero Hendricus Wyrmstriker."

This name was unknown to Lord Winston, but Kel'shorie said, "I knew him well. Over five centuries ago we fought side by side in the war. I was pleased to learn that his legacy continues to this day."

"The blood of a hero runs through him?" Sarentha seemed quite forgettable, and blended into the background most of the time. Lord Winston found it hard to imagine him performing any great feats worthy of legend.

"If that is surprising to you, perhaps you should have a seat for this next news." Pau'sien's face, normally expressionless, twitched slightly. Lord Winston took her advice and sat down.

She looked down at him. "Thomas is the descendant of Matthew Strongblade."

Erwin missed Pau'sien's next words – his mind went blank. In his private chambers, locked away in a chest hidden in a false wall, was an ancient stone tablet. The tablet was Erwin's link to a past long forgotten by most. On that tablet, written by a long-dead king during the war of which Kel'shorie spoke, amongst all of the history that had been left for future generations to find, only one name had been carved. *Matthew Strongblade*. The writer had not even inscribed his own name. Only the hero who led the forces of mankind, Matthew Strongblade, was vital enough to take up what little room there was on the stone fragment. Erwin had read the name a hundred times while committing the tablet's writings to memory. To hear the ancient hero's name spoken aloud, to learn he had the hero's living, breathing heir in his employ, was unfathomable.

"'Tis not possible," he whispered softly.

"I never had the privilege of fighting alongside Matthew Strongblade," Kel'shorie said, his voice full of regret. "I wish I had. The stories they told–"

"But you know of him?" Erwin was on his feet in a flash, his eyes wild with anticipation. "Tell me! I must know!"

Kel'shorie drew back a step, appearing uneasy with Lord Winston's manic look. "But I am sure they were just stories, Lord Winston. No man is capable of the things I heard."

Erwin was not about to back down. Even if they were false, he needed to know. He might never meet another living being who could tell him anything about the legendary hero.

Kel'shorie replied, "Well, it is said that in a distant land Matthew Strongblade alone rallied the forces of mankind and fought very dark, powerful, and ancient forces to find freedom. During the war he held back an entire army so that others could escape. He was loved and admired by all who knew him. I have heard that he was involved in the original alliance between men, elves, and dwarves. It is said he could slay giants and dragons single-handedly, and smote mountains with his gleaming blade."

"The Strongblade," Pau'sien interjected, "is a potent magical weapon, but certainly not powerful enough to perform such miracles."

Lord Winston paused briefly as the weight of Pau'sein's words hit him. "*IS* a powerful magical weapon? It exists still?"

"It is in our care," she confirmed.

"When he fell, the blade was spirited away by Hendricus Wyrmstriker. He brought it to our elven camp where we were recovering from another pitched battle. Before turning back with the main human forces and our remaining elves for their final battle, Wyrmstriker handed the blade over and ordered me to flee. He knew they were doomed, and did not want the Strongblade to fall into enemy hands. I hid it in the jungle with our elders, where it remains," Kel'shorie said.

"It belongs to men," Lord Winston said, with a tinge of ire.

"It belongs to the heir of Matthew Strongblade," Kel'shorie

corrected earnestly, not backing down. The force of his voice gave Erwin pause, and the three shared a long moment of silence.

"Thomas is not ready for such responsibility," Erwin said at last. "Yesterday he was a lumberjack. Even if Matthew Strongblade's blood does run through him, it may have been badly diluted over the centuries. Surely we could give the blade to someone more fitting. I have a commander who—"

Pau'sien stood and raised her hood over her head, hiding her identity. Her form appeared to waver slightly before Erwin's eyes. The magic in the cloak gave her nearly perfect invisibility in nature, but did not function well indoors. She spoke. "As caretakers of the Strongblade, we have the final decision. But we will discuss your request with the elders. They are older and wiser than all of us and will know what the best course of action shall be."

Lord Winston had no choice but to acquiesce. Kel'shorie clasped the noble's hand, and they shared a searching look. Erwin wondered how many times this warrior before him had wanted to take up the Strongblade himself and test the legend of felling a mountain, but had refrained because of the will of his elders.

Kel'shorie put up his hood, and shimmered faintly. "We will be swift. First we must join Shah'lao in Khrymyre to consult with the dwarves. The lost sword Fallia must be reforged. As soon as the elders make a decision, we will send word of the Strongblade."

Lord Winston bowed and said, "Thank you." He moved to the front doors and pushed them wide open, warmed by the afternoon sun as he watched the two figures fade from sight. Their magic would whisk them away momentarily, and the fate of the sword and mankind would be debated by elves. Lord Winston felt a pang of indignation, feeling that human fate should rest with humans, but he had no choice. Even so, the elves' news brought him hope for his cause. With the heir of Matthew Strongblade on his side, he felt they could not fail. He realized he must not treat the two peasants like expendable help any longer. If Thomas and Sarentha could live up to the legends of their lineage, he would need them in his schemes. If everything went according to plan, the lumberjacks would soon prove their worth.

Chapter 5: Thurzin Trollbane

Lord Winston stood before them in the grand dining hall, brought the wire-wrapped emeralds up to his eyes, and looked around the room through the green gems. "Interesting," was his terse report, before handing them over to the heavily armoured dwarf Sarentha remembered from earlier. "What do you make of them, Thurzin?"

The dwarf removed his spike-covered steel gauntlets before handling the gems, holding them closer for inspection. "Bah, they be emeralds. I don't see nothin' special about 'em. Back home we'd dig up a dozen o' these a day from the belly o' the mountain."

"So you could get us more?" Lord Winston asked.

Thurzin nodded once, handing the stones back. "Will cost ye a pretty penny, o' course. An' t' get 'em like these ones are will be takin' a wizard's touch, an' we dun have no wizards back home."

"I know some wizards in Tamor," Lord Winston said casually. He turned back to the emerald-hunting party, and said, "Ben, Eliza, Thomas, and Sarentha, you have my thanks. Ben, you may pass on my gratitude to the soldiers as well. The glasses are everything I had hoped for."

Ben saluted, turned, and left the room.

"What sort of trinket did they fetch you, Erwin?"

Sarentha turned to see a handsome, tanned man, with a slim, firm frame covered in translucent silks. His coppery hair hung half-way down his back, and his hazel eyes flicked over the others before settling on Lord Winston.

"Just these emeralds, Your Grace," Lord Winston said. He retrieved them from the pouch, and brought them up to his eyes once more. "I had heard that a local goblin possessed a set of glasses made from them, and I thought it was a waste for mere goblins to hold such wealth."

The Duke snorted with derision. "Goblins do not even deserve the air they breathe. Filthy maggots." He glanced dismissively at the emeralds, before turning his attention to the others in the room. "Who are these newcomers? I told you I wanted to know everyone in your compound."

Lord Winston bowed deeply. "Where are my manners? Until recently, Thomas and Sarentha were lumberjacks from the east side of town. They have been helping with our mission."

"What part have they played?" The Duke approached slowly, staring them down as though mentally measuring their worth. "How much do they know?" he whispered.

"Nothing," Lord Winston answered smoothly. "They entered the tomb and retrieved the Amethyst of Arythia for me, and have just now returned from guarding Eliza through the goblin camp incursion. Now that they have proven their worth, they are ready to learn more of the quest."

The Duke looked them up and down again. "*They* retrieved the stone? Perhaps they are not as useless as they appear. Yes, I suppose we can tell them as much of the plan as concerns them. And I care little for your own personal missions to slaughter goblins."

Winston smiled, waving for everyone to be seated. "Ten years ago my father, Samuel Winston, was judged to be a traitor and executed." Sarentha's memories instantly surfaced of that day in the tree, when he had witnessed the soldiers of Tamor behead a noble. He had never been able to shake that image from his mind.

Lord Winston continued. "At the time, my father was harbouring elves from distant lands who had stolen valuable objects from the nobles of Tamor. My father had no knowledge of the elves' greater plans, but nonetheless was found guilty of collaborating with them. The nobles of Tamor were most displeased, and demonstrated their power by murdering my father. They left without finding their belongings, but not before questioning my sister and me about our knowledge of the thefts. Neither of us knew what the elves had planned. It was good that we were innocent, for a wizard who had accompanied the soldiers cast a spell to determine whether we were speaking the truth. It was fortunate that they did not pry deeper, for there were indeed some things I knew.

"When the elves first arrived they were disguised as humans until they could be sure who was worthy of their trust. They spoke to my father at length about his attitude toward Tamor and found him to be displeased with his station as a mere lord in Whampello. The elves entrusted him with a stone tablet inscribed with the final thoughts of a long-forgotten king. My father allowed me to read it. If the soldiers of Tamor had known about this tablet and my knowledge of it, I would have died alongside my father ten years ago."

Silence hung in the room as Thomas, Sarentha, and Eliza digested the news. Eliza appeared shocked, and she looked with hurt-filled eyes to her uncle.

"I am sorry," Lord Winston said, appearing shaken by Eliza's fallen gaze. "You have to understand. My father was killed for harbouring elves. I could not jeopardize your life. I did not want to involve you until you were older and would not do something rash in your grief over losing your father."

Eliza nodded her understanding, pain flashing over her face with the mention of her father. "I know you would not deceive me unless it was necessary."

Lord Winston said, "I want to strike back at the nobles who unjustly executed my father. However, to do so I require the creation of a special artefact. Thomas and Sarentha, you have helped retrieve the focusing stone, and I thank you again. But I need more."

The Duke asked, "And the map: does it exist?"

Sarentha stared at the Duke. The only words the Duke spoke were either to belittle others or to ask pointed questions. It was easy to understand Lord Winston's motivations, but why was Calarin involved? He treated Thomas and Sarentha like lowly beings. Sarentha doubted he would ever learn very much about the Duke.

"The Map of Foodle exists, and has been located in Tamor," said Lord Winston. "It contains the details that we require to continue."

The Duke nodded his approval, although his face never cleared of its constant scowl. Winston continued, "I am sending Thurzin, Thomas, Sarentha, and Eliza to Tamor to buy the map and find the tree. Ben will remain here, and continue training our soldiers. I am also looking at recruiting more."

"You will need to increase your numbers," said the Duke with the faintest hint of approval in his voice. "If we were intelligent we would wipe out every other noble house in this city and take their soldiers as our own. And still we would need more.

The noble houses of Tamor are powerful."

"We have no reason to kill anyone in this city," Lord Winston replied in even tones. Sarentha nudged Thomas subtly with his toe, making a face that silently said, "See? I told you he's not a war-crazed psychopath!" Even so, Sarentha held some reservations, seeing that Lord Winston planned to avenge his father's death by attacking the nobles in Tamor. Lord Winston said, "Iggy assures me we have allies in our mission, and Thurzin has also offered assistance."

"Dwarves and gnomes?" the Duke frowned, causing Thurzin to scowl fiercely back. "Desperate times, I suppose..."

"I'd chop ye down t' size in a second, ye fluffy duke!" Thurzin yelled, standing on his seat, and slamming his hands on the table.

Winston raised a hand imploringly towards the dwarf. "The dwarves have long proven to be powerful warriors and loyal friends. The gnomes are quite crafty in their own right. I expect no help from the elves of Tamor, and especially not the halflings. We could not afford their prices."

"Those capitalistic midget mercenaries are not worth the gold they demand," said the Duke.

"Perhaps not," Winston conceded. "However, we should make haste and dispatch our team. We will have time to discuss alliances while they are away."

The Duke nodded, and Lord Winston turned to the others. "I need you to find the cartographer in Tamor. Eliza, you can use the funds the goblin leader rejected. Once you have purchased the map, open this envelope and follow the instructions within." Lord Winston lifted a plain envelope from the table, and handed it to Eliza. "Thurzin Trollbane, a chest awaits you at the stables with enough payment for everything we will need from your homeland."

Thurzin nodded eagerly, rising once more. He was obviously ready to leave the sight of the Duke. Thomas, Eliza, and Sarentha rose and followed the muttering dwarf from the dining hall.

"Desperate indeed," Thurzin fumed audibly as he stumped outside and started towards the stables. "Damnable nobles be a lot o' idiots! Takin' hard-earned coin from their own t' line their pockets an' make fluffy clothes that ain't no good fer fightin' in. Errr, yerself excluded, me lady," Thurzin said, bowing awkwardly towards Eliza. "An' yer uncle. E's a good sort. I be thinkin' in a past life 'e might 'ave been a dwarf 'imself."

"You are too kind," Eliza said, smiling down at the dwarf. "So, we are off to Tamor. I have not been there in several years. I was but a girl when I saw the wizard's tower, and the city's castle."

The smell of the stables hit them like a wall. The odour of manure and wet horses filled the area, as stable hands worked to clean and groom the horses that had just returned from the goblin expedition. Thurzin called out for his mount, and a stable boy went running. In moments, a few lads were leading out fresh horses, one for each rider and a pack horse for supplies.

Thurzin's black mare was shorter than the rest, and wider, much like the stature of a dwarf. Like Thurzin, it was covered in black metal barding with rows of spikes protruding in all directions from the head guard. "C'mere ye stinkin' horse," Thurzin said, grabbing the reins and yanking it outside, despite its resistance. "I don' care if ye like it in there better than on the road with me, ye're comin'!"

The beginning of the ride out of town was a battle of wills

between the dwarf and the mare. She would stop for no reason, toss her head and gnash her teeth at passersby. Her jerking gait almost threw Thurzin several times, but somehow the dwarf clung on. Several times Thurzin whacked the horse on her headpiece, the ringing of metal sounding loudly from his armoured fist. "Stupid horse! She likes it, I swear! Won't go nowhere without gettin' a good beatin' first!"

The other three looked at each other skeptically, but the horse did appear to calm down after a few altercations with her rider. By the time they were on the road out of town, the mare was trotting along merrily.

"Tha's the problem with these damn dwarven horses," Thurzin said gruffly, with a hint of affection in his tone. "They got the brains o' orcs, an' the stubbornness o' dwarves! Ye're better off standin' on yer own two feet t' meet a chargin' group o' orcs. Damn horses take too long t' get ready, but if ye got the time t' be gettin' 'em set, there ain't a more terrifyin' sight!"

After considering the black metal-clad mare, the three agreed they would not want to cross paths with an angry horse like her. "This one time in the depths o' Trahllen, it was just me an' blasted Khrakhoom here ridin' along mindin' our own business when a group o' stupid goblins came runnin' up screamin' some durn fool stuff in their stupid speak. Well, Khrakhoom here went ballistic! I couldn' swing me axe fer nothin' in the tight hall, but she damn well trampled the little beasts over and over again. Took me three hours t' settle 'er down. Weren't nothin' but paste o' goblin left on the floors when she was done with 'em! She woulda ate the damn crap off the floor if I hadn' been there t' beat 'er half t' death afterward. Stupid horse. But they be good enough when ye need 'em."

"I have not heard of Trahllen before," Eliza said, while Sarentha was still trying to figure out what the story was about. The heavy dwarven accent on every word made his stories difficult to decipher. "Is it like the city of Khrymyre, southwest of Tamor?"

Thurzin yelled, "Bah!" He stopped his mount and glared at Eliza. "Ye fool girl, tis nothin' anywhere near the same. Khrymyre be more like yer filthy human city, built above groun' with walls o' stone an' buildin's popping up all o'er the place. Ugly as sin, too! Nay, Trahllen be a gem amongst goblin shite! In yer human ways, Trahllen be meanin' Stone Home, but t' dwarves it be meanin' a great deal more 'n that."

Eliza asked, "And what *does* it mean to a dwarf?"

Thurzin nodded towards her, his hardened features softening. He started up his mare again, with only a light kick to her flanks this time, and said, "Well, I guess it won't be hurtin' t' tell ye the sum of it. The name Trahllen be like a dwarven hymn in the heart o' any dwarf who hears it.

>Dwarven halls o' stone 'n steel,
>hard o' touch but home it feel.
>Dwarven voices yell an' cheer
>in times o' strife an' times o' beer!
>Dwarven hammers, what a sight,
>ringin' true throughout the night.
>Dwarven grit in times o' war,
>that's what we're created for.
>Dwarven might shall ne'er fail,
>we'll all fight on, tooth an' nail.
>'Til end o' times, when mountains fall,
>the dwarves will last, outlive ye all!

It be an old, old song among the dwarves. 'Tis said every dwarf knows its tune from before birth, an' every dwarf's heart sings it when 'e falls."

"It is lovely," Eliza offered, but Thurzin's steely look told Sarentha that he did not approve of the descriptor.

"So dwarves like to drink and fight," Sarentha said. "I know some of our own people who are like that."

"Hah!" Thurzin laughed. "I'd match the best o' yers with the worst o' ours, an' I'd still put me bet on the dwarf! Ne'er met a man who could drink a mug o' dwarven ale without throwin' up all o'er himself! Hah!"

"I'm not much of a drinker, but I bet Thomas could handle it," Sarentha challenged.

Thurzin shook his head and guffawed. "Well, we won't be testin' tha', anyway. Dwarven ale ain't allowed outside the gates o' the mountain."

It was Sarentha's turn to mock. "Oh, why's that? So you can boast about how no one else can stomach it, and not actually offer it up for proving you wrong?"

Thurzin shook his head, thoughtfully running a plated gauntlet through his long black beard. "Nay. Last time we snuck a keg out t' Khrymyre some men stole it an' sold it t' the damn bastard halflings. Short shrimps died when they drank it. Figured it's just best fer everyone if we be leavin' the drink at home. I canno' wait to go back, an' 'ave a pint."

"Well, maybe you could take us to Trahllen after we've finished our business in Tamor?" Sarentha sounded hopeful. He had never imagined an entire city built into a mountain before.

In response, Thurzin turned and opened up the chest strapped to his horse. He pulled out the wire-wrapped emeralds, and looked through them briefly. He also pulled a two-foot long metal cylinder from the chest. The silvery metal glinted in the sun; Thurzin looked over it quizzically, before putting it back. Sarentha was about to ask about the strange object when Thurzin finally answered his earlier question. "I do think I'll be headin' back home after our stop in Tamor, but I doubt that's where Winston'll be sendin' you lot. I heard 'im mentionin' a tree or some such, an' there ain't no trees in Trahllen! I do know Foodle flew o'er our mountain home when 'e was makin' 'is map abou' twenty years ago, or so. Damn near shot the stupid gnome outta the sky! Thought maybe it was a damn dragon comin' t' finish the job."

"Dragon!?" the other three all chorused as one. Eliza said, "But dragons are just a myth!"

Thurzin's face went dark and he turned away. "Aye, dragon, wyrm, drake. Three words meanin' the same thing. A couple o' centuries ago the damn things came callin'. They made a right mess, too, but ain't no force can break into a dwarven hold when the dwarves inside don't mean to be lettin' 'em in! They left after a while, but we worried they'd be back t' try t' take the mountain. Seems they're content so long as we be stayin' in there, though."

Eliza asked, "Well, what would dragons do if they found you out of the mountain?"

Thurzin nodded gravely. "I've asked the same question many o' time, young lass. I just have t' hope they be as stupid as I think they are, and just think I be from Khrymyre. I need t' be real sneaky on me way out o' the city, and on me way t' the mountain. If any dragon saw me headin' out that way, I might ne'er come back, if ye know what I mean."

"So there are real dragons near Khrymyre?" Eliza asked,

wonderingly.

"Aye," Thurzin answered. "There be all manner o' beasties between 'ere and there. But enough abou' that. How'd ye like t' hear some stories o' goblin smashin' in the deep holes beneath me lovely hometown, or perhaps a tale or two from the good book o' Throkden?"

"Smashing," Sarentha said, at the same time Eliza said, "I have not heard of this book you speak of." Eliza's imperious glare humbled Sarentha and he said nothing. The trip had just begun and he did not want to get on Eliza's bad side.

Thurzin chortled at the exchange and reached into his saddle bag to take out a worn and battered volume. *Holy Book* was written on the outside cover in faded gold letters. Thurzin tossed it to Eliza. "It be the holiest text from Trahllen's first king, Throkden. Before then, our stories were only passed down orally, as all them in tha' book still are. But the king felt the stories be too important t' be leavin' up t' memory, so he got the Archclerics o' the time t' put the most important ones down on stone. O' course, carryin' around chunks o' stone ain't too practical, so they eventually been transferred t' parchment. But the original stone version still sits in Trahllen."

"I never had much use for religion," Sarentha said, looking skeptically from the dwarf to the book.

"Every dwarf be religious," Thurzin said with confidence. "We be faithful t' the first dwarves. Why, we even named our finest metal, Adamantium, after the two of 'em. Adaman, the first dwarf, and Tium, the first dwarm. Ye can read about 'em in the first few pages o' the book. Got tricked into talkin' t' a giant by a wyrm an' were kicked out o' paradise. Fyuhrllhen. None's e'er found the old halls o' Fyuhrllhen since."

Eliza flipped the cover over and read aloud the Decree that was written on the first page. "'Work with love, and love to work.' This is the rule that dwarves live by?"

"Aye, The Mithril Rule," Thurzin said, nodding sagely. "Ol' Throkden 'imself climbed up the craggy trail o' the Black Peaks t' the south t' meet Adaman's ghost an' learn the foundation o' what it means t' be a dwarf. Dwarven clerics used t' 'ave pilgrimages t' the Black Peaks long before I was born. But after the world trembled, none's been able t' get back. They've since been renamed the Terror Peaks, on account o' people sayin' they be cursed. It's a true pity, since them mountains were considered our holiest grounds, even if the black stone was no good fer craftin' or minin'. Anyway, as fer the Decree, if ye stick t' yer work, an' love what ye do, ye'll ne'er need t' stray t' darker things. Ye'll ne'er find harder workers than us dwarves, on account o' that Decree."

"And what is your job?" Sarentha asked, trying hard to picture Thurzin wielding a hammer and working over a forge.

"Fightin'," Thurzin said, winking. "An' ye better believe I love me work!"

"Our religions have creation myths, too," Thomas said.

At the orphanage they had been required to study the various deities, and their own accounts of how everything had begun. Sarentha had never before heard a story where dwarves were created first.

Thurzin's brow dropped menacingly. "Ain't no myth, lad. Them stories 'ave been passed down since the first dwarves, an' they hold true. Don't ye be doubtin' it. Ye humans may 'ave made up some young pup gods that can't be helpin' ye, but dwarf clerics can summon up the power o' the first dwarves strong enough t' bury ye quick."

Eliza, who was reading the first few verses, broke in, "I have not gotten to the first dwarves yet, but I do not understand why you do not worship these first gods or the titans they created. Certainly they must be more powerful than the first dwarves."

"Aye, an' perhaps they be, but we dwarves ain't ne'er heard nothin' from 'em. Back when dwarves started prayin', it was Adaman himself who came t' answer our needs. Nearer the end o' the book there be a section about a war tha' shook the very foundation o' the world. The clerics said Adaman warned 'em t' stay in their new homes deep in the mountain, an' he'd keep 'em safe from the Gods' War. Ne'er went into much detail about it, but Adaman kept 'is word, an' the dwarves stayed safe enough. It might be that war is the reason ye humans ne'er hear nothin' from no gods. Or maybe the titan that created ye just ain't that interested in ye."

Sarentha wisely kept his doubts to himself. The idea of being magically created by some unknown higher power sounded like the stuff of children's stories, and the dwarf's unshakable faith was not about to convert him.

Eliza read until the book turned into a genealogy of dwarves and closed the cover. "So from what I see the dwarves have included humans and elves in their creation story. But what about halflings and gnomes?"

"Ye didn' read far enough," Thurzin said with a small chuckle. "I wouldn' recommend it, neither. Yer eyes'd go crossed after a few more pages, I'd be guessin'. I'll just spoil the story for ye and tell ye. The dwarves passed down stories o' Fyuhrllhen, which means First Home. One day they decided t' dig into the mountains t' try t' find it again. They dug an' they dug. They got pretty deep, too! But then the strangest thing happened. A third o' the dwarves grew small, weak and insane. Them be the gnomes. 'Course they weren't actually insane, but dwarves didn' know no better back then. Another third got bigger, tougher and angrier. Them be the dwarves ye'll meet these days. The other third got small, weak and greedy. Them be the halflings. There be some debate as t' what happened at that point. Some say the three groups tried t' keep workin' together t' find the First Home, an' as they continued diggin', they split off again into goblins, orcs, an' ogres. At that point, there weren't no way diggin' would get it done, an' the whole project got scrapped. Others think we were all given different ways o' talkin', an' none o' us could understand the others. Unable t' work together, everybody just stopped diggin'."

Sarentha slyly asked, "Well, where does that second group say the goblins, orcs, and ogres come from then?" He continued half-seriously, "And now that there is a common language, why don't the gnomes, halflings, and dwarves start up where they left off?"

Thurzin laid a dark glare on Sarentha for a moment before turning in his saddle back toward the road. The dwarf reached into a saddlebag and pulled out a sack of nuts and dried fruit, chewing slowly before speaking again. "Enough about the Good Book. How about I tell ye all some o' me personal adventures in the deep caves near me home o' Trahllen? Wherever them green-skinned uglies came from, I've done me fair share o' smashin' 'em back t' their creator!"

Following his example, the three friends also took out the food and flasks of water that had been packed for them back at the Winston manor. They all sat back in their saddles, relaxed, and listened to Thurzin's wild tales while they rode.

Chapter 6: Tamor

"An' that's how I got this 'ere dent in me helmet," Thurzin finished. The sun was starting to set, shadows were lengthening, and the forest trail was growing darker; for some of the forest creatures, it was their time to scurry about in a hunt for sleeping prey. Thomas had lost his appetite early on in the story-telling, for Thurzin was beyond gruesome in his recall of every single detail of every single battle he had ever taken part in. The dwarf seemed to have a story for each dent, notch, and scratch in his gear. Even the horse had war stories to make seasoned soldiers seem like green recruits.

"How many years have you been fighting?" Sarentha asked in exasperation, while pulling on a piece of smoked jerky.

"Oh, about two hundred an' forty years now, I think," Thurzin said, scrunching up his face in thought. "Let's see. I was only twenty-three, I think, when me father took me out t' kill them rodents in the south halls. Aye, about two hundred an' forty years."

Thomas stared at the dwarf, who, he thought, looked fairly young, not that he had seen any dwarves before Thurzin. But there was not one strand of grey in the dwarf's thick black beard. "I had no idea dwarves lived so long!"

"Well, most would be old an' feeble by me age," Thurzin admitted, winking. "But I got a secret t' keep me young an' kickin'!"

"Let me guess," Sarentha said sardonically, "The same liquid you use to clean up oily messes, put babies to sleep, light fires, kill goblins, and get drunk with."

Thurzin released a belly laugh that was far too loud for the quiet woods. "Nay, but I'm glad ye've been keepin' count on some o' the wondrous uses fer dwarven ale! Nay, I be keepin' a wizard as a friend. Ol' Ramar Wettias, who ye'll find in Tamor, has been brewin' me this concoction fer a while now. We been friends fer a long, long time. 'e wandered 'is way into our mountain with a group 'o adventurers lookin' fer mithril dust. No doubt they weren't ready fer what was in them caves. Lucky fer Ramar I happened t' be in the area an' knew a thing or two about fellin' a mountain troll. Can ye imagin' goin' into a cave with a mountain troll, an' not havin' any ale t' light on fire t' kill it with? Fools! Anyway, after I saved the scrawny wizard's hide, 'e said 'e owed me 'is life. 'e cast a spell that bound us together as e'erlastin' friends. He can brew this concoction that extends life unnaturally. Works like a charm, too! 'Course, a couple hundred years ago 'e fergot me, but 'is magical oath held, and 'e still makes me the brew t' this day. Pity 'e don't remember that scrap with the troll, though."

"Did the potion do something to his memory?" Sarentha asked.

"Nay." Thurzin continued in soft undertones to Sarentha, "'Twas somethin' much more sinister an' menacin'." His countenance suddenly brightened, he looked up, and pointed ahead. "There we go, the gates 'o Tamor at last. We'll find ye a good tavern fer the night, an' tomorrow ye can meet the cartographer. Might be that I'll introduce ye to old Ramar, too! But don't be tellin' 'im I told ye that story about 'im! I just remembered it's a secret."

The three smiled a promise. Thurzin turned and muttered just loud enough for Thomas to overhear, "At least I didn' tell ye the most *important* part."

Outside the gate the light of torches showed off the imposing, high stone walls and lofty wooden drawbridge. A small stone guardhouse stood on the outside of the wall. Light poured from the windows, illuminating the road for the approaching travellers. Two guards could be seen inside, eating dinner at a table. A third stood guard and eyed the newcomers warily. Travellers from Whampello were rare, especially at night. Not many had the nerve to venture down the dark road.

"Thurzin Trollbane o' Khrymyre, seekin' t' enter the Grand Streets o' Tamor," Thurzin trumpeted, reining his horse to a stop. He muttered more quietly, "Grand in the scale o' their filth, anyway, ye dirty ground dwellers. Errr, no offence meant to ye three, o' course."

"Welcome, friend Thurzin," came the hesitant reply from the guard. "You come late this night. What business do you bring?"

"I be here t' be seein' Ramar, errr, the Wizard Wettias. An' these three be here t' be lookin' t' buy a map."

The guard appeared skeptical. "Three of them for one map?"

"They are my protectors," Eliza chimed in, flashing a smile to the guard. "I never travel anywhere without them."

The guard peered in the darkness and nodded his head. "Normally I'd say such protection wasn't necessary on the road, but these are strange times."

"Problems in Tamor?" Thurzin inquired casually.

"Strange disappearances," the guard confirmed. "Nobles and politicians have been leaving the city and not returning when scheduled. Don't get me wrong, many remain, but it is odd that the missing are of higher station."

Thurzin muttered a soft curse into his beard, but nodded. "Aye? Ye don't say! Well, seein' as we're not no noble family o' Tamor, shouldn't be no bother t' us then, eh? If anythin', ye should be glad we be bringin' a noble lady from Whampello t' yer city."

"I suppose," the guard answered, motioning the guards to open the iron portcullis that barred the way. "At any rate, I hope you enjoy your stay, Master Dwarf. And you as well," he added hastily, bowing his head to Eliza and her companions.

The horses' hooves clopped loudly across the drawbridge as they entered the city. Inside, one- and two-storey stone buildings lined a street barely wide enough for two carts to run side by side. The buildings were crammed together with only very narrow alleyways between every fifth or sixth structure. The second storeys jutted out slightly overhead, giving Thomas the feeling of being loomed over. Every second lamp along the street was lit, giving them enough light to find their way. Periodically they passed a patrol of city guards.

"Now," Thurzin said in a whisper, watching a troop of guards move out of sight. "Don't any o' ye go snoopin' into the missin' nobles thing. It ain't none o' yer damn business. Ye're here fer a map, an' that's that. I'll be pinnin' one o' Ramar's boys on ye, t' be makin' sure ye're not pokin' yer noses where they don't belong, ye understand?"

The three nodded obediently, and Thurzin looked away, satisfied. "I be headin' t' the middle o' town, t' the wizard's tower. It's a big ol' metal monstrosity, if ye're needin' me. Ye can't miss the bloody thing. It ain't far from the cartographer's place, neither. But fer tonight, ye can stay at the Purple Potion

Inn, right o'er there." Thurzin nodded his head again, and turned to them. "I'll be takin' me leave now. Ramar hasn't the patience fer lateness, an' it already be late enough!"

"Thank you for sharing the road with us," Thomas said. At the inn door, a young lad stifled a yawn with his fist, and held out his hand for the horses. Without another word, the dwarf and his broad little mare plodded away.

The Purple Potion Inn was quaint. A picture of a bubbling potion hung over the doorway, though the purple had long since faded to grey. Inside, the common room was quiet, with the fire burning low, and only a few people still awake and drinking. A thin man with a pointed beard and long moustache greeted them quietly at the bar, which he was wiping with a towel. "Welcome to the Purple Potion. It's late. You must be looking for a room."

"Two rooms, please," Eliza corrected. "One for me, and one for my companions."

"Very well, miss. That'll be a gold coin, please." Seeing Eliza's shocked expression, the man said, "Prices here have gone up lately, on account of the missing aristocrats. There are rumours, people are muttering things, wondering where the nobles are off to. We haven't been getting much business lately."

Eliza nodded, and handed over a coin in exchange for two brass keys.

The trio headed up the stairs to a narrow hallway with several rooms on either side. Thomas and Sarentha bade Eliza good night, entered their cramped quarters, and looked at their two small beds. It was obvious that Sarentha was not thinking about sleep. "Why would the dwarf tell us not to go snooping around unless he actually wanted us to?"

Thomas frowned. He had a feeling what was coming. "Maybe

it's none of our business. We are here for a map, and then we're leaving. I'm sure if it is important, the king will have his own men looking into the issue."

Thomas lay down on the bed, stretching his weary muscles, but Sarentha paced back and forth as best he could in the small room. "It feels like another adventure, don't you think? There's this great unanswered question before us, and you just want to sleep?"

Thomas nodded, weary from the ride to Tamor, and Sarentha frowned. "If nobles are leaving, perhaps they have left with their guards! Think of it, Thomas! We could find some empty noble's house and—"

"We're not here to rob anyone," Thomas said quickly. "Besides, you heard what Thurzin said. He's assigning someone to watch us."

"I'm going to check things out," Sarentha stated stubbornly. "I can't just leave without trying to find out what I can. If I leave now, Thurzin won't have had time to set his guard on us yet."

Thomas removed his riding clothes and tossed them on the lone stool in the corner. He crawled under the sheet and fluffed the flat pillow. It was not long before his snoring filled the air.

Determined not to let Thomas dampen his adventurous spirit, Sarentha quietly opened the door and left. He slipped softly out of the inn, and into the night streets. Standing out in the cool night air, he realized he had no idea where in Tamor the nobles lived. Tamor was easily ten times the size of Whampello.

Nevertheless, he hastened in the direction that Thurzin had gone earlier. His feet padded soundlessly over the cobblestones. Keeping to the shadows, he narrowly escaped being seen by a passing patrol. The guards in the unit were quiet, their eyes moving slowly and methodically over the streets, looking for signs of trouble. Sarentha grinned to himself after they moved past without noticing him.

Sarentha sprinted down the road and came to an open square with merchant stands closed for the night. A raised platform surrounded a fountain spouting water high up into the air. Sarentha paused, his gaze falling on a high stone ring wall. Standing atop the ring was a sculpture portraying a human, elf, dwarf, halfling, and gnome linking hands and gazing skywards, smiles etched into their faces. Sarentha could not decide whether they were gazing with rapture at the heavens, or simply overjoyed in their unity. He did not notice the person behind him, until a hand grasped his shoulder and pulled him backwards into the shadows. A gloved hand covered his mouth before he could make a sound.

Sarentha's eyes widened to see another patrol enter the square and check the market stalls. Once they were sure everything was as it should be, the patrol moved on. The grip on Sarentha's shoulder relaxed. He stepped away from his captor, and his hand moved to his belt for his dagger. Instead, the stranger held the dagger up in the light, examining it curiously. "Average blade for an average troublemaker," a man's voice spoke from the darkness under a brown hood. He tossed the dagger up and down a few times before handing it, handle first, back to Sarentha. "I don't recognize you. What are you doing trespassing in my neighbourhood?"

Sarentha took back the dagger and kept it ready in his hand. He did not like the man's tone. "Just looking around. I'm new here. I'm from Whampello."

The other man snorted. "That explains the smell, then. We

A Noble's Quest

don't get many visitors from that little hole in the ground. What are you doing here?"

"Sight-seeing," Sarentha lied. "I've always heard about how grand the city is. I thought I'd come see it for myself."

"It looks better in the day-time," the man said with a chuckle. "So, were you looking to loot the stalls? They're locked up tight. There's never anything of worth left in them anyway. Can't imagine why not," the stranger said in a snide tone.

"Rupert, is that you?" Another figure emerged from the dark, gripped the first man and spun him around so hard he stumbled. "Ah, why don't you move on out of here? Leave this one alone. I'll make sure he's not worth your time."

Without another word Rupert was gone, running for a dark alley. Sarentha turned to this newest stranger, a tall man with long brown curls hanging down to his shoulders. The man's pale eyes examined him. "Sarentha? You must be Sarentha. You fit the dwarf's description of a 'roguish country bumpkin' perfectly. Old Thurzin certainly does have an eye for detail."

Sarentha straightened and tried to look dignified. "And you are?"

"Where are my manners?" The man nodded curtly. "Richard Winston, here to escort you back to your room, where you will remain."

"Winston?" Sarentha looked harder at the face, and noticed the family resemblance. "You're related to Lord Winston of Whampello?"

"His son," Richard answered, opening his cloak to reveal a long sword bearing the family crest on the hilt. "He sent me here a few years ago to train with the guard. Very boring, and not for me. Wizard Wettias intervened with an offer to relieve the tedium.

And now here I am, doing surveillance on the door of an inn. But the job has its rewards. I certainly never would have learned magic with the city guard."

Sarentha's eyes flashed with longing at the thought of learning magic. The men exchanged a long look, and Sarentha's mind raced as he tried to think of a way out of the situation. "Well," he said, "you don't need to worry about me. I'm just looking around. I've heard there have been some disappearances."

"Oh, don't you be concerned about that," Richard said, his chain-clad hand shooting out to grip Sarentha's shoulder tightly and turn him back toward the inn. "It's been nice travelling weather lately. A few of the noble families have decided to tour the countryside, and some are checking on their holdings in other cities."

Sarentha's eyebrows rose. "Really? Because I got the feeling people were uneasy."

"It's nothing," Richard insisted, more forcefully this time. "You know, you're quite sneaky for an unknown. People like you tend to be snatched up pretty quickly. It'd be a shame to waste your talent. I wouldn't be surprised if Rupert was looking to take you in."

"Well, I already work for your father," Sarentha said loyally.

"I am referring to darker markets," Richard said smoothly. "I was watching the inn door before you left. I also had my eye on a comely young woman in a guard patrol, so you're lucky I noticed you leave. Rupert is not kind to little thieves entering into his domain. I don't *think* he's ever killed anyone for it, but I can't be certain. He belongs to a thieves' guild – very unsavoury types. You would do much better falling in with Wizard Wettias' crowd."

Curious, Sarentha turned, but Richard's hand was on his back and kept him moving. "Not now, of course, since you're working for my father. But if a time comes when you are no longer under his heel, you might consider doing something a little more interesting. The pay is quite good, and you get amusing little assignments like skulking around in the wee hours, herding young would-be adventurers."

"Hey, now–"

"Here we are," Richard said. They rounded a corner and stopped at the entrance of the Purple Potion Inn. "Seriously though, I'll mention you to Wettias, and see what he thinks. He's always looking for new recruits to his little band of misfits. Those are his words, not mine. We are a diverse group, although small, and are quite capable of handling ourselves in tricky situations. Think on it. Now, head back to your room. I'll be keeping a much better watch this time, and if I see you wandering about again, I will be far less gentle."

Without a sound, Richard disappeared before Sarentha's eyes. The place where he had been standing was empty. Sarentha noticed another patrol moving his way, and decided it would be best to heed the advice of Lord Winston's mysterious son. Quietly he returned to his room. Crawling under the sheets, he reflected on the goings-on of the night. A thieves' guild, and a strange group hired by a wizard: Sarentha was intrigued. But he had not really learned anything about the nobles. He did not for a moment believe Richard's story about them going away for mere pleasure. If that was the case, people would not be emanating this worry and suspicion in their voices.

Something was going on in Tamor, of that Sarentha was certain. But what could it be? With mystery on his mind, Sarentha drifted off to dreams of dark alleys and pockets full of gold.

Chapter 7: Cartography

Sarentha woke the next morning to the sound of Eliza rapping at their door. Thomas, already up and dressed, accompanied her down to the tavern for some breakfast. Sarentha leaped out of bed. He had expected to be tired after the long ride and his late-night wanderings, but found instead that he was brimming with energy.

From the small window, he could see the morning mist rising from the grass, making Tamor look like a city built on clouds. Robins and larks sang in the few trees lining the streets, and from his vantage point he spotted several early merchants wheeling carts of all manner of goods out to the square. While most were bringing in produce from outlying farms, other wagons carried furniture, weapons, armour, jewellery, clothing, children's toys, and marble, brass, and glass knickknacks.

With a splash of water on his face and a quick comb of his fingers through his unruly hair, Sarentha was dressed and ready to go. He practically flew down the stairs to find Eliza and Thomas chatting at their table. A young woman about his age came and took his order, and when he turned back to his companions he wished he had not. Eliza was staring daggers at him, her fingers drumming on a piece of paper covered with a flowing script and the seal of Wizard Wettias.

He was reluctant to ask, but had no time to consider his options because Eliza spoke first. "Find anything interesting last night?" She pushed the paper across to him, and Sarentha read the words from Eliza's cousin describing Sarentha's roving during the night prior.

Sarentha frowned in thought. It would be hard to explain his way out of this one. Thomas kindly interrupted, "I was hungry, but the kitchen was closed. He just went out to see if he could find a bite of food for us."

Eliza harrumphed and snatched the note back, folding and tucking it in her satchel. "Next time ask first, since I am in charge here."

"*You're* in charge?" Thomas and Sarentha asked together.

"Of course I am," she replied briskly, her look daring them to argue. "You two are *my* bodyguards, after all. That obviously places me in charge, since you are just the hired help. I hope you remember that in the future so I can avoid receiving mocking notes from my troublesome cousin. I can see him in my mind sitting back and howling with laughter that my *underlings* do not know how to listen to simple instructions."

A tense moment of silence passed between them, but Sarentha could not find a way around her logic. Finally he asked, "Okay, so what's the plan for today, *boss*?"

Unfazed by the sarcasm, Eliza smiled and received her title at face value. "The cartographer is located near the merchant's square. We will head there after breakfast, purchase the map, and find this tree Uncle Erwin is so interested in. I imagine we will be back in Whampello before dark, and then you two can be on your way."

Three mugs of water were placed on the table. Thomas took a swallow while Sarentha reflected, "Well, so far these jobs for your uncle seem pretty easy and pay extremely well. After we find this tree, I'm not about to disappear from our lordly employer. He may have more money to throw our way."

"Well, come or go, I cannot imagine you will ever work for me again after Uncle Erwin sees how careless you were, walking the streets alone at night. You cannot guard me if you are thrown in jail for ignoring the city's curfew, Sarentha."

"Curfew? Well no one told–"

"Sarentha?" a ragged male voice spoke from behind him.

"Yeah," Sarentha said, thankful for the distraction. Too late, Eliza's and Thomas' startled and puzzled faces told him something was wrong. Sarentha spun around out of his seat a second before a thunderous boom sounded from behind his chair. The chair's back board splintered apart, and Sarentha saw smoke emerging from a strange metal cylinder held by a scruffy stranger and aimed at his back. The other pair of patrons screamed and ducked for cover while the waitress ran for the door to alert the city guards. The stranger cursed and stepped backwards, trying to adjust the tube. Thomas hurled his pottery mug at the stranger, hitting him square on his crooked nose.

The man cursed again, dropping the strange weapon and clutching his bloodied nose. In an instant, Thomas had followed the mug right over the table and tackled the stocky man to the floor, his fists smashing where the mug had hit. Eliza was beside him after two slugs and clutched at an arm, trying to restrain Thomas. Sarentha, shaking away his daze, caught the other arm just as Thomas was readying for another swing.

Pulling Thomas away, they could see the stranger was unconscious. Blood ran from his nose and mouth, and his long brown wool coat lay splayed open. Thomas shook off his companions, but did not continue his assault. His protective instincts settled when the attacker was no longer a threat.

"What in the hells was that?" Sarentha paled, surveying the

damaged chair, thinking about what his back could have looked like had he stayed there.

"A sort of musket?" Eliza responded, picking up the still warm handgun and examining it, before handing it over toward the shocked innkeeper. She checked the assailant's pockets for any sort of clue, and found a folded note. "The weapon is gnomish, I think. They are extremely rare, and I cannot imagine why someone with the wealth to purchase one would bother using it on the likes of you." She noted the hurt look on his face, and added, "No offence."

"None taken," Sarentha replied sardonically. "And I honestly have no idea why anyone would want to use something like that on me, either. I don't have any enemies that I know of." His thoughts went to Rupert of the night before, but he could not believe that this man he had met once would send a hit man for him. His desire to explore more of Tamor suddenly faded.

Eliza unfolded the note and skimmed it. "Do you two know someone named Frank Grimbling?"

Thomas and Sarentha stared wide-eyed at each other.

"Actually, that name sounds familiar," she said, folding up the note. "Does he not own a lumber…" Eliza noted her companions' frightened expressions. "You know him, then."

"He was our employer," Sarentha squeaked.

"If he gets word that this assassination failed, he will probably send another," Eliza deduced. "The note is quite explicit. You must have angered him greatly."

"I killed his son," Thomas whispered. "I sort of blacked out in a rage when he assaulted Sarentha."

"Well, I think we should get out of here, and catch up on our meal later," Eliza said.

Thomas nodded in agreement, and Sarentha said, "Attempted murder *does* cut a fellow's appetite. Let's go."

The trio walked away and soon noticed guards entering the tavern, summoned perhaps to investigate the explosion. The companions increased their pace, knowing they would be unable to explain the reason for the attack. Besides, if they were searched, how could they explain a purse full of money and gems, or Eliza's private letters from Lord Erwin and Richard Winston, or the note from Frank Grimbling.

The streets were quiet, with only a handful of people going about their early morning business. Farmers were selling eggs, fresh milk and cheeses, and a variety of vegetables and fruits in their stalls. Some merchants were unravelling fabric rolls to display small weapons, jewellery, or flashy trinkets. Eliza pointed to a sign over a nearby doorway that said "Winkle's Maps," and the three companions made their way there. Before they could enter, a large burly green-skinned orc barred the way, his hands hidden in the wide sleeves of a deep-red robe. Two small tusks jutted up from his bottom row of sharp teeth, and he wore a gold hoop pierced through his left nostril. His head was shaved bald to reveal a scar running from the top of his cranium down to his right cheek. Amidst the farmers and merchants in the square, he most definitely stood out, so tall that even Thomas had to look up at him.

"Sarentha," the orc said fluidly.

"I have a feeling I'm going to start hating the sound of my own name," Sarentha muttered, his hands moving cautiously toward his hidden daggers.

"Are you injured?" the orc asked.

The question gave him pause, his look turning to one of

curiosity. "Umm, no," he replied.

Nodding, the orc pointed toward the inn. "Good. From afar, I saw the assassin entering the Purple Potion Inn. I heard the explosion and was terribly worried. Richard had alerted me of possible trouble, but I was too late to stop him."

Eliza shot Sarentha a knowing look, which he ignored. "Well, it was nice of Richard to spread the news so liberally."

The orc was not listening, instead surveying the area looking for anyone suspicious. "I forget myself. My name is Feng, and I am a wizard studying at the tower. Your safety has been made a priority by Wizard Wettias. I will stand guard while you procure your map, and I will then escort you out of the city. No one else will interfere while I am with you."

The certainty behind Feng's claim helped to settle Sarentha's frayed nerves. He had never felt so jumpy in all his life, but having a big orc on their side made him feel much safer. Wordlessly, Feng stepped aside and motioned for them to enter.

The interior of the shop was unlike anything Sarentha had ever seen, covered from floor to ceiling with dusty shelves containing all variety of maps, protective tubes, reams of blank paper, quills, coloured inks, and bizarre mechanical gadgets with directional gears and knobs. A narrow path meandered through the chaos to a small desk, where they could glimpse a shiny bald head bobbing up and down. The shopkeeper whistled a merry tune while he worked.

Eliza stepped forward and coughed lightly, to no response. The whistling continued. Eliza said, "Excuse me? I am looking to purchase a map."

The head did not rise any higher, but a wrinkled round face tilted to look up at the three customers. The little gnome grinned and his eyes squinted behind too-large glasses. "Oh, hello! I'm Theodonious Winkle! I didn't hear you come in. Strange, as I have such sharp hearing. Are you here to buy a map?"

Eliza nodded, about to point out that she had already said as much when the little gnome slapped a tube down on the counter. "Only three gold pieces will get you this amazing map of Tamor's hot spots! You can find all the celebrities on here!" The little gnome opened a tiny hand for payment.

Eliza frowned, not having expected the sales pitch. "No, I do not want that map. I have a specific–"

"Huh? You don't want a map?" Theodonious looked confused. "Didn't you say you were looking for one? Well, I guess not. If you're not looking for a map, how about a trusty compass? They're great for getting you where you need to go!" The proffered map disappeared behind the counter and was replaced by a little round device with the letter N scratched into it.

Visibly reining in her ire, Eliza said, "No, I do want *a* map! Just not that one–"

"You don't want that one, either, eh?" The compass disappeared, and a large blank parchment with an ink pot appeared. "You say you wanted to make a map? Here you go! It's a steal for a single gold piece!"

"No," Thomas finally broke in. "We're looking for a *specific* map!"

"Well why didn't she just say so?" The little gnome tucked away his wares. "What map are you looking for then? I have them all!"

Eliza leaned forward and whispered, "The map of Foodle."

"Poodle?" Theodonious looked terribly perplexed. "You're looking for the dog sanctuary across town. I don't have any poodles. I sell maps!"

"*Foodle*," Eliza hissed.

"Do you mean Mitzy?" Theodonious asked, his look of bewilderment giving way to recollection. "Well yes, I did have a poodle named Mitzy back quite a few years ago now. She wasn't mine, mind you. She was my wife's, bless her soul."

"Foodle is what she said, sir," Thomas tried again.

"Are you sure she said Foodle? I heard her say Poodle! Tell me dear – actually, best if you just nod or shake your head. Do you have any elven in you?"

Eliza looked quizzical, but nodded her head slowly. "I am half elven. My father is an elf."

They were not sure whether Theodonious understood, but he nodded in response and cut in, "That would do it. You have an elvish accent, which I have a devilish time comprehending. That makes sense. No offence to you, but I'll just talk to your full human companion here." He turned his attention back to Thomas, and leaned forward with a gleam in his eyes. "So, you want the map of Foodle, eh? Are you here for that Winston fellow out of Whampello? I had a gnome in here the other day trying to get a look at it. I gave him enough of a peek to see it's the genuine article, but no more!"

"Yes, we're here to purchase it," Thomas said.

Theodonious beamed. "Very well, that will be five hundred gold coins."

Sarentha choked and dropped the compass he had been playing with. Thomas paled. Eliza calmly lifted her bag over the counter, pulled the drawstring, and spilled out the contents. Golden coins and precious stones dropped from within, which the gnome promptly scooped up, closely examining each piece.

After a few minutes of counting and calculating, Theodonious nodded. "Would you like change? This is rather more than I've asked for, I believe."

Eliza shook her head, and the gnome bowed graciously. "Well, at least let me throw in some extra paper and an ink pot. Maybe you'll bring back a grand map like old Foodle one day, and I'll pay you some of these coins back if it's something I've not seen before."

Two tubes and an ink pot appeared on the desk. The first tube contained blank paper and the second, the Map of Foodle. Theodonious said, "Thank you, have a good day!" His head bent down again, and he returned to his whistling and his work.

The trio exited the shop with Eliza carrying their new purchases. Feng greeted them, and led the way toward the eastern city gate closest to Whampello.

"I didn't know you were half-elven," Thomas said to Eliza while they walked. Morning shoppers were arriving for the freshest goods, and the square was steadily growing louder with shouts of merchants touting their wares.

Eliza shrugged. "It usually does not come up. My father was living in our manor, working with my grandfather. He fell in love with my mother, and I was the result. He told me the elven elders gave him an ultimatum of staying with my mother and me, thus losing his long elven lifespan, or returning to the elven lands of the north. I was only eight years old at the time, and was devastated to lose my father. It broke my mother's heart when he left. She was never happy again. That sort of sorrow takes a toll on someone. Her only request before she died was that Uncle Erwin take care of me. She left me this crystal dragon from my father. I have worn it around my neck ever since."

Thomas laid his hand gently on hers, with a kind look.

"I did not mean to upset you," Eliza said, gently removing herself from his touch. "It was long ago, and I have grown stronger from my circumstances. I learned to be self-sufficient, for although others might come and go in my life, I need to be able to fend for myself."

"I could smell the elf in you," Feng stated plainly, his eyes roaming over the crowd. "I honestly don't know how you humans survive with such poor senses."

"Speaking of races," Sarentha interrupted. "I have never seen nor heard of an orc being in civilized lands before. How did you come to be in Tamor, Feng?"

Feng smiled wistfully, baring rows of sharp teeth. His long strides and wide frame caused people to jump out of his way. "Wizard Wettias found me several years ago. I had become separated from my tribe during my rite of passage into adulthood. After fasting for two full days, I had a vision of a tall metal tower. After, as I was trying to return to my clan, I became disoriented and lost. Wizard Wettias was gathering wild herbs for his potions when he came across me stumbling through the woods. Imagine my wonder when he led me to the same metal tower I saw in my vision. He took me in until I could gather my strength, and since that moment, I have learned magic with Wizard Wettias. I think he is unsettled by my ability, but I'm not sure why. He accidentally calls me by another name on occasion, but when I ask him about it, he grows confused. Wizard Wettias is brilliant, but sadly his mind becomes a bit addled at times."

Eliza asked, "And what has Wizard Wettias called you?"

"Shump. Also, he has called me Wizard Imsh. He seems to think both names belong to the same person, just as he is sometimes called Ramar, and sometimes Wizard Wettias. But he cannot remember the origin of the name, and can summon no image of the wizard to whom it may refer. Shump Imsh certainly sounds like an orcish name, but I do not know it. If I could have found my tribe, perhaps the elders could have solved the riddle. But my people are nomadic. When I returned to where I had left them last, they were gone. I fear I may never see my tribe again." Feng paused before apologizing, "I'm sorry, I'm not usually this talkative. Here we are at the city gate, and none of you have had a chance to say much."

"Think nothing of it," Eliza assured him, placing her small hand on Feng's thick forearm. "It was a pleasure to meet you and hear your story. I hope we will meet again."

"You are too kind, Lady Eliza," Feng responded, bowing his head slightly. "Safe travels to you all, and may fortune be on your side." When he finished speaking, he vanished from sight.

"I must learn how to do that," Sarentha breathed, looking around in wonder. He moved his hand through the space where Feng had been, but it was empty.

"Come on," Eliza said, giving Sarentha a gentle push. "Let's exit the city, look at our new map, and find the tree."

Unlike the previous night, the gates were wide open and unguarded. A few soldiers surveyed the roads and woods from atop the walls, but they seemed at ease. The road to Whampello was empty of travellers, which was not overly surprising. The three companions left the city, ready for adventure.

Chapter 8: Not So Fast

Far away in the wooded city of Amaroh, Pau'sien and her companions attended a gathering where elven elders joined them in the Hall of the Sky. The walls were tall jungle trees growing together to form a ring, broken only by the space that formed the doorway for the elves to enter. The canopy of broad green leaves formed a ceiling high above their heads. Inside the natural halls, the floor was cobbled stone with a bubbling fountain in its centre. Surrounding the fountain, the twelve elders sat down cross-legged and looked up at their young wards.

Pau'sien looked to her left and right making sure Kel'shorie, a renowned warrior, and Shah'lao, a fierce druid were ready. Their travels to the Tamorran Empire had been successful, but Pau'sien waited patiently for Sief, the elves' frail, wise leader, to ask them to speak.

After more than five centuries, Pau'sien still recalled Sief's vivid tales of sights unseen in over two thousand years. She had fled her ancient elven homeland when a foul undead plague devastated the land. She sailed across the sea to found a new sanctuary. None of the elves who had travelled with her still lived. Sief's terrifying memories would show in her haunted eyes whenever she was asked about the distant past. She never spoke of the nightmares that still invaded her sleep, although many elves had overheard her cries in the night. The raging hordes of undead had been gone for nearly one thousand years, but Sief would never forget their howling screams.

After fleeing her homeland, Sief helped found Amaroh, a beautiful organic city. The trees listened to the guidance of druids, also known as Forest Born, to bend their trunks and branches to provide shelter. Some of the trees had been shaped over centuries, and their unnatural twisting bodies were a marvel to behold. It was a testament to the strength of leadership, and harmony of the council that had existed since Amaroh's coming.

Now that the council was convened and prepared to listen to their young wards, Sief lifted a spindly arm, and motioned for the report to begin.

Shah'lao bowed deeply for a moment before straightening. "It is an honour and a privilege to have been chosen in the name of the council. We three thank you for entrusting us with secret passage beyond the boundaries of our people."

The elders nodded their heads slightly in unison, graciously accepting the praise. Finwe, the Raja Forest Born, asked, "And tell us of your travels, my student."

Turning towards his teacher, Shah'lao replied, "My trip to Khrymyre was successful. I found an old dwarf crafter who was sympathetic to our cause. Although his own fires burned out long ago, he assigned his greatest apprentice to reforge Fallia. The shards are without power, but Wizard Wettias will perform the arcane rituals and restore Fallia's song."

Aarti, the leader of the Brahmin caste's wizards, turned her gaze to her pupil, Pau'sien. "Why would you allow a human to imbue an elf's sword?"

Pau'sien bowed very low, her hair touching the stones at her feet. Leaving the sword with Wizard Wettias had been her decision, and Pau'sien hoped her reasoning would convince the elders. She remained bowed and said, "I apologize for making this judgement without first addressing the council, Aarti." She straightened and explained, "I thought that the less we travelled to and from the Tamorran Empire, the better it would be for our cause. I dared not risk detection, and Wizard Wettias was more than willing to offer his aid."

Aarti, about to protest further, was silenced by Sief's raised hand. "Caution is wise," the leader softly advised.

Pau'sien beamed with the compliment, before remembering her place and turning her eyes down humbly. There was silence while those present reflected on Sief's words.

Kel'shorie stepped forth. "Pau'sien and I were welcomed into the home of the human noble, Lord Erwin Winston. We traced the genealogy he requested, and the council will be interested to know that the two chosen men are of the bloodline of heroes. The Wyrmstriker and Strongblade lineages live on."

The council murmured in shock, waves of disbelief passing from elder to elder. All knew of humanity's legendary heroes, and some had even led elven forces to fight alongside Hendricus and Matthew in their cause. More than five centuries later, it was still a contentious point, for many elves had lost their lives. Unlike humans, who had the capacity to replenish their population quickly, elves could not mate as regularly due to their much longer fertility cycles. Thus, their numbers had severely dwindled in the war, and even over five centuries they had not fully recovered.

Pau'sien recalled the stories of that time, where the war's outcome had been preordained by their prophet, Ellie'soushah. Even so, the council had decided they could not sit idly by, and had sent their warriors to offer strength. The elves experienced a schism. Ellie'soushah's followers left the great city of Amaroh and formed their own commune at the northeast jungle's edge, far from the eyes and ears of the council. Since that time, Ellie'soushah had become the elder of his clan, and leader of his commune. It was customary for the most senior elf to drop the given name, for the eldest was believed to be the shining example of all the family stood for. Thus, Ellie'soushah had taken on the name Ellie. Pau'sien had been too young to remember the betrayal, but she knew there were some who blamed the humans for the division. Hearing that the line of heroes remained unbroken was not good news to all gathered before her.

"Lord Winston has requested that the Strongblade be given to his commander, Ben Okar," Kel'shorie finished, when the mutterings subsided.

There was an uproar. The elders demanded to know how Lord Winston had learned of the Strongblade's continued existence. They were outraged that some minor, human noble would make such a presumptuous and unprecedented demand of the elven council.

In the middle of the storm's fury, Sief raised her hand, and the circle was immediately silenced. When a sense of calm had once again settled over the council, Sief lowered her hand and looked up to the three younger elves. "The Strongblade is not to be wielded by just any mortal. The sword was created for the greatest protector of all humanity's hopes and aspirations. I believe that Lord Winston has spoken in haste, without reflecting upon the situation's gravity. To break with tradition and pass Matthew Strongblade's estate to someone not of his lineage would be sacrilegious. Only the heir is worthy. Any other decision would be a breach of nature."

The rest of the council quietly supported their leader's choice, although Pau'sien noted that some faces still held traces of anger. The three young elves bowed their acceptance of the verdict.

Kel'shorie asked, "How should we convince Lord Winston of the error in his judgement? I have no doubt he will be displeased with the council's decision. He views Thomas and Sarentha, because they are mere peasants, as unworthy. Shock was readily apparent on his face when he learned that the blood of heroes ran in their veins."

Sief replied, "Their social status is unimportant. We shall draft a letter to Lord Winston. In it, we will explain our decision, and if he chooses not to honour us, he will not receive the Strongblade. It is that simple. If the lineage of Matthew Strongblade continues to this day, it is very likely that his bloodline will continue for many generations to come. The strength of his ideals will never quietly lie down and die. The sword does not *need* to be dispensed at this time."

Murmured assent once again filled the hall. Sief haltingly rose to her feet. The rest waited until she was fully standing before they too arose.

"May the spirits guide you on your travels back to Lord Winston's home," Sief said to Kel'shorie. She turned to Pau'sien and said, "We will honour Wizard Wettias by allowing him to perform the enchanting of Fallia. Let the ties of our friendship bloom and grow once more. And let our enemies tremble in fear when our alliance once more stands united."

The council of elders was dismissed, and they filed through the opening between the trees. Pau'sien, Kel'shorie, and Shah'lao waited for all to leave before turning and speaking to each other.

"I am envious that you once again are chosen to travel to the human lands, Kel'shorie," Pau'sien said, unable to hide the bitterness in her voice.

Shah'lao smirked. "You might not be later. We will see how well or how badly Lord Winston takes the news that the elves will not bow to his wishes."

"The way Sief speaks of alliances being rekindled, I believe she has faith in Lord Winston's judgements," Kel'shorie mused.

Pau'sien thought back to how animated Lord Winston had become at the idea that elves would determine the fate of mankind's heirlooms. "I just hope the letter they draft is exceptionally diplomatic."

* * * * *

With the map unfurled on the ground, Eliza was having a hard time deciphering Foodle's writings. The sheer size of the map was daunting, but the tiny hand-written notes scrawled over the entire surface made it worse. To the southwest a message read, "I think those little things are dwarves, and I think they are shooting at me!" To the north there was a green blob with a note, "Some strange winds stop me from flying over these woods. Perhaps there is some powerful magic afoot!" To the distant eastern coast another message wondered, "Are those halflings? Are they eating a halfling? Barbaric savages!"

There were dozens of such markings but very little in the way of relevant details. There were numerous names, but no symbols or explanations beside them. There were no indications of what the names might refer to, or where the areas in question were located. Sarentha wondered aloud how anyone could justify calling the paper a map at all.

By persevering, Eliza finally located what Lord Winston's note indicated they must find. She pointed to a poorly drawn tree to the southeast, and read the note, "A golden tree! My, how

A Noble's Quest

beautiful! I wonder if it is real gold? I must return and investigate further in good time." Just south of this, overlapping writings observed, "Strange ruins. The whole town is filled with flowers. I wonder who used to live here? I see carvings in a stone wall that spell 'Cephae.'"

Unfortunately, none of Foodle's questions had been answered. Eliza referred to Lord Winston's note, which included a brief summary of the map's history. According to the note, Foodle returned to Tamor with his entire continental map in hand, and was soon stricken by a strange malady that took his life. His map went missing, presumed destroyed by those who spoke of conspiracies. But these theories proved false when the map resurfaced several years later. Theodonious had purchased a terrible self-portraiture of Foodle at an estate auction, presumably because he enjoyed the dark wood frame. When he removed the painting of the eccentric gnome to make room for a portrait of his dearly departed wife, to his surprise he found the map. Lord Winston noted that it seemed far too coincidental that Theodonious, a map merchant, should stumble upon such a find. Lord Winston surmised that, through some mysterious gnomish connections, Theodonious knew where Foodle's map had been hidden. Clearly, Theodonious was smarter than he appeared.

Some assumed that Foodle had caught a deadly foreign illness during his mapping expeditions, and others whispered that he had been murdered for knowing too much. Whatever the cause, no one dared follow Foodle's map lest it be cursed.

"Cursed?" Thomas sounded uneasy.

"Bah," Sarentha grunted. "There are no such things as curses. This map is a gold mine! Think about it! That gnome gave us paper and ink! I could redo Foodle's map if we went to all the places he described, and make a fortune by putting names to the things he saw. If there are old ruins, there may certainly be clues as to the names of those lost cities, and their inhabitants. We could be rich!"

"Well you can do that on your own time," Eliza moved on. "For now we are only interested in the golden tree. Apparently it is much further than I initially thought. If the scale of this map is right, it is over a week away on foot."

"I don't suppose you have any money left over for horses, after blowing five hundred gold on the map?" Sarentha asked.

Eliza grinned, but shook her head. "We could go back to the Purple Potion for the horses if you are that desperate."

Sarentha paled and shook his head vehemently. "No, walking will be good for us. I'm done with assassins."

Before an hour had passed dark clouds rolled in, and a light rain began to fall. Eliza's mood sank, hearing the nearby rustlings of hawks and fox mingled with the distant howls of timber wolves in an eerie melody of hungry animals. They plodded along through the tall field grasses, each looking distinctly uncomfortable.

When the clouds parted around midday, the trio unrolled their map and took another look.

"How did you figure out how far away the tree is?" Thomas asked, squinting at the squiggly lines.

Eliza sighed and Sarentha piped in, "Well, there's Whampello. And it was about a day's ride from there to Tamor."

Eliza looked down at the map, attempting some quick calculations.

"About seven days," Eliza confirmed, even as Thomas said, "Two days," and Sarentha groaned, "eight days." Eliza looked at the two men and sighed.

Frowning again, she said, "Wait a moment. I forgot. That was a day on horseback. How long would it have taken to walk on foot?"

Again Sarentha groaned, and Eliza's sore feet likewise dreaded the long journey ahead.

"There's a town in the south near the edge of the woods," Thomas offered hopefully, pointing at the map. "Cynil?"

"It's Foodle's home-town, where gnomes live," Eliza said, looking curiously at the note. "I do not understand why he wrote this in gnomish, when the rest of the map is written in the common language of the allied races."

"I wonder what a city of gnomes looks like," Sarentha wondered aloud, gazing into the distance. "If gnomes can make that weapon we saw in the Purple Potion Inn, I'd hate to think what other horrible things they might construct."

"Gnomes are mostly peaceful," Eliza said, folding up their map. After Sarentha's near-death experience, she felt the need to comfort him. "Uncle Erwin says they are a curious bunch, constantly inventing new gadgets. Probably that little musket was made for hunting rodents, until someone imagined using it for much more."

"The thought of a whole town filled with *potentially* deadly inventions doesn't make me feel any safer than a town full of *known* deadly weapons," Sarentha spoke uneasily. Despite surviving the incident, it appeared that his invincible, adventurous spirit had been tamed by the truth of his mortality. "Maybe we should just avoid Cynil."

Eliza agreed, stowed the map, and continued walking. It was not long before the rain returned to dampen her spirits for the long trek still ahead.

The clouds darkened, and the low rumble of distant thunder rolled across the plains. The rain came down harder, and turned into hail. The trio, battered and exhausted, had no choice but to keep moving, when the downpour stopped unexpectedly. They glanced around at the storm still raging everywhere, save the place where they stood.

Eliza looked up to see three horses and a man floating gently down to the ground. The horses were theirs from Whampello, but the man she did not know. His grey robes settled as he alighted, his long light brown hair undisturbed by the rampant rain or winds. When he drew close she noticed strands of grey and white hairs, which complemented his grey eyes. The horses whinnied nervously, but calmed moments after their hooves touched solid earth.

"Sorry for dropping in like this," the wizard said, bowing. "Feng told me you were in a hurry to leave town, and had no time to collect your horses. I thought this would be a good opportunity for us to meet."

In a rare turn of events, Eliza was unsure of what to say. Here was a stranger descending from the sky in the midst of a thunderstorm. How did you greet someone who could do something like that?

"My name is Ramar Wettias," he continued, oblivious to the awkward silence. "Archmage of Tamor. I think Thurzin may have mentioned me."

"Yes," Eliza said, regaining her composure. Despite feeling like a half-drowned sheep, she held herself regally. "It is a pleasure to meet you, Wizard Wettias. I am Eliza Winston, cousin of Richard Winston, and these are my bodyguards Thomas and

Sarentha."

The wizard's face broke into a wide smile. "I thought for such a long journey you might want your horses. I also hoped we could speak briefly."

"How did you – *do* that?" Sarentha spluttered, staring in awe at the sheets of rain pouring down everywhere but on them. Lightning streaked the sky, and thunder boomed.

The wizard wiggled his fingers, saying, "Magic! I have been alive a long time, and possess knowledge of many arcane tricks. Well, it is not all magic, actually. It was quite simple to find three people walking south toward the golden tree."

"Wait," Thomas interrupted, "If you can just fly there, then why did Lord Winston send us?"

"I am rarely unwatched. Indeed," the wizard responded, looking about the storm-raked fields, "even for the short time I am out, my absence may be observed. The king is quite demanding of my time, and prefers to know where I am, always. Apparently he does not trust his wizards to walk around unattended." The wizard's smile faded then. More serious now, he continued, "So I must be brief. This mission that Erwin has sent you on is of the utmost importance and necessarily secret. It may seem but a simple task to retrieve a single tree branch, but for the majority of us who would go in your place this is quite impossible. Powerful preventative forces are at work. Fortunately, Winston has a talent for finding people who suit his needs. I heard your story, Thomas and Sarentha. The inn keeper at the Purple Potion Inn is an old friend. He has been vocal about your alleged assassinations. Sarentha's run-in with Rupert gave us a believable cover, and will not raise alarms. The actual assassin has since been silenced, so there is no one to doubt the claims that he was Rupert's man. In fact, it is said that he killed you both. The forces that overheard your interest in discovering the truth about the missing nobles now believe you to be dead. And Eliza, lamentations of your being waylaid by goblins on the road to Tamor have been spreading through Whampello. Your uncle is currently mourning your loss, and sending Ben and his men out to find your captors. They have been told to bring back bodies from the goblin camp that you all attacked the other day, and then come home to report that they could not find you."

Eliza stood dumbfounded.

Wizard Wettias continued, "So you see there is more at stake here than you three may have realized. You must be cautious in your travels. If certain forces realize that you yet live and are working on a clandestine series of quests to construct the artefact, your lives may come to a sudden and unfortunate end."

Sarentha and Thomas shared a stunned look, while Eliza could not help wonder what this artefact could be. What could be so secret and important for Lord Winston to fake the death of his own niece?

Eliza gulped back her conflicting emotions, and quietly asked, "What will we do with the branch, then?"

"Sarentha, Richard spoke of your stealth," the wizard said, clearly impressed. "You will slip back to the outskirts of Whampello. West of the Winston estate is a small, dense grove of oak trees where Lord Winston will wait for you. Eliza, he said you know the place, as the two of you have picnicked there. Once Lord Winston receives the golden branch, he will send you on your next mission." Ramar noted Eliza's argumentative stance and added, "No, you must remain hidden, Eliza. You are too well known amongst the estate owners, and cannot be caught. It must be Sarentha."

She nodded her consent, although it was not Sarentha's part she was going to fight, but rather another journey. This one was already not going as planned, and she did not relish the idea of further travel.

Ramar looked up and smiled, as though he had not just delivered grim news. "It appears the clouds are breaking. I wish you good speed and ease of travel. I must go. I told King Dalmethias I needed to perform a complex magical experiment to restore my faulty memories, and I am certain he will be expecting my failed results soon. Good luck!"

Without another word, Ramar zipped through the air, his outstretched arms motionless like hawk wings, his robe and hair fluttering wildly as he sped north back to Tamor. The rain had ceased, and the earth and grass squished wetly beneath the travellers' feet when they turned to watch him fade into the distance.

"I need to learn how to do that, too," Sarentha said softly, and Thomas and Eliza nodded in awe. They resumed their journey upon their trusty mounts. Before long, Sarentha spoke again. "I don't like any of this," he said. "What sort of forces could there be to cause a wizard so powerful to be frightened?"

"He didn't really seem–"

Sarentha cut off Thomas, "The fear may not have been visible, but it was there. Why else would he be in such a rush to get back, and why would he lie to the king about where he was going? He is afraid of something."

Eliza pondered this. The more involved she became, the less she seemed to know. Thomas agreed that something was wrong, but had no idea what. Eliza's mind focused less on the problem, and more on the solution.

"Sarentha, do you think you could show me how to move around unnoticed the way you do?" Eliza asked, interrupting Sarentha's train of thought with this rare and unexpected compliment. "I would dearly like to speak to my uncle about all this, and I do not like that wizard telling me where I can and cannot go."

Sarentha shrugged. "I don't know if it's really something I can teach. I can show you what I do, I suppose."

Eliza said, "Well, you must have quite the skill to impress Wizard Wettias. I *would* like to hear more about this Rupert, the fellow they are framing for sending Grimbling's man after you."

Eliza looked at him sharply. Sarentha sighed, holding his hands up in defeat.

"Fine," he exhaled, exasperated, before telling them the story of the stranger named Rupert who had accosted him at the market.

"Why did you not just tell us the truth from the beginning?" Eliza asked.

Sarentha hung his head in shame. "I thought you'd be mad, and I wanted you to trust me."

Thomas rode his horse close, clapping a large hand on Sarentha's shoulder. He said, "You don't need to lie to me. You heard what the wizard said. We're all dead now, so we have to watch out for each other."

Thomas' words sank in. They were alone. If they got themselves into danger, they would have only each other to rely on.

"How long do you figure we'll be pretending to be dead?" Sarentha asked, uneasily.

Eliza disliked the idea, and did not want to dwell on it.

"Maybe when we have completed our missions my uncle will spread the news that we have returned alive. This golden tree quest seems straightforward. What could possibly go wrong with collecting a limb from a tree?"

"Let me tell you a tale of Sarentha having problems with a tree," Thomas grinned. "When we were born, around eighteen years ago, we were dropped off at the orphanage. It is a not uncommon story in Whampello. The people are poor, and a new baby meant another mouth to feed and back to clothe. We were playing outside around ten years ago…"

"I want to climb the tree," Sarentha said, pointing to the large maple in the corner.

"Again?" Thomas asked. He had no interest in trees. They were everywhere, as far as the eye could see. Whampello had been founded in a forest, and provided wood for the rest of the Empire. Thomas had learned this in school. The problem was, not everyone wanted wood, so Whampello's people were often poor. This last part he had figured out on his own.

Sarentha ran ahead, and Thomas followed. Thomas never let him down.

Thomas caught up with Sarentha, who held his arms up, unable to reach the lowest branch. The priests at the orphanage had in fact cut off the lower branches of all the trees to discourage Sarentha from climbing. He had a propensity for falling and injuring himself. Thomas, a head taller than Sarentha and strong for his age, easily boosted his friend, and Sarentha scrambled up the tree.

"I'm going to tell on you!"

Thomas turned to see Clara, a girl their age, pointing up at Sarentha. Everyone knew that tree-climbing was forbidden. The priests said so with every branch they took off. However, Sarentha was not one to worry about such arbitrary rules.

Higher he climbed, until he could see well past the yard of the orphanage and out to the western manors. There were not many nobles in Whampello, save a few wealthy families who had been living there as long as anyone could remember. Perhaps at one time they had owned lumber mills, back when lumber was in high demand. No one remembered anymore.

Sarentha liked to imagine living in a manor. He had confided to Thomas that he hoped a noble would come one day to the orphanage and adopt him, taking him away from the dull routines within the orphanage walls. Classes were easy for him, and he preferred hiding in the small library to read and reread the only book of fantastic adventures. Clifford and the Ogre, *it was called, and he had read it dozens of times. Clifford, a young man with no particular talent, was thrown into unlikely circumstances. He became a hero in his village when people believed he had slain a marauding ogre. The ogre had actually slipped and smashed its thick head open on a rock, but Clifford never did own up to the truth because he rather enjoyed the praise and attention. Sarentha held no illusions that he would ever be as lucky as Clifford, and he certainly could not overpower an ogre, but still he daydreamed about one day being rich and famous.*

He peered off toward one of the distant manors, and saw something out of the ordinary. Usually it was pretty quiet, with only the odd guard patrolling the grounds, or horses being walked, but through the trees on this day Sarentha spotted a large group of soldiers standing at attention. He recognized their flag as the one from Tamor. He had learned about all the cities of the Tamorran Empire in his classes, and he certainly could not mistake the colours of the capital city. The banner was divided diagonally with a white triangle on the top left, and a black triangle on the bottom right. In the centre was a brilliant golden crown, adorned with three rubies. The flag shone brightly in stark contrast to the plain standard that flew over the manor, with a tilted black arrow surrounded by a circle on a field of white. Sarentha had memorized the city flags, but he did not recognize the symbols of individual nobles.

Sarentha called down, "Hey Thomas! There's something going on at one of the manors!"

Father Timothy hollered, "Get down from there!"

Clara had told the priest that Sarentha was up the tree again. He looked cross, and Sarentha was sure to receive another beating. Even so, he did not heed the summons, but continued looking off into the distance.

Sarentha saw a man being dragged through the manor's front door and forced to kneel. A loud voice shouted that the man, Lord Samuel Winston, was the accomplice of traitors and must now be put to death. Sarentha heard screams and saw people fighting their way closer to the kneeling man, but the soldiers of Tamor held them back. An axe swung up, and then down, severing the noble's head.

Thomas concluded, "Sarentha froze and lost his grip. He fell out of the tree right on top of me."

"I was in the courtyard that day," Eliza whispered. "They beheaded my grandfather. Our whole family was forced to watch."

Thomas apologized profusely for reviving hurtful memories. He had not connected the story with Eliza, and had forgotten the lord's name.

The interconnectedness of their stories did not escape Eliza. She was not sure she believed in fate, but it *was* a strange coincidence that she should wind up on the road with the man who was likely the only child in Whampello who had witnessed her grandfather's execution.

She looked more closely at the slender young man and noted his gaunt appearance. He turned to her and attempted a smile, but it faltered.

"After that incident, the priests cut the tree down," Thomas said.

"Yeah," Sarentha mused, "what could possibly go wrong with cutting a branch off a tree?"

Chapter 9: Famous Last Words

A week of riding passed uneventfully. To their good fortune, Ramar Wettias had filled their saddle-bags with packets of a mysterious spongy substance the colour of bread, but by the squishy texture Sarentha knew it had to be something else. It was extraordinary how just one piece filled him up as though he had eaten a large dinner. The flavour changed depending on his appetite, which meant he never grew tired of eating the magical substance.

The weather had held for the duration of their trip, with only a few sprinklings of rain here and there. After crossing the river at a shallow point, their route followed the forest edge, so they simply rode their horses in the cover of the broad-leafed trees for protection. Overall, it appeared that Eliza's assessment of the job's difficulty was correct.

Even so, Sarentha was more and more watchful, the closer they came to their destination. He kept expecting the group to be waylaid by something at any moment. If this job was so vital, certainly they would not pull it off unscathed. After all, even their first relatively easy job of procuring the purple stone had a deadly catch.

Finally, in a distant valley the weary trio spied the tip of a golden tree, gleaming in the morning sunshine. It was immense.

Arriving at its base, Sarentha looked up and up but could no longer see the top. Thomas dismounted and circled the trunk, inspecting it with the professional eye of a lumberjack. The diameter of the base was more than twice his height. He pulled out his axe and surveyed the land for a safe place to drop the tree.

"Do not cut it down," Eliza said, consulting her uncle's letter. "My instructions say we need only a single branch, roughly six feet long, good and sturdy. It should look like it would make a good walking stick." Eliza read, "And it is imperative that no harm come to the tree before the branch is removed."

"You're kidding, right?" Sarentha looked at the note. "We came all this way to find a walking stick? That's the mission? Let me guess, your uncle lost a bet with Ramar, and now he owes him a gold walking stick. This is ridiculous. At least he said not to harm the tree before we get the branch. Maybe afterward we can cut the whole thing down and sell it in Tamor!"

"As you said before," Eliza said, frowning, "Wizard Wettias seemed fearful. Be serious, Sarentha. Ramar would not be afraid if all this was just about a gambling debt." Putting her hands on her hips, she asked imperiously, "So, who will climb the tree?"

Thomas and Sarentha exchanged a look. Obviously, Sarentha. He was the natural climber with experience. Sarentha pulled on his hole-filled work gloves and eagerly approached the tree's base. Although he had climbed many trees, he was certain this would be a unique experience.

Calling over his shoulder, Sarentha asked, "How high do I need to climb to find the right branch? Do the instructions say?"

Eliza shook her head, poring over her uncle's words once more. "No. You will just have to use your best judgement."

Sarentha muttered that his best judgement was sometimes questionable, but as soon as he touched the tree's surface, he relaxed. The golden tree bark was quite rough, and Sarentha's smaller fingers had no problem finding holds for the first twenty feet. When he disappeared from sight into the leafy branches above, Thomas called up, "Be careful! I'm not catching you if you fall this time!"

Sarentha ignored the jab. The climb from that point was simple, and he lifted himself deftly, higher and higher into the thick branches. After a few minutes and no suitable branch, Sarentha began to wonder if he would ever find one. He looked down, but immediately regretted it as a sense of vertigo hit him. In desperation, he wrapped his arms around the trunk. He had never been so high before, and he still had further to go.

Thomas and Eliza were calling, so he waved his arm in reassurance. Looking up once more, he continued his ascent. After some time the branches thinned. He was certain that Thomas could not have made a climb like this, for the branches at this height might not have borne the heavier man.

The climb went more slowly now, as Sarentha made sure to choose only the sturdiest branches to bear his weight. When the wind blew even gently, the top of the tree swayed broadly, forcing him to cling on and wait. Looking up, he spotted the perfect branch at last. Sarentha was certain its long, gnarled, and twisted shape would look impressive as a walking stick. He might as well make the climb worth his while and take the best branch he could.

Sarentha rested for a moment on the limb below the one he was planning to claim. From this vantage point, he could see the ruins of a city far to the south. He remembered the note on Foodle's map about ruins filled with flowers. He squinted to see whether he could identify any details, then decided to get on with the job at hand. Perhaps he could convince the other two to go down and look at the ruins with him later.

Reaching to his belt, Sarentha slid a knife from its sheath. He suddenly noticed an eerie silence, no breeze, no birds. Trying to ignore the unnatural calm, Sarentha's left hand gripped onto the branch above. He swung his right arm back, careful not to touch any other branches, and took his first hack at the branch's base. To his shock, the knife cut through the branch in one clean stroke.

Far below, Thomas and Eliza gasped. Although Thomas could not see what Sarentha was doing, he knew something must have gone wrong, for the tree itself seemed to be undergoing a violent physical reaction. First the branches twirled in a dizzying pirouette. Tens of thousands of leaves flew from the branches, leaving the great tree bare and revealing Sarentha high above. The trunk writhed, and Thomas watched his best friend struggle to hang on for dear life. But when the tree unexpectedly became brittle, the branches and leaves disintegrated beneath his clutching fingers. Sarentha's scream was clear as he and the leaves and the branches plummeted, the golden limb in his arms.

Thomas gauged Sarentha's position and ran with outstretched arms to catch his friend, heedless of his own welfare. Memories of Sarentha as a boy falling from trees on top of him raced through Thomas' mind. His feet pounded through the golden flakes, but he was too late.

Sarentha hit the giant heap of debris with a muffled thud, golden dust erupting around him. He was instantly lost to sight as yet more flakes floated down to earth. Where once there was a majestic tree of radiant gold, there was nothing now but debris.

Even as Thomas searched, burrowing through the remnants for his friend, the flakes were losing their golden hue and turning a rusty orange-brown. Thomas' hand struck something firm, and he heaved Sarentha out of the rubble. His heart pounding, Thomas checked for signs of life. Sarentha was unresponsive.

Thomas carried him clear of the branches and flakes and laid him gently on a patch of grass. Eliza leaned down to take a closer look at Sarentha. She touched her fingers to his neck and gave a sigh of relief. "He has a pulse." They hurriedly examined him and were pleased to find no signs of broken bones. Without warning Eliza slapped Sarentha hard on the face. He sputtered and gasped, his hands gripped his chest, and his eyes fluttered open, then looked around wildly.

"You are fine," Eliza said, standing up and shaking her head. "You just passed out from fear. The tree's remains must have cushioned your fall."

Thomas smiled broadly, embracing his friend and lifting him to his feet. Sarentha whistled, looking around at what had become of the tree. Almost nothing was left. Even the flakes had turned to dust, and were floating eastward on a gentle breeze.

"The branch?" Sarentha asked, searching around for it. "It didn't break on the way down, did it?"

That set the three of them in motion, kicking their feet through the dust, until Thomas discovered it. He lifted up the gnarled, six-foot length of gleaming golden wood and marvelled at it. Although the rest of the tree had disintegrated to nothing, Sarentha's branch was still perfect.

"We must be careful with it," Eliza said, taking the branch from Thomas and examining it. "I imagine it would take hundreds of years to grow another tree like that." She tenderly tested the length of golden wood, trying to bend it, but it would not budge.

Thomas tried, with more muscle behind it, but still the branch did not flex. Sarentha gave a low whistle and admired the unmarred branch. "Unbreakable wood? That's incredible! I guess that's why Lord Winston didn't want the tree to be harmed. All the strength of the tree went into one branch. So much for my idea of selling the rest."

"We do not know that it cannot be broken," Eliza corrected. "We only know that even Thomas cannot break it."

"It's definitely unnatural," Thomas said, fascinated. He rested the branch across his thigh and pushed down with all his might. Still it did not bend.

"Unbreakable," Sarentha reaffirmed. "How much do you think something like that would sell for?"

"It is not for sale," Eliza said, taking it from Thomas and wrapping it in a blanket. "We were sent here to find it for my uncle. I am certain he will pay you handsomely."

Sarentha did not push Eliza on the point. Thomas knew Sarentha well enough to understand how his mind worked. Sarentha probably figured if he could keep getting employment from Erwin Winston, he would likely make more money over the long run. Besides, who else would want it? Thomas imagined the market for such a special piece would be small.

Changing the subject, Sarentha turned towards the south. "From up in the tree I saw the ruins of a town. I think they are the ruins Foodle marked on his map. It's probably not more than an hour or two away. Let's take a look."

Eliza firmly shook her head, as she tied the safely wrapped branch to her saddle. "We should get back. I am sure the ruins will last until you have the chance to come back one day. I do not want anything to go wrong so long as we have this branch."

Thomas was also curious about the abandoned ruins, but since Sarentha did not pursue his idea, he let it go too. There was already enough tension between his best friend and Eliza without him putting his thoughts out there. In part he agreed with Eliza: The sooner they completed their missions, the happier he would be. He just hoped the next mission would not involve any more vanishing surprises. But seeing their track record with odd quests, he suspected that they would witness more bizarre sights before they were through.

Before leaving, Sarentha took out the tube with paper, the ink pot and quill pen. He unfolded the map of Foodle.

"What are you doing?" Eliza asked, looking over Sarentha's shoulder as he dipped the quill in the black ink and began to mark the blank sheet.

"I might as well start a new map, even if I don't get to go everywhere," Sarentha said, marking three dots in an equilateral triangle for the ruins to the south. He also marked a dot where the tree had been and labelled it "Magic Vanishing Tree." He filled in the city of Tamor and town of Whampello on the map based on the distances Foodle had used.

Thomas noted Eliza's thoughtful look before she helped Sarentha outline the forest edge. Was she using this opportunity to smooth things over with Sarentha? Her tone softened when she spoke to Sarentha, and Thomas saw Sarentha's shoulders loosen up, losing their tense tightness.

"I am unsettled by the idea of my uncle spreading stories of our deaths," she stated after Sarentha finished marking up the paper. "The golden staff is not a simple quest item to me anymore, but my ticket back to confront my uncle. I have pointed questions to ask. He may not divulge any more information, but I need to try."

"Ramar said Sarentha should be the one to talk to him," Thomas said. He was not certain who he would rather get in trouble with, Eliza or Ramar.

Eliza's cold gaze settled on him, and he was transfixed by her green eyes. "Perhaps you do not understand. I have always loved and trusted my uncle. There have been many times when I have spoken up for him, telling others that he was a good, honourable man. Certainly he lives a secluded life, but even if he does not attend the other nobles' social functions, he is truly kind to others.

"Or so I had thought," she said, her voice taking on a dark edge. "Perhaps I was wrong? Staging my death in order to cover up... what? What is it we are even doing? Why are the three of us out here, and not a regular hired soldier? Certainly he could have faked the death of someone who was not as near and dear to him, or as well-known, as I am."

"We're as in the dark on this as you are," Thomas said. While he was uncomfortable with the idea that people were being told he was dead, he realized it was a much more personal blow to Eliza. While he was used to being treated like his life mattered little, she was a noblewoman, and might not have ever been betrayed before.

Eliza offered Sarentha kind words on a job well done while he folded up his new map. Thomas saw that she was trying her hardest to smile convincingly, but the smile faded as soon as Sarentha turned. A bitter look came over her before she turned away to the north.

* * * * *

Far away in a long forgotten place, twenty hooded figures gathered in the darkness of a damp cave. The distant sound of running water echoed about the cavernous room and the figures silently formed a circle.

The head of the group, shrouded in white, stepped forward to address the attendees. "Sarsha-meshail has informed me that the end of an age approaches. He tells me all the knowledge of our ancient tomes cannot prevent what is to come. It is, he says, this very knowledge that shall usher in the new age. What have you fair nobles heard from your cities?"

The hoods moved slowly back and forth, each waiting for someone to speak. Eventually, a short figure in forest-green robes stepped forward. "There is no news at all in Themat, and I am well connected with all those in power. If there were even slight murmurings of rebellion and change amongst the halflings, I would know it. They have loose tongues when enough gold is put in their palms."

"The elves of Pothice are as feeble and impotent as ever," another blue clad figure offered. "They are no danger to our ways."

The white hood turned to another member of the circle, and motioned. The stout silvery-robed woman took a step and said, "The hammers of the dwarves of Khrymyre pound ceaselessly in their work. There has been no disruption in their tune to indicate any trouble."

A very small member in purple robes stepped forward and said, "The gnomes are too foolish to think of the future. They are focused only on making ridiculous gadgets."

The white-hooded leader leaned closer and asked, "Are you certain? Your disdain for them has not driven you so far away that you would not hear the rumblings of war, has it?"

The purple hood dipped in a bow of reverence. "No, certainly not. I maintain the illusion of friendship with several high-ranking gnomes. They accord me great status among them and would never exclude me from such plans."

"There is nothing from inside Tamor itself," another spoke, clad in pale blue robes, from outside the circle. "I have my agents with their ears to the ground. However, I did learn that an outsider – a human – was foolishly looking into our whereabouts. He has been silenced by a mercenary for hire. Unfortunately, overly zealous city guards killed the assassin."

"A corpse shares no secrets," the white-robed figure said. He then turned to another who had thus far remained silent, "Calarin! Why are humans snooping around? I thought that hole in the ground you call Whampello was so thoroughly crushed and devoid of hope that their kind would be unable to come to Tamor."

"Such would normally be the case," the Duke of Whampello said, stepping forward in golden robes. "Those two were desperate. They had been involved in a fatal struggle in a lumber camp and fled town. I cannot even feign surprise that their foolishness got them killed in Tamor."

The others in the circle sniggered at the Duke's disdain for Whampello's human population. As the levity faded, the assembly's leader stood in the centre of the circle. "The odds of such secrets being kept from us in all cities are remote. A single city could not muster the strength to stop us. It would appear that either Sarsha-meshail is incorrect in his precognition, or the inhabitants of the Tamorran Empire are far craftier than we give them credit for. But having seen how smoothly the Empire runs, I doubt there is any concern. Even so, we would be wise to keep our ears open and to pry into the goings-on of the residents. Increase taxes. Crush their hope with debt. Starving people cannot fight back."

With their orders given, the circle split, and each figure left the cave. The Duke of Whampello smirked as he moved out of sight of the other nobles on his way back to Whampello. They had swallowed his lie whole. He had fulfilled his duty and protected Thomas, Sarentha, and Eliza for the time being. It was entirely possible one or all of them could yet die on their path, but this was not his concern. The vanishing nobles would soon return to Tamor and ease the worries of the populace.

Chapter 10: Shadowed Return

The stars were masked by an overcast sky, making it unlikely for anyone to perceive the shadowy form darting from tree to tree. The figure tried to stay out of sight, pausing regularly to find its bearings, hiding deeper in the gloom of the trees and bushes, ensuring no one would follow its slow but steady progress to the forest grove northwest of Whampello.

The soft drizzle of rain veiled any sounds the hooded interloper might make. Ahead, within a circle of tall trees, stood Lord Winston, the hood of his cloak pulled up to protect him from the rain. He peered around cautiously, and the stranger hunched down behind some bushes, carefully concealing a six-foot-long package.

No guards were in sight. Lord Winston had left his compound unaccompanied for the first time in years. He glanced around at every small sound, obviously nervous about being unguarded, possibly fearing an opportunistic foe sabotaging his plans before they came to fruition.

A well-thrown rock caused a loud noise that made Lord Winston jump. The stealthy rogue darted closer, dashing for cover behind one of the grove's thick oak trees. Lord Winston turned in all directions, but the source of the noise could not be found. The cloaked figure hid for another moment before peering around the tree to work out the timing of its next move.

As Lord Winston moved slowly in a full circle, the stranger sprang forward and grabbed Lord Winston around the waist. Lord

Winston started and turned. He offered a wry smile and clapped his hands. "Well done, Sarentha, well done. I had received word of your return from my scouts, and yet I was quite nervous to be so exposed." He tapped the wire-wrapped emerald lenses he wore. "These allow me to see clearly at night, so I knew you were near, but when I heard an unexpected sound I feared there had been a mistake."

The figure pulled its hood back to reveal eyes of green and very feminine features. Erwin blanched slightly at the sight of his niece.

"Do not worry, Uncle Erwin," Eliza said, grinning. "You do not need your guards this night. I have learned a few tricks on the road. I asked Sarentha to teach me his moves, and although I do not feel I am as qualified a sneak as he, if you had not worn those glasses I am sure I would have been good enough."

"Indeed," Erwin replied, regaining his composure. His smile returned when Eliza unstrapped the long package from her back, and handed it to him. He unwrapped the top, glimpsed the golden shine, and whispered, "The Branch of Life. The staff is nearly complete." His eyes turned up to his niece again, and she saw his tears shimmering in the moon-light. "Years of planning have gone into this, Eliza. You cannot comprehend the magnitude of this quest that you, Thomas, and Sarentha are completing."

"I have some idea," Eliza stated coldly, walking past her uncle, and kicking the stump they sat on to tell ghost stories around a campfire in her youth. The grove was dark, illuminated only by a cloud-streaked moon. Eliza knew the woods well, for she had come picnicking here with her family many times over the years. Though the sun was down and the grove was dark, the place still felt welcoming and familiar to her.

When Erwin followed, she said, "Wizard Wettias came and told us just exactly how important all of this is to you. So I am dead, am I?"

Erwin grimaced slightly, but nodded in affirmation. "For now, I am afraid it is a necessity, my dear. Of course my soldiers know the truth about the events at the goblin camp, and have been sworn to secrecy. But outside my compound you are believed to be dead. I have received many condolences expressing sorrow and love for you, Eliza. I can only hope that these same people will not feel betrayed when they discover you are alive and well and that this was an elaborate charade. I would hate for their friendly overtures to sour."

"Well right now there are soured feelings, I assure you," Eliza said, shrugging off her dark cloak and taking a seat on a log near the cold fire pit. "What is this all about, Uncle? You always promised there were no secrets between us. You said I was like a daughter to you. I trusted you."

She hoped the past tense was not lost on him, and knew she had hit the mark when Uncle Erwin closed the distance to sit with her. He reached over and tilted her chin up to look into her eyes. The moonlight illuminated their shared pain. "Never doubt that I love you like a daughter," Erwin said with conviction. "I love you as I do Richard, my own son. Speaking of whom, he wrote to tell me of his meeting with Sarentha in Tamor. I had hoped to speak with Sarentha about this encounter, and I thought I had made it clear that he was to be the one to meet me here in secrecy. Why did you come in Sarentha's place?"

"I need to know what this is for," Eliza replied. "Something does not add up. Why not just send Thomas and Sarentha on these fool errands? Why involve me at all?"

Erwin's mouth tightened and he turned away from Eliza. After a moment of thought, he sighed. "As much as I wish I could tell you, Eliza, I cannot. I am sorry. If anything were to happen to you or your companions, this information must not fall into the hands of the enemy. There is too much at stake. I sent you because I am still not certain of your companions' loyalties, especially Sarentha's. I know that his judgement can be swayed by money. I could not yet trust him with the sum required to obtain the map of Foodle. Besides, what would you have done with your time, at home in Whampello? Gone to parties, practised your marksmanship, just frittered away your youth, I suppose. This was the opportunity of a lifetime, and I wanted to give you the chance to grow as a person, rather than spend your time doing frivolous nothings with your vapid friends."

He turned to her then, ignored the indignant look on her face, and said, "Imagine, if you can, being lied to your entire life. Imagine that the very foundation of everything you knew was false. Not only that, but that your ancestors had lived under the same delusions. Would you not want to do everything necessary to uncover the truth? We are coming to the dawn of realization, Eliza. Ancient tomes and manuscripts are nearly in our grasp which will tell us – everyone – the truth."

Eliza asked, "What does this branch have to do with knowledge?"

"Everything," Erwin answered reverently, uncovering the branch from its blanket. In the dim moonlight the wood shone like a gift from the heavens, casting dancing golden light about the forest grove. "This branch is unique. I was not even certain of the tree's existence until Iggy told me of the detail on Foodle's map. It is one piece of the artefact that will reveal the truth, and chase away the fog of uncertainty."

Eliza pondered this statement for a time, thinking about uncertainty. Two unanswered questions came to her mind, and she asked, "Like how Ramar has lost his memories? Or how the nobles of Tamor have disappeared?"

"The nobles have returned. I am not certain about Ramar's memory. The truth I speak of is far more present and dangerous. Ramar may regain his memories if our quest succeeds, but if so that is only a by-product of the greater cause. We must learn the truth of our past."

"I do not understand the role of what went before, Uncle Erwin," Eliza said, confused. "If, as you say, everything we know now is a lie, how did *you* come to know the truth?"

"The historical tablet in my keeping is the only known record of our collective past. It is frustratingly lacking in detail, yet its words are powerful. Your father brought it to my father before you were born. During his years with us, Lorrie'nar tried to devise a plan to reveal the truth. In the end, he realized he needed more information. The elves decided to risk a venture against the nobles of Tamor to see if they could uncover anything powerful enough to help their cause. They failed, and their trespasses did not go unnoticed. It was my father who paid the price."

Eliza paused to digest the information. After a moment of reflection she asked, "Then how can you be certain your plan will work any better than theirs? The elves live long lives, and have great wisdom. If they failed to reveal the truth, how can you hope to succeed?"

"Greed is a powerful force," Winston answered cryptically. "We would never have come this far were it not for the insatiability of Calarin. After my father's death, the Duke approached and asked if I knew anything of any hidden relics that my father owned. Somehow he knew that I had seen the tablet. I believe he saw in me a spark that he could fan and eventually use to revolt against the other nobles of Tamor. He knew more of the artefact than I ever could have. I have always known that Duke Calarin is not all he says. Recently my suspicions were confirmed. There are plots within plots that we cannot speak of now, my dear."

Eliza asked, "Well, how did Calarin come to learn of the truth, and know so much about the artefact?"

Erwin smiled then, and nodded, appreciating his niece's perceptive mind. "Not all of us have been living the lie. A few know the truth, and those few do not always agree with each other on how to maintain the secrecy. But it is my–" Erwin quickly corrected himself, "–our mission to shatter the lie and lay bare the truth. I am sorry I cannot tell you more, my dear. I may have already said too much by mentioning the Duke. You must leave this place, and return only when this last mission is completed."

"Why must I leave?" Eliza asked. "Where are you sending us?"

Erwin straightened, thinking. "It will take time for Ramar and me to alert our allies. In the meantime, you must go to your father."

Eliza's eyes widened in shock, and she stood up. "How could I? He left, and we do not know where he went."

"I have learned of his whereabouts," Erwin said, stepping closer to her. "Your map will show a forest to the northwest. I believe this is where the elves fled. The reason Foodle could not give more detail because it is a forest that is magically warded. He could not enter it, or even fly over it."

Eliza was surprised by the revelation. "Fly? You mean like Ramar?"

"Yes, just like that. Foodle was a powerful wizard. You did not think he could have created a map like that by walking, did you?" Erwin chuckled. "At any rate, I think you will find your father in this forest. Tell the elves that the golden staff has been assembled once more, and that some of us know the truth."

Not liking the cryptic phrasing, Eliza asked, "They will know what that means? What if they ask more questions?"

Erwin said, "Then tell them the truth. Tell them you are a messenger, and do not know any more. This should be enough for them to rally to our call."

Eliza nodded, although the uncertainty bothered her. She knew her uncle was not lying, but at the same time she felt uncomfortable in her own lack of knowledge. Finally, she pulled her cloak over her shoulders and flipped the hood up to cover her features. She turned toward the ring of trees. With Lord Winston unable to see her face, she asked in a neutral tone, "How is Ben?"

"I think he misses you," Erwin replied, with the hint of a knowing smile. "He would never say as much, but I see the loneliness and worry on his face when he thinks I am not looking."

Eliza hung her head, picturing Ben sulking around the manor. She was torn. She always tried to envision him stalwartly standing by, continuing his training and keeping busy. Hearing about his vulnerability touched her heart.

She waited until she could be sure her voice would not break and said, "Tell him I am well. I will give your message to the elves. When I return, will you tell me the truth in its entirety?"

"When you return, I will show you the truth first-hand, my

dear," Erwin replied gently, running a thumb over the base of the branch before covering it for his return to the manor.

Eliza slipped out into the night to rejoin her companions with the news of their next mission.

* * * * *

Meanwhile, in a ten-foot by ten-foot doorless room in another dimension, an orc, a halfling, and two men sat around a table tossing dice. The walls were dark and unadorned, shimmering softly in the light of a magical glass globe on the table's centre.

The orc, Feng, laughed heartily following a toss of the dice and scooped up several gleaming silver pieces. Feng's crimson-robed arm slid towards another coin from the halfling's pile as well, but Lyle Greenbottle had sharp eyes and quick reflexes. With a pointed glare he pushed Feng's sleeve away and pulled his silver coin back.

One of the men, Richard Winston, grimaced and flipped another silver coin onto the table. "Remind me again why I play this damnable game with you lot?"

"Because you have no friends," said Denton Marks, the second man, smoothly sliding his own coin onto the table for the next round of throws.

"Which again begs the question," said Richard, "why do I roll dice with you, if you're not even my friends? I could give this money to charity or something, rather than the Charity of Feng's Pocket."

"I'll remember that the next time you need a protective potion or spell," Feng said, simpering.

Something about the orc's smile always left Richard feeling unsettled, perhaps because of the way the little tusks deformed his mouth. Whatever it was, although he knew that Feng was friendly, he still felt uneasy. Richard responded, "I will remember *that* the next time you request your own personal Secret Guardian who'll protect you from all the forces in the world that would like to stomp your orc body into mush."

"Ah, what a terrible lover's quarrel," Lyle piped up, taking the first toss of the round. The deer-bone dice clattered across the wooden tabletop and stopped at a two and a three. Lyle frowned, appearing to attempt to will the dice to explode.

Lyle received a similar look from Richard. "Look, short stuff, just because I've sworn an oath to protect this big lout does not mean we are romantically engaged. You *know* that."

"He still makes you flustered though, after all this time," Denton observed, scooping up the dice and blowing on them for luck. "That's why he makes such crass remarks. You react." The dice skittered across the table, into the bumper at the far end, bounced back, and stopped at two fours.

Richard leaned over to pick up the dice and idly shook his hand, taking his time before throwing them. "It's my job to react. If I let my guard down, you'd all have died years ago." The clatter of the dice settled on a one and a two, eliciting a curse from Richard.

"Yeah, yeah," Lyle said, waiting for Feng to take his next turn. "Look at the pretty noble boy wanting to be the star of the theatre. You would love it if we all bowed down and praised you for your wonderful job of attracting attention and weapons, wouldn't you?"

"A little appreciation now and then wouldn't–"

Richard was cut off by Denton's emphatic cursing when Feng's roll showed a five and a six. Feng pulled in the coins and Denton said, "I swear you're using your damn magic to influence the dice! No one is that lucky!"

Feng shrugged, bringing in his considerable winnings and stacking them with the rest. "You know as well as I do that the only magic that works in this place is Wizard Wettias'. I can't cheat. That's why we play here."

Denton grumbled, "Maybe you found a way around the room's magical protection."

"Not possible," Richard said, shaking his head. He was equally disheartened to lose so much money to Feng, but he knew the room had been created with Wizard Wettias' arcane power in a supernatural dimension far removed from their own. Only Ramar's magic worked there. The only way in or out was with a simple silver ring that Wizard Wettias had specifically enchanted to bring them to the room whenever they wished. The ability to vanish was a handy magic trick, and Richard enjoyed using it to impress outsiders. It made him appear much more powerful than he actually was.

Before the dice could be rolled again, their boss materialized in an empty chair. Wizard Wettias huffed, picked up the dice, and rolled double sixes. Richard frowned and put his coins away. He *knew* Ramar cheated at dice every chance he got, and that the game was over.

"Denton and Lyle, I need your services." Wizard Wettias slid five silver pieces to each of them. "I have received word that my old friend Lord Winston has managed to get his hands on the Branch of Life, as well as the Amethyst of Arythia. Obviously I cannot ask Richard to watch his tongue around his own father, and Feng blends in about as well as a sunrise. You two must bring me the branch and the stone so I can begin the process of combining their components. As usual, do not be seen. The roads are dark, our enemies watchful. Trust no one."

Lyle and Denton vanished. Richard looked expectantly at Wizard Wettias, awaiting orders.

Instead, Wizard Wettias said, "I promise not to cheat. How about just one toss?"

"You really think we're going to fall for that again, Ramar?" Richard asked.

Wizard Wettias shrugged noncommittally, "It was worth a try. You know you will get the coins back eventually. Think of it as helping your poor employer."

Feng giggled and pulled a silver coin down from his stack. Richard asked, "You're not serious! You know that coin is as good as gone!"

"I have won many coins tonight," Feng said, picking up the dice and shaking them in his big hands. "I am feeling lucky."

The dice rattled to the table, their tops showing two fives, then floated up into Wizard Wettias' waiting hand. He shook the dice for several seconds, appearing to ponder some great mystery. Finally he released them and they rolled around and around the table. At last they settled on double sixes.

"I couldn't help myself," Wizard Wettias said unapologetically, collecting Feng's silver coin. "Now, I had better go back to work. You two have the night off. I advise you to hone your skills. Stay sharp. I will soon have work for you, and you will need to be at your best."

Wizard Wettias disappeared, leaving Richard and Feng alone together in the small room. Richard stood and stretched, although he did not feel the least bit tired.

Feng asked, "How would you like to train, my pompous protector?"

Richard laughed, which ruined his stretch. Eying up his companion, the thought of getting revenge for his lost coins was too much to pass up on. "I'll meet you in the basement of the wizard's tower in two minutes. We'll cross swords."

"We will use magic, correct? I doubt that basic weapon training is what Wizard Wettias had in mind," Feng said.

Richard shrugged, "Fine, you can throw spells around. Just try not to batter me so badly that I'm not ready for whatever Ramar has in store for us."

"I am sure you will recover," Feng offered ominously and left. Richard winced, but followed.

Chapter 11: A Long Road

Disbelief was plain in Sarentha's voice. "He didn't tell you anything? What happened?"

Eliza frowned at Sarentha before turning her attention back to the path through the dark woods. She had fully intended to learn what the quest was all about, but when she saw her uncle's resolve she knew she must be patient. Besides, he had dangled a very large carrot by sending her to reunite with her father. She remembered almost nothing about him. Her mother had told her precious little, and her uncle had even less to say.

The first light of the dawn was filtering through the trees to illuminate their path. Robins were awake and singing. Watchful rabbits held their ears up and alert. Sarentha pointed out a deer standing stock still in the bush a short distance away.

Eliza had been awake for far too long, and was not feeling as perky as the creatures that enjoyed the early dawn. When the sun peeked over the horizon, Sarentha led them off the path into a clearing where they set up camp. Before settling down for some sleep, Eliza unfurled the map of Foodle and they gathered around it.

She said, "My uncle said this last mission is going to take us up to the forest northwest of the Empire, where Foodle could not go. I am not at all sure how we are supposed to get in considering a powerful wizard could not. Perhaps the elves will allow us to enter."

"Elves?" Sarentha breathed.

Eliza looked over and knew he was definitely interested in meeting the elves. During their travels, Sarentha had made no secret that the idea of travelling outside the Empire to the home of another race thrilled him. He shared bard stories of elves who moved like shadows and cast powerful magic.

Eliza smiled at his wistful gaze. "Yes. I have a secret message for them."

Studying the map, Sarentha measured the distance from Whampello to the Golden Tree, then calculated that it would be even farther to the forest of the elves. "Maybe ten days? That's a long trip just to deliver a message. How much will he be paying us? Did we get paid for delivering the golden branch?"

"I forgot to ask," Eliza confessed. "Anyway, where we are going, we will not be needing money. You know my uncle is good for it. But yes, it is a long trip, and I know it will add a few days, but I think we should head north first before going west. The halflings are traders, and the road from Themat to Tamor is well travelled. I do not want to cross paths with anyone on our way. Uncle Erwin stressed the secrecy of this mission."

Sarentha and Thomas groaned in unison. At least two weeks to make the journey to the forest of the elves, and another two weeks to return. A month away from civilization and still they had no idea of their purpose.

"I don't like this," Thomas said. He backed away from the map and unrolled his bedroll.

"I like it even less, since we haven't been paid," Sarentha agreed.

Eliza had to get them back on task. There was no way she could make this trip alone. She put the map away and looked pleadingly at the two men. "Fine, you do not have to trust my uncle. But will you come to the elves with me for *my* sake?"

They looked at her warily. Even travel-stained and road-weary, Eliza retained her regal nature. Despite the grime of the road and the tangled hair, she was always beautiful, and she was not above using her charm to get what she wanted.

The three of them had grown close, whether any of them wanted to admit it or not. She and her companions came from totally different backgrounds, but they had come together under one common banner. They were alone and they had only each other to rely on. According to the world, all three of them were dead. They could not help but bond given such isolating circumstances.

Sarentha and Thomas shared a knowing look and she saw them come to a silent agreement. They would not abandon her now. The trip would be long and gruelling, but they had come too far to turn back. Besides, where else could they go? What could they do? And if they let her down and Lord Winston discovered it, what fate would await them? No matter how they looked at it, Eliza knew Thomas and Sarentha would be joining her to meet the elves.

Pleased at the outcome, her mind turned to other topics, and she asked, "Do you think me shallow?"

Their eyes opened wide. Eliza knew their minds before they could answer and said, "My uncle said as much. He thinks that if I had stayed in Whampello, I would have spent my time going to parties, reading, and practising my crossbow. He think I need to grow, but that is the problem: there's nothing I really yearn for. What is it you two strive for in life?"

Sarentha's answer was immediate. "Wealth! I want to be rich beyond my wildest dreams."

"Why?" Eliza asked.

"I've never had money," Sarentha said. "All my life I've looked at the nobles' manors from afar, now that I've visited your uncle's estate, I know that's the kind of life I want. You want for nothing; you said so yourself just now. I can't imagine a life like that – so privileged... so *easy*."

Eliza frowned in thought. "Well, it *is* nice to have *things*, but these past few days have brought more excitement than I have ever known, and I have not spent a single coin."

"Just five hundred of them for that map," Sarentha pointed out, offering a wry grin.

"You know what I mean," she grumped. "Out in nature, exploring the countryside with no one to answer to, all of us counting on each other, I feel I am discovering a part of myself that I never knew existed. Before this, going more than a day without a warm bath was unthinkable!"

Thomas laughed, drawing her gaze. "The closest I've come to a warm bath is in midsummer when the water in the lake heats up in the noonday sun. I can't begin to imagine the luxury of a bath every day."

"You must think me quite silly," Eliza said, casting her eyes down. "Here I am, pining after things I miss that you two have never known. I wish I could see life from your eyes."

"No," Sarentha replied, "you don't."

They sat in silence for a time before Eliza turned to Thomas and asked, "What about you? Do you aspire to a noble's life, too?"

Thomas shook his head and grinned. "No, nothing like that. I think one day I'd like to build a cottage in the woods, settle down and have a family. I've always pictured a bunch of kids around me, laughing and playing. Since I grew up without parents, I'd like to try to give my children all the things I never had."

"Knowing your parents has its good points," Eliza said, "but..." She pictured her mother, heartbroken and downcast without her father.

Sarentha poked Thomas with a stick. "When have you ever known a mere peasant to own land? How would you get it, steal a patch of forest from under the Duke's nose?"

"Am I more likely to stumble upon a treasure chest heaped with gold?" Thomas said, snatching away the stick and poking Sarentha back.

Sarentha grabbed another stick, and Eliza watched the two friends battle for their honour. Sarentha poked Thomas in the stomach, and he doubled over in mock pain. He gasped, "All my hopes and dreams of a family – dashed by your cruel blade!" Collapsing into a heap, he feigned death and Sarentha struck a heroic pose over him.

Eliza laughed and said, "Well, perhaps back in Whampello, you two will receive the rewards you seek." She prepared her bedroll, and was overcome by a yawn. "After all, my uncle is paying you well, compared with what you made before. The Duke might even grant you a piece of land for your part in this adventure."

She was glad to see the two men smile, their eyes gazing into the distance. Maybe one day she too would have a dream.

Resting her head, aware of the lumpy hard ground under her roll, Eliza knew it would all come in time. She thought of her uncle's rough relationship with her cousin, and of her parents. Perhaps she did not aspire to have a family life, but there was surely something out there she wanted.

A Noble's Quest

* * * * *

In the dining hall of Winston manor, the Duke of Whampello met with Lord Winston and one he did not recognize. The servants had not yet risen; it was the perfect time for them to convene. The Duke's narrowed hazel eyes inspected the newcomer. He was not tall, fairly slender, and had a few strands of blond hair peeking out from under his dark, hooded cloak. The Duke's gaze did not rest long on the stranger, however, before alighting upon the golden branch in Lord Winston's hands.

"Right on time," Calarin said, reaching out and snatching the branch from Lord Winston. He examined the piece of wood carefully, and tested its strength to make sure it was legitimate. When it did not bend under his full strength he was satisfied. "It appears your faith in the peasants may have been well placed after all, Erwin."

"It will take some time to fully assemble the staff," Lord Winston said, gently removing the branch from the Duke's grasp. "Denton here is an associate of Wizard Wettias. He will take the branch and the stone back to Tamor."

"Ah, Denton Marks," the Duke said. "Of course, I should have known. Ramar would not entrust the couriering of such rare and precious items to anyone less than his best servant."

A cough from the side of the room caused the Duke to spin around with his hands raised defensively. A diminutive fellow stood next to the door. His curly brown hair and bare feet told the Duke all he needed to know. A halfling with Denton Marks could only be one person. "No offense meant to you, Lyle Greenbottle."

"None taken," Lyle piped up as he sauntered over. "I know I'm better than Denton, so it's a sort of sideways compliment, isn't it?"

Calarin knew the two sneaks made a deadly pair. Denton, a roguish devil, was most comfortable skulking around the busy streets of Tamor. He had been a legendary thief until he crossed paths with Ramar Wettias. No one knew how Wizard Wettias had convinced Denton to leave his ways and join his merry band of misfits. Lyle, on the other hand, was a skilled hunter and marksman. He was as at home in the woods as Denton was in the cities. He might be small, and use a short bow, but only a fool would underestimate his deadliness.

Calarin ignored Lyle's egoism and pushed on. "I trust both Erwin and Ramar have told you how vital it is that you are not seen with these items." The Duke removed a small sack from his belt and handed it carefully to Denton, who immediately tied it to his own belt.

"Yes," Denton replied.

The Duke waited a moment for the rogue to elaborate, but he said no more. Calarin continued, "You must not be seen by any living thing from here to Tamor. Without the staff our mission will be a failure and all of my – *our* – planning will have been for naught. If we are discovered I will personally see your lives ended. Am I clear?"

"Yeah, yeah," Lyle said with a shake of his head. "We get it. We ain't idiots. All we have to do is get to Tamor, and Ramar'll take care of the rest. Not to worry, Duke. There's good reason Ramar chose us."

The Duke still felt wary about relinquishing control of the relics to others. Had it been possible for him to make the journey himself he would have, but for the time being he needed to maintain a low profile. Reluctantly he stepped aside, and motioned for the pair to leave.

When they were gone, the Duke glared at Lord Winston. "Why was I not informed that there would be *two* couriers? I do not appreciate being made to look like a fool."

"I apologize, Your Grace. It slipped my mind," Lord Winston said, bowing humbly. "There are so many things happening now, I try to say as little as possible. It would be a grave misfortune if our plans were heard by the wrong person because I spoke too liberally."

The Duke grunted, not convinced. "Ramar should have come himself. I do not like dealing with these middlemen. The more people involved, the greater the chance of our plans being undone."

Lord Winston frowned. "I trust only a few, but Ramar Wettias has my full acceptance. If he has confidence in Denton and Lyle, then I do as well. Do not concern yourself, Your Grace. Such worry causes premature aging."

The Duke's eyes narrowed to slits as he glared at Lord Winston. "I hope your trust is well placed for your sake, Erwin. We cannot fail."

"I understand that perfectly well," Lord Winston said levelly, meeting the Duke's heated gaze. "Ramar will soon have the pieces of the staff, and in a month's time we will have the completed work back in our hands. We will not fail."

The Duke pivoted on his heel and left.

Lord Winston exhaled deeply and sat down. His hands were shaking with adrenaline. The truth was one step closer to being revealed, but he needed all his concentration and guile to make sure everything moved forward according to plan. He agreed with the Duke that there might be too many players involved, yet each was necessary. It was a dangerous balancing act telling people only as much as they needed to know. Only himself, Calarin, and Wizard Wettias were fully aware of the process. Certainly Thurzin and Igatiolus knew enough to gain allies, but even they were not wholly knowledgeable of the situation. To confuse the matter even further, Thurzin and Igatiolus knew certain things that even the Duke and Wizard Wettias did not. Lord Winston meant it when he told the Duke that he spoke as little as possible. What he had failed to mention was that there were plots within plots, and the closer they came, the more careful he had to be. Nothing could be leaked.

The first servant came into the dining hall, surprised to see Lord Winston already at the table. He immediately set to work preparing breakfast.

But food was the last thing on Lord Winston's mind. He had not been eating much lately. He looked at his hands and noted how thin and frail they had become. Worry certainly did lead to early aging, as he had warned the Duke. He himself was living proof. Paranoia some called it, but his was not an unfounded fear. Many lives hung in the balance, and depended on his ability to stay sharp and in control. If the plan was to come to fruition, Erwin needed to maintain his focus and energy for at least another month. He wished he could speed up the process.

Chapter 12: Action

William Cob was not, by any measure, a smart man. Nor was he particularly good-looking. He most certainly could not read. Really, William had almost no useful skills at all. That was why he had signed up to be a guard in the capital city. Tamor was ringed by a high stone wall, which was exactly where William was stationed on this fateful night. William did have eyes, though with slightly less than average vision, so he had been assigned the duty of standing in the dark atop the city wall staring out into the pitch-black forest.

Nothing ever actually came out of the forest. Nothing suspicious, anyway. There were a handful of occasions where he had spotted a deer walking along the border of the woods. Rabbits would often hop out and nibble on some grass and leafy weeds. But if his job was to watch out for danger, then his job was the easiest in the entire kingdom. No one had ever attacked Tamor. He had never heard of a single instance of anyone even attempting any sort of aggressive action against the city.

So guard duty was pretty dull. Because it was so boring, William had polished up his sleeping skills. He liked sleeping. Sometimes he would lean over the wall and slumber, so that if passersby happened to see him they might think he was examining something below very closely. Sometimes he sat atop the wall and leaned against a tower. If he was really tired and needed to stretch out, he would just lie down and cover his eyes with his metal cap.

But tonight he was going to try something new! He would

attempt to sleep while standing, like a horse. Propping himself up on the haft of his spear, taking care not to impale himself, William wedged the end of the spear into the wall's heavy stones. He tested it, putting weight on the shaft, and decided it would hold him. After a few minutes of leaning on the spear, William was forced to accept that this was not a good idea, for when he nodded off he nearly tumbled backwards into the city. There was no way he would be able to come up with a reasonable excuse if that happened.

Tonight would probably be a sleeping-against-the-tower night, William concluded. As he shuffled off toward the gate, something curious happened. William heard a loud *snap* from the woods. Thinking he might get lucky and see another deer, he leaned over and squinted into the darkness (he found that squinting helped him sharpen his focus).

An arrow came whizzing from the forest and whistled over William's right shoulder. He nearly jumped out of his skin. He spun around to see where the arrow had gone, but it was nowhere in sight. Turning back to the woods, he heard his fellow guards beginning to stir.

"What was that?" Kelly called from William's right, far down the wall.

Now that the others were looking to him for guidance, William thought he should get a better hold of his spear and look prepared. "I dunno," he hollered back. "Think it mighta just been a bird." Sure, it could have been a bird. To him, this made sense. Maybe it was a screech owl, or something similar. He pointed his spear toward the woods and gave it a shake, cursing the birds who had caused such alarm. He relaxed his grip and rested the end of his spear against the top of the wall, feeling that there was nothing more to be done.

Another arrow, silent this time, flew in and forced the spear from his loosened hold. "Hey!" William shouted reflexively, before he could stop himself. The spear clattered onto the cobblestone walkway behind and below him. He turned, saw his weapon lying in the middle of the empty city street below and muttered a curse.

There was no doubting it – someone was shooting arrows at poor William, and now he was literally disarmed. Other sentries approached, looked at their spearless colleague, and peered out into the woods. "What's all the racket? It's pretty late for games," Kelly commented as he came closer. Kelly was twice as thick as William, in both body and mind.

"It ain't a game when someone's shootin' me!" William sniffled, realizing he should duck down behind the wall's protection.

"You're shot?" asked Jim, the third guard. He crouched down beside William. "Are you sure?"

"Well, no," William said after a pause. "But something shot my spear right out of my hand. Now it's gone."

Kelly started when his spear also went tumbling down to the streets, an arrow jutting out of the shaft.

The three guards huddled behind the protective wall, looking suspiciously toward the woods. Only Jim was armed now, and William were perplexed. When they tried to brainstorm the correct response to a threat, all they achieved was a braindrizzle. The captain would know what to do, they concluded.

"But he's asleep," Kelly said, looking worriedly back across the slums in the direction of the barracks. "Might get mugged walking to wake him."

"Might get shot if we don't go," Jim argued.

"And someone's got to watch the wall," William said.

William sat in silent contemplation for a while.

Mark, their supervisor, approached with a scowl on his face. He disliked most of his night-shift guards, for they were typically the stupidest and ugliest. The smarter, better-looking guards were purposely posted during the daytime so that the people of Tamor would see a shining example of security and feel safe in their homes while they slept. Jim, William, and Kelly were better unobserved.

"I thought I told you three to work in different sections of the city," Mark hissed from below. He picked up their spears and noticed the arrows protruding from them. "What's going on up there?"

"We were shot," William and Kelly said, almost in unison. The combination of their slightly asynchronous speech and clumsy tongues made their words difficult to comprehend, but Mark thought he understood.

"What!?" Mark exclaimed in stunned disbelief. If they had been shot, why had they not fallen from the top of the wall?

"Well sort of," Jim clarified weakly. "Someone shot the spears outta their hands. I'm keepin' mine down just in case."

"Is this some witless prank?" Mark asked. The muscles in his jaw tightened, his next words coming out like a hiss. "If it is, I'm not amused! The security of this city is not a joke!"

"No prank," William said. "I thought the first one was a bird cuz it made such a sound, but then another quiet arrow came and hit my spear. 'Nother one hit Kelly's. Someone's out there shootin' at us!"

A Noble's Quest

"And none of you thought to sound an alarm?" Mark fumed.

"Oh," Jim said, nodding toward the other two in belated comprehension. "*That's* what we're supposed to do!"

By the time the alarm finally sounded, it was far too late. Denton had climbed over the wall as soon as William had been disarmed. Lyle was far away setting up his camp deep in the woods. Wizard Wettias already had the stone and branch in his possession and was commencing the process of magically joining them to form the golden staff bathed in violet light.

William, Kelly, and Jim were fired.

* * * * *

Thomas took the lead after they cleared the forest and cut across country. According to Sarentha's sums, it was going to take an extra three days to skirt around the border of the Empire in order reach the elves' northern forest. Figuring that the road to Themat could not possibly be constantly busy, Sarentha convinced Eliza that they could make it across without drawing attention to themselves. He reasoned that the only people who might see them would likely just be merchants.

The ride was fairly uneventful through the long grass of the flat plains. The odd tree here and there marked shady places where various animals escaped the heat of the day. Thomas was surprised when he suddenly stumbled upon a road in the middle of the grassy plains. A quick glance from north to south showed that no one was currently within eye-sight.

"See?" Sarentha looked triumphant. "We would have wasted three days for nothing!"

"You were right," Eliza conceded graciously.

Thomas could not tell when the packed-dirt road had last seen use, and he relaxed knowing that the road was not as busy as they had feared.

Without fanfare, they continued on their path to the northwest.

But moments later, the calm was broken when Eliza pointed out two figures. They were mounted and riding fast. "We're alright," Sarentha said. Despite his assurances, they watched the pair riding north toward Themat.

The riders veered off the road, and turned in their direction.

"Can we worry now?" Thomas asked, turning his horse back toward the road. He checked his axe and hoped it would not come to a fight.

"We are just taking a pleasant ride in the fields to gather flowers for my wedding bouquet," Eliza said pointedly. "Nothing more."

Sarentha asked, "Which one of us are you marrying?"

"*Neither* of you," Eliza hissed through her teeth. She kept smiling for the benefit of the approaching riders.

The companions tried to wait as calmly as possible while the strangers drew near. The first rider, a human, wore a chain shirt with leather breeches. His long sandy-brown hair whipped in the wind and his grey eyes examined each stranger in turn. The other rider, a little gnome, wore a simple white robe and had a staff resting across his lap. His head was bald, and his dark brown eyes appeared too big for his head. The small stature and lack of armour forced Thomas' mind back to the little goblin shaman Ben had nearly cleaved in two. He wondered if this gnome also wielded arcane powers. If he did, Thomas hoped that he would not use his magic to strike them all down off their horses. He remembered Ben mentioning some casters who could level entire buildings, and he gulped nervously.

"Travel off the roads is forbidden," the man said curtly, as he brought his horse to a stop.

"Really?" Eliza asked. "We were just–"

"You heard me. Get back on the road."

Thomas asked, "Why is it forbidden?"

"Orders of King Dalmethias," the man said, pointing to the road.

Thomas looked at his friends. Why would the King ban off-road travel? Thomas was unfamiliar with the military mindset of following orders without question; Eliza spoke on their behalf with some understanding.

"I am a noblewoman and friend to King Dalmethias. Perhaps you could turn a blind eye just this once?" Eliza suggested, offering a regal smile. Whether it was her grimy face, or his unshakable loyalty to the crown, he would not waver.

Instead, his hand moved to his sword and he asked, "What part of 'forbidden' do you not understand? I do not wish to use violence, but I have my orders. Come back on the road, and we will escort you back to wherever it is you hail from."

Time slowed in Thomas' mind. Here it was. They could not go back. If they went with these two, questions would be asked. They had to protect what little information they possessed, but if they remained silent they could be locked up for treason. They would spend the rest of their lives chained in a dark, dank dungeon and never taste freedom again.

Movement woke Thomas from his gloomy reverie. The gnome was straightening his staff. Thomas remembered Ben's words about how to combat those who could control the forces of magic. Hard and fast.

Thomas' white and brown courser leaped instantly, charging

the gnome, whose eyes widened with surprise. Arcane words emerged from his lips, but too slowly. Thomas' arm swung across, tearing the little gnome from his saddle and sending him sailing to the ground.

The human swore and drew his sword. His mount also charged into battle, and Thomas turned in time to see Eliza deftly steer her horse aside and out of reach. Sarentha stood on his horse's back. With his daggers crossed, he leaped through the air, deflected the soldier's swinging sword, and tackled his opponent to the ground. Sarentha rolled and shot up to his feet. In an instant he closed the distance to the supine soldier, and his blades pierced the other man's exposed neck.

Thomas stared, uncertain what to make of the violence, when he saw the gnome rising to prepare a spell. His hands wove mysteriously and unleashed a blinding bolt of light.

A crossbow bolt hit the gnome in the shoulder, sending him spinning before he could attack a second time. Thomas was vaguely aware of Eliza's scream when he slumped off his horse, smoke ascending from his chest. He hit the ground on his front, grunting with the impact. Looking up, he saw Eliza racing to load her crossbow as the gnome began casting another spell.

Thunk. Eliza was faster. The second bolt hit the little gnome squarely in the chest, sending him spiralling down to the ground in a heap. Relieved, Thomas' head fell to the ground and he moaned in pain.

Sarentha untangled himself from the fallen soldier and sprinted over to Thomas. He rolled his friend over and saw the scorched front of his leather armour. Thomas groaned and coughed, "Ow."

"You need to get over your fear of death," Sarentha

admonished. He helped Thomas sit up and said, "That little gnome certainly wasn't holding anything back when he laid into you."

Thomas sighed. "I thought maybe we didn't have to kill them. If we just injured them and spared them, maybe they wouldn't throw us in prison."

"Unlikely," Eliza said. She kneeled down beside Sarentha. "Assaulting a soldier of the king is almost as bad as killing one. Once you cross that line, from a legal standpoint, you may as well go all the way. And given the secrecy of our mission, we cannot risk incarceration."

"I don't think the gnome had imprisonment in mind," Sarentha said, examining Thomas' injury. Thomas reached up and felt the breastplate. The large blackened mark on his armour had nearly burned through the leather chest piece. A second attack surely would have burned his flesh underneath, and might have been fatal.

Thomas asked, "What do we do with their horses?"

Eliza considered their options. "The innocent creatures could easily be seen from the road. While grazing horses would soon be discovered if someone came to investigate, our enemies' lifeless bodies will be otherwise impossible to spot in the tall grass."

"I hate all this killing," Thomas muttered.

Eliza reflected on Thomas' feelings and decided, "We will take them with us, and leave them at the edge of the Empire. If off-road travel was illegal, surely no one would go that far."

With boosts from his friends, Thomas managed to get back up on his horse. Sarentha and Eliza ran to mount theirs and they were on their way, with two extra horses in tow.

The trio with five horses were out of sight when the gnome, Zanderboot Pickly, finally stirred. His little hands again made a series of complex motions, and a white light enveloped him. Holy power coursed through his little body, until he found the pain more bearable. With two loud grunts he slid the crossbow bolts from his body. Another spell of healing sealed the wounds and he was almost as good as new. The same could not be said for his companion. Once someone died, they were beyond the healing magic of the gnome priest.

Zanderboot would have to walk back to Tamor. He swore an oath that the strangers would pay for their actions. The King would bolster his guards and the three would be put to death.

Chapter 13: Reunion

The forest's edge had been visible for miles, but up close they were awed by its wildness. The warm, humid air caused sweat to drip from their noses. They looked up at soaring, exotic trees. Winding vines and brilliant orange and red flowers seemed to reach out in every direction in odd shapes. Sounds of animals unlike anything they had ever heard emanated from deeper within.

"It's a jungle," Sarentha marvelled. Fables told of jungles with huge wild cats and hairy humanoids. They were said to be teeming with unknown life that was both beautiful and dangerous.

"You are certain there are elves in there?" Thomas asked doubtfully, peering into the jumble of trees. "It looks pretty wild. I would have expected a forest that a civilization calls home to look tamer."

Eliza nodded in confirmation, unfolding the map and checking it again.

After tethering their horses outside the jungle, Sarentha took the first step in, his hands parting the thick foliage. "It is gorgeous compared to our forest back home," he said. "And it sounds more populated as well. It should be easy for us to move around unnoticed with so much noise from the wildlife."

He took two more steps and suddenly stopped. An elf stood not five feet away with a bow in her hands, the arrow drawn and pointed directly at his head. She was diminutive in stature, and extremely slender. Her rough, animal-hide jerkin left little to his imagination, and her matted golden hair hung over her shoulders in wild unkempt locks. Her green eyes were slanted slightly, and despite the weapon and openly hostile face, he thought her the most beautiful woman he had ever laid eyes upon. Sarentha stared, frozen, and Thomas, following close behind, collided with his friend. Eliza narrowly escaped being part of the jumble at the edge of the jungle.

Eliza ignored the threatening weapon, smiled, and bowed to the elf. "Hello, my name is Eliza Winston. I come from a small town called Whampello. My uncle, Lord Winston, has sent me here to speak with your people."

The elf looked as though she were about to order them out of the jungle when her eyes flicked down to the sparkle of the tip of Eliza's crystalline dragon. On their way north, Eliza had removed her studded leather breastplate because of the humidity and heat. The shirt underneath allowed just the tip of the pendant to be exposed to the sun's rays. The elf woman clearly recognized it.

After several seconds of silence, the elf slowly loosened her hold on the bowstring and put the arrow back in the quiver at her hip. She said, "I am Lief'senshai, the Stalker for this region. Come with me, Eliza Winston. Your men can accompany you as well." Lief'senshai turned and motioned them to follow.

After exchanging uncertain looks, Sarentha struggled to push through the undergrowth and vines. The lithe elf, in contrast, seemed to dance through the jungle. She moved as if walking down a clear path, whereas the outsiders could not seem to keep their footing. Sarentha had the easiest time, nimbly avoiding vines and roots, and his slender frame helped him glide past branches and bushes. There were muffled curses when Thomas or Eliza slipped on moist greenery and slick rocks, taking tumbles along the way.

They could not tell time in the jungle's filtered light, and the sounds of the insects and animals were a constant presence. Eventually, they gained some coordination in negotiating the lush growth. They were certainly not as graceful as Lief'senshai, who often paused to let them catch up, but at least they were no longer tripping over every snag.

While crossing a river they soaked their feet, and Thomas had to stop to retrieve a boot he lost to the muddy bottom. Continuing on, they were surprised to see Lief'senshai suddenly sprint up the thin rotten trunk of a tilting tree and continue walking along the outstretched branches of higher, healthy trees.

"I don't think I can follow her up there," Thomas said wearily, pausing to catch his breath.

Sarentha eyed the trunk of the dead tree, and viewed it as a personal challenge. He was not much bigger than the elf. Without warning, he ran at the trunk and dashed up. But the tree would not bear his weight, and the bark crumbled under his feet. Half way up, the trunk groaned and wavered, and Sarentha's balance faltered. With a deep resonating crack, the trunk shattered under him and Sarentha dropped to the jungle floor amidst a hail of old splintered wood and bark.

The two halves of the broken tree settled nearby and Eliza chided, "Someone has problems with trees. Perhaps you should try to climb something that will not disintegrate beneath you."

Sarentha, brushing away the fragments of bark and wood, was about to retort when he suddenly straightened. His eyes darted about the bush. Three more silent elves had materialized.

The middle one appeared to be the leader, wearing a colourful feathered headdress and a long artfully tattered robe. The other two elves were dressed in leather tunics and leggings and each had a hand on a slender sword.

The leader offered a deep bow before speaking. "Welcome, children. I am Finwe, Raja Forest Born of Amaroh. I understand you seek an audience with the elves. Erwin Winston has sent you here."

Sarentha was taken aback. He had not seen their elven guide say anything to the newly arrived elves. Finwe answered his puzzled expression with a slow wave of his hand to the trees. "The trees speak to me, and this news has travelled quickly. The jungle wonders what it is our old friend could want from us."

"I am Eliza Winston." Eliza bowed just as low as the elf had. "My uncle sent us here to seek my father. The staff is nearly complete and the truth will be revealed."

The jungle itself seemed to energize around them, the tree tops rustling fiercely in response to Eliza's statement. The elf before them remained composed, and offered them a small smile. "This is good. When will it be ready?"

"I do not know," Eliza admitted. "I was not told very much. My uncle was extremely cryptic, and gave me little information in case misfortune befell us. He said too much was at stake to have his plans revealed to ears that should not hear."

Sarentha suddenly comprehended Erwin's caution, looking up to the trees that apparently understood their every word. If Finwe could communicate with the trees, perhaps someone more nefarious would also listen to their excitement at the news Eliza had just revealed.

"Your uncle is wise, Eliza," Finwe said, nodding his approval. "I will take your father to the woods east of Tamor to meet you when all is ready."

As Finwe turned to leave, Eliza sputtered, "But I thought we were to meet with him!"

"Your father is very sick," the elf said, not meeting her gaze. "And the path to Amaroh is fraught with danger. You may have elven blood in you, Eliza, but the forest has perceived how dominant your human side is. You lack the grace of the elves to travel the rest of the way."

"He's sick?" Eliza sounded shaken. "How bad is it?"

"His mind has difficulty focusing," Finwe replied, his eyes lifting to the forest ceiling. "When your mother died, he shattered his sword in grief. He never stopped mourning the leaving of his family, and your mother's death was a terrible blow to him. A Bladesinger without a blade is only half an elf. Without a purpose, your father's mind has grown foggy. It is my hope that his thinking will be restored when the truth is revealed."

Eliza said, "I thought he had to return to the jungle to be well. How could he have fallen sick when he was where he needed to be?" She faltered, and drew a deep breath. "Could he have stayed with us in Whampello after all?"

The elf turned back to her, shaking his head sadly. "Lorrie'nar was a hero, Eliza. Your father faced many grave dangers to safeguard our people. Many owe their lives and continued health to him, but in the end, he could not save us all. Have you seen the elves of Tamor, or their city Pothice to the west of Tamor?"

Eliza shook her head.

"They are changed," Finwe said, pausing over that last word. "The grace you see in us is gone from them, much as it is from you. Their minds are not whole. Unlike your father, who is lost in sorrow, those elves do not know why their minds fail them. It is worse for the oldest among them. Some of the younger elven adults appear to be fine, according to your father, but the older generation has gone astray. They are ghosts of their old selves, and I fear their minds will never be restored."

Sarentha joined two streams of thought together. "Have they lost their memories, like Wizard Wettias?"

Finwe nodded. "I do not know your wizard, but yes, their memories are gone. Elves live for thousands of years, therefore the oldest among us has the most to lose. They survive, but so much has been erased. Their minds are not youthful enough to learn anew. The slums of Pothice are devastating, where the elders languish without hope or thought in their blank eyes.

"So to answer your question, as a hero to our people, Lorrie'nar sought allies amongst the shorter-lived races, who would not be so irreversibly damaged. That was when he met your mother, while he was disguised as a human. Although he lived in hiding for several years, he shared the truth with your mother about who and what he was. She accepted him, despite his initial deception, and grew to love him as he loved her.

"Lorrie'nar never forgot his mission, but was unable to leave. You see, his love for you and your mother was so powerful. Lorrie'nar was a valiant warrior of unmatched courage and grace, but one day his mission took him to the very precipice of disaster. He finally had to leave.

"What's more, he had to lie to your mother so that she could not be accused of aiding his escape. It was a terrible choice, having to leave his child and love, but to stay would have meant your deaths. These many years later, he grieves still. He left the spoils of his final mission with your mother, and the forest rejoices to see that she passed on this pendant to you."

Eliza held the crystalline dragon pendant in her hand, sensing the meaning behind it. This was a link to her past, the last gift her father gave her mother. Emotion shook her body and tears streamed down Eliza's face. Thomas and Sarentha were there to hold her upright while she wept.

"I am sorry, Eliza," Finwe said. "When the trees convey your readiness, I will lead your father to the woods near your home. Once the truth is revealed we can help your father find his way, and then perhaps you and he can be united once more."

Eliza nodded through her sorrow, and offered a small hopeful smile to Finwe. She choked out a "Thank you" before he turned and disappeared into the jungle's darkness.

Sarentha stood in silence waiting for Eliza to regain her composure. After some time, their guide dropped lightly out of the trees and motioned them to follow. The return trek went much more smoothly than their efforts to enter, and by nightfall they were at the jungle's edge bidding farewell to Lief'senshai.

Thomas looked at his friends when the nimble guide faded back into the jungle. He felt that their journey was almost done. The last of their quests had been completed. Despite his initial reluctance, Thomas found himself looking back on their journey wistfully. He realized he would miss travelling and experiencing strange new things more than he ever would have imagined.

"There is no reason for it to end yet," a voice spoke from behind, and Thomas spun to see a small elf lad. His shoulder-length blond hair was silky and smooth. He wore plain beige robes that hung to the ground. With his hands folded into the sleeves, all Thomas could see of him was his face. His eyes shone with a strange inner silvery light.

The other two were startled, but Thomas had the impression

that his silent thoughts had somehow been read by the boy, who nodded to Thomas in confirmation. Thomas' eyes grew wide.

"Fear not," the boy spoke aloud, with a slight tilt of his head. "I do not share what I sense. I have learned over the years to keep my knowledge to myself."

"Who are you?" Thomas asked, before either Sarentha or Eliza could speak.

"My name is Ellie'nethise... for now," the boy answered. "I come from a blood line of prophets, and have the ability to see things that others cannot. For you I see greatness." The silvery eyes locked with Thomas', and Thomas knew in his core that the message was meant for him. "I am sorry, I spoke out of turn," the boy continued. "I was too excited to meet you. I could not stay home and let this moment pass."

Sarentha chuckled. "Are you talking about Thomas? You were excited to meet a lumberjack playing at guard duty for a lady?"

The boy nodded, before his eyes turned toward Sarentha. "And you and Eliza of course. Your exploits will be legendary as well. But even among your heroics, Thomas shines like a beacon in your presence."

Eliza and Sarentha shared an incredulous look. Thomas was sure what to make of the elf's pronouncement.

"I forget myself," Ellie'nethise continued. "I am not here to speak of your futures. I bring a gift for Wizard Wettias." He opened his hand and showed them a large golden coin. Sarentha gave a low whistle, but the boy handed it to Thomas for safe keeping. "Make sure the wizard gets this. Tell him it is the key that will harness unlimited magical powers. Give him the name 'Arus Borneam of Cephae', and he will set you all on the road to an astonishing legacy."

"Who will? Ramar or this Arus Borneam?" Eliza asked.

The elf stood quietly for a moment before nodding enigmatically. "It was good to meet you all. We will meet again. Good fortune in your travels."

Although not quite as graceful as their guide, the elf boy quickly hopped back into the jungle and in a moment was out of sight. The trees seemed to swallow him up, leaving no trace of his ever having been there. The only tangible proof of their jungle mission was the heavy gold piece in Thomas' hand.

Looking at the coin, Thomas saw the profile of an aged, robed man, and the name Arus Borneam pressed below. On the other side was a skull.

Sarentha found their horses nearby, dug distractedly through the saddle bags, and emerged with the map of Foodle. He scanned quickly over it and looked up triumphantly. "I knew the name sounded familiar! Cephae was the name of the ruins we were near when we were at the golden tree. I told you we should have checked them out! Can you imagine the riches in that place, if they had large golden coins like that one?"

Thomas held it up for them to see. "How would an elf boy have gotten this coin? Those ruins must be almost a month's travel away. And why would his parents let him wander the jungle alone like that to come see us?"

"That 'boy' is probably older than all our ages combined!" Eliza said. "Elves have incredibly long lives, and age much slower than humans. My blood is a mix of elven and human. Although I age at the same rate as you, my uncle seems to think I should outlive everyone I know."

Speaking of her heritage brought a reflective expression, and

Eliza idly touched the dragon crystal at her neck. Thomas was quiet so as not to interrupt her thoughts. Eliza broke the silence. "You won't tell anyone."

"Tell them what?" Sarentha asked.

Eliza started to respond when she noted Sarentha's cheeky smile. Thomas nodded in assent, implying he had heard nothing in the first place.

They mounted their horses and headed for home. This time they would take the long way around the Empire's borders to avoid any more trouble on the roads.

Chapter 14: Returning

After the difficult walk through the jungle, the grassy plains were a welcome relief. On horseback they flew.

They travelled with haste, pushing their horses to take them home. After the words of the mysterious Finwe, Thomas sensed that their quest was coming to a close. Soon they would learn the truth that Erwin Winston spoke of; soon they would discover the greater purpose beyond their secret tasks.

But as they rode closer to civilized lands, their rapid pace drew unwanted attention. Thomas was surprised when he spotted three riders on horseback approaching from the south. Nowhere near the roads of the Empire, he did not expect to meet anyone. The strangers were human males. The leader raised his hand, motioning them to stop, which they did.

"Identify yourselves," he ordered, reining in his horse. His dark blue eyes stared at them commandingly from behind the metal nose guard of his cap. Thomas felt uneasy when he noticd the soldier's right hand rested easily on a sword at his hip, while his companions held upright lances bearing the banner of King Dalmethias.

"We are travellers," Eliza said smoothly. "We were simply out for a ride into the plains to see the sights."

The scout grimaced. "Riding in the outlying lands is forbidden. And in any case, there is nothing of interest for you to see out here."

"We have seen gazelles and a lion pride, actually," Eliza lied.

In truth, Thomas had seen nothing more than a few rabbits and snakes. But stories of lions had been told to young children to dissuade them from wandering too far from civilized lands.

The leader smiled and pointed south. "You will come back with us to Tamor. I'm sure the inquisitors will find your northern stories very interesting. They might also find the tale of murder on the road to Themat worthy of attention. Drop your weapons to the ground for confiscation."

Eliza's horse snorted and side stepped, as though sensing her rider's unease. When the leader's eyes turned to her, Sarentha moved his hands to his daggers. With a quick toss, Sarentha's blades spun furiously through the air, shining in the sunlight. One struck a lancer, the blade sinking deep into his unguarded leg. The other rider had spotted the motion. Mounted as he was, his movement to dodge the missile cost him his saddle, and he fell with a sickening crunch to the ground. His neck broke on impact.

Thomas froze. He watched the lead rider snarl, his eyes angry with protest. Eliza brought out her small crossbow, which she kept loaded, and fired a bolt into the lead rider's shoulder. As the rider on the ground slumped lifelessly to the side, the leader's horse reared in panic and unseated him the moment his hand reached up to the bolt protruding from his shoulder.

The third rider, scowling with pain from the dagger in his leg, lowered his lance. With a howl of anger, the man levelled the lance's point at Sarentha and began his charge. In an instant, he learned about Thomas' fierce protective instincts, when all one hundred and ninety pounds of flesh and bone slammed into the man, dragging him from horse to ground. The two toppled over each other and rolled through the grass. Thomas came out on top, and his fists pounded into the man's face, knocking him unconscious.

Thomas turned just in time to see the leader rising, drawing a long sword and advancing. On his knees, Thomas felt his muscles tighten, and he bellowed in anger. The savage fury of the yell caused the leader to falter, giving Thomas enough time to rise up and bring his axe into the melee. If anyone there had hoped for a long battle, they were disappointed. The man brought up his blade to protect himself from Thomas' powerful downward blow, but his single sword arm was no match for Thomas' two muscled limbs powering the axe home. The sword flew to the side. The blade of Thomas' axe crushed through the metal cap and buried itself in the man's skull.

Silence.

Eliza sat poised upon her horse, crossbow reloaded and ready in case any enemies moved. Sarentha watched in awe. He was unarmed after throwing his two daggers in his opening move. Thomas had barely exerted himself in the battle, yet he found his breathing laboured as he pried his axe from the leader.

Three corpses. Thomas' thoughts of killing Hank Grimbling came back to him. At least Hank had picked that fight. With time, Thomas had been able to justify his actions. But this? These soldiers had been planning to take them away for murder: murder they had actually committed.

Turning on his companions, Thomas asked, "Why did we just kill these men?"

Eliza slung her crossbow over her shoulder and stuck to her canned answer. "Our mission is a secret, and therefore we must be extremely secretive. I signalled to Sarentha that I would distract them so he could give us an advantage."

Thomas had missed that signal. Still, her answer did not sit well with him. "We could have tried reasoning with them. These were men of Tamor! Certainly they will send more to find us. Now we've murdered two groups of soldiers."

"They did not sound eager to negotiate," Eliza commented. "And it was not murder, it was self-defence. They wanted us unarmed and easy to take. For all we know, they were bandits disguised as soldiers of Tamor who would have robbed us the instant we laid down our arms."

Thomas rolled the leader onto his back, averting his eyes from the gaping head wound. He pulled a pouch from the man's belt. Inside was a paper with the mark of Tamor ordering them to patrol the outskirts for trouble. They had known about the murder off the road of Themat. With these two pieces of evidence, Thomas was certain they were not simple bandits.

Sarentha thought fast. "Well, we couldn't just let them take us into custody. What if they had learned what we were up to?"

"What *are* we up to?" Thomas asked, his voice breaking with hysterics. "I wouldn't even know what to say to anyone who asked! Maybe I could say we're collecting weird little bits of strange artefacts for an unknown purpose? Or that we're returning from a failed mission to find Eliza's father? What interest would any of that be to the city of Tamor? They'd let us go out of boredom!"

"Calm down, Thomas. Stop and think," Eliza said in soothing tones. Thomas felt his blood pressure go down. Something in the way she spoke and her tone calmed him. "Soldiers of Tamor killed my grandfather ten years ago," she said, "My relationship to him is likely known, and would bring questions back home to my uncle. We carry with us the map of Foodle, which is said to be cursed and highly valuable. You saw the sum my uncle paid for it.

Wandering the wilds with this in our possession might be enough to draw suspicion. And what about the coin from Cephae you have been entrusted to safeguard for Wizard Wettias? Some might think that a strange errand too. All of this is difficult to understand since there is much we do not know. We cannot chance running into someone who is better informed than we are and who could piece together whatever my uncle wants to keep secret."

Everything she said was true. Still, Thomas was finding it hard to convince himself that such wanton violence was the only possible response. "Do you honestly believe this secret truth is worth the lives of these three men, and the two before?"

Eliza sighed, shaking her head slowly. "I am not sure, to be honest. All I know is my uncle was adamant that this remain a secret, and he was terribly worried about the consequences of any information falling into the wrong hands. We cannot take any chances. By the time this patrol is missed, we will be long gone. We might even be back in Whampello before these men are discovered. I do not know where we are exactly, but I am certain that we are far away from civilized lands."

Thomas wiped his axe blade clean, and hooked it back on his belt. With these reflex motions he realized he had become very used to having a weapon at his side. His axe, like the tool he had carried for work, was a deadly instrument. A chill ran down his spine with the thought of being hardened to battle and death. He was not sure he wanted to become so cold and cynical.

In his saddle once more, Thomas signalled his horse to ride on ahead of his two friends. While Eliza and Sarentha spoke of the necessity for violence and death, Thomas could not help believing there must be a better way. He hoped their days of killing were behind them.

* * * * *

    If Thomas thought his own travels were difficult, he could not have withstood Thurzin's trials on his journey home to Trahllen. The tunnel from Khrymyre to the edge of the southern Witchwood Forest took a day on foot and was a tight squeeze for a dwarf and his stubborn war horse. The dark forest on the other side was treacherous. Stinking bogs and foul marshes dotted the way, which Thurzin took great care to avoid. Trolls, giant lizards, and wicked warlocks lived in those woods, and were quick to strike any intruders. Thurzin had to kill only one lumbering swamp troll, where he was challenged to keep the beast on fire long enough to properly kill it. If they were not incinerated, trolls had a habit of rejuvenating and holding lifelong grudges against those who attempted to kill them.

    After clearing the evil forest, the mountains were even more sinister. Giants ranged in height from three to six average humans. Cunning and brutal, they waited to ambush anything that would make an easy meal. Dwarves, who rarely roamed from their mountain homes, were a delicacy. Enormous feral cats and canines patrolled the mountains in packs, and were capable of bringing down mammoths and simple-minded dragons that could feed them for days. Altogether it was a tense and terrible ride, and Thurzin was glad to be home.

    The grand Gates of Kranoth led to the mountain chambers and halls of the dwarves. Crafted of mithril, the towering gates were light enough that dwarves could easily push them open, but strong enough that no attacking force had ever been able to break through.

    Thurzin's eyes adjusted quickly to the darkened halls of the mountain kingdom. He could see as much in pitch black as

A Noble's Quest

humans saw in bright daylight. The sound of hammers echoed all around, to the accompaniment of deep singing voices. Industrious and proud, for centuries the dwarves had defined themselves by their craft. Thus was the way of the dwarves.

Thurzin's heavy metal boots crunched along the stone floor, adding to the chorus of hammers on metal. Thurzin stalked unerringly through the halls of Trahllen, his black armour a spiked shadow in the dark depths. Dwarves along his route paused in their work, offering him a smiling salute. Thurzin's armour told them what he did, and every dwarf admired a Rager. The Rager was always the first into the fray, and often the last to leave it. Watching a truly gifted Rager in action was the stuff of legends, and in battle Thurzin lived up to these visions of pure brutality. He had torn apart entire groups of goblins single-handedly in such a ferocious manner as to make even stout dwarven soldiers blanch.

The hall curved gradually downward, until he reached a large stone arch carved from the earth. Once inside the underground kingdom, there were no doors, and the opening to the King's Keep in Trahllen was no exception. A dwarf was always welcome anywhere. As for dwarven enemies, they never had the chance to see the great cities of stone. Great metal doors guarded every entrance to the kingdom, and a dozen guards stood ready to sound the alarm should any threat approach.

So it was that Thurzin entered King Rhell Stonearm's quarters without preamble. The royal guards, outfitted in the drab armour suitable for lightless halls, all knew Thurzin personally. Thurzin recognized a few that had even expcrienced the great honour of fighting alongside him. Thurzin, a friend and advisor to the king, was the eyes and ears of the dwarven nation in the surface world.

The wizened old king turned at the sound of the familiar metal boots. His aged face crinkled up with delight, making his black eyes disappear in the folds of his wrinkled skin. "Thurzin me lad! So good t' be seein' ye! I had been worryin' ye'd been et up by some beastie!" The king's robes were plain and grey, with a black axe symbol embroidered onto his chest. His grey hair was neatly braided down to his waist, and his beard consisted of two grey braids tucked into his belt.

"Nay!" Thurzin chortled. "Dunno if there be a beastie big and bad enough t' be eatin' me. But somethin' may get me yet!" He lowered his tone. "And perhaps soon, me King."

King Stonearm's thick black eyebrows shot up. "Ye be meanin'–"

"Aye," Thurzin said, nodding soberly. "They'll be needin' every hammer an' axe arm we can spare. War be comin' t' the surface dwellers soon enough."

The king jumped up eagerly and ran to a carved stone shelf. From out of the cubbyhole he pulled out a glorious bejewelled axe. The double-headed weapon had dwarven runes engraved on both blades and its leather wrappings of the haft were rumoured to have come from the nastiest creature of the lowest levels of the cavernous mountains: a Draykul. Draykuls were said to have no sight at all, and breath that could kill a dwarf at a hundred paces. They were black as midnight, and cold-blooded so as to be undetectable in the lightless depths by creatures with infra-red vision – not a problem for dwarves who saw in black and white. In living memory, no dwarf had fought one and lived to tell the tale. The Axe of Dwarven Lords had been crafted by the first king of Trahllen, Throkden Mithrilweaver, and passed down to subsequent kings through the centuries.

A Noble's Quest

Unlike other monarchies where the king was born into his position, dwarves competed for the crown with three challenges: The Craft, The Wisdom, and The Battle. Each contender had to showcase his greatest creation, which was then judged by field professionals for superior quality. The few who crafted well enough to satisfy the judges moved on to the next stage. The Wisdom challenge entailed the telling of old tales to demonstrate the prospective king's appreciation for the rich oral dwarven history spanning the ages. The ten most knowledgeable dwarves were then selected to compete in the final phase. The Battle required the would-be king to go alone into the depths of the caves and bring back the head of the most powerful creature he could slay. Needless to say, the competition was not for the faint of heart. The battle to become king was so fierce that many did not return from this final challenge. It was said that any dwarf who died in his attempt to be king was given a seat in the ever-living earthen chambers of the dwarven lords of old to watch over his people and bring them long life.

Knowing all this, even the sturdy, battle-hardened Thurzin felt a chill to see his king take up the ancient axe of his people. A dwarven king in battle was the stuff of song for generations.

"War, ye say," King Stonearm said, hefting the axe with one hand and admiring its perfect balance and quality. "I'd be up fer that!"

Thurzin grinned, and slapped the king's shoulder. "Aye, I would be too. An' that wizard friend o' mine made me a little surprise t' help even the odds."

The king spat. "Ne'er trust a wizard!"

"Bah," Thurzin argued. "Wettias be a good man. He's been keepin' me kickin' fer two kings, now!"

King Rhell grimaced. "Hopefully not long enough t' see a third!"

"Says you!" Thurzin laughed loudly, the sound echoing through the halls of the castle. "Anyway, ye better be gettin' over yer squeamish feelin's, fer ye'll soon be fightin' alongside a few wizards. Tamor's got a whole tower full, an' most of 'em will be standin' with us."

The king bellowed, "I'll mop up them that ain't!"

Thurzin shook his head. "Nay, me king. Wettias has a plan for them that ain't with us. Just you be gettin' yer stuff an' our people ready. There'll be more 'n enough heads t' bash fer all o' us."

The king backed up a step when Thurzin held aloft a small shining tube of metal. "That yer wizard toy?"

"Aye," Thurzin nodded, wistfully turning the object over in his hands. "I plan on findin' some particularly tough heads t' be gettin' with this 'ere trick. Wettias be a good friend, an' an incredibly dangerous enemy. We be lucky t' be on 'is side!"

King Rhell puffed out his chest. "An' he be lucky t' be on *our* side! Dun ye be fergettin' it, neither!"

"Ne'er, me lord," Thurzin said, bowing his head respectfully.

Appeased, the king nodded, patting down his beard. "So, we be ready t' be headin' out? That damn alarm taken care of?"

"'T'will be soon, not t' fret. We got some o' our best boys on it as we speak. No one'll be the wiser t' the march o' the dwarves!" Thurzin proclaimed.

* * * * *

Thundering snores obscured the approach. Ten stout soldiers crept up the mountain trail as quietly as dwarves could creep. Luckily for them, the 'alarm' was a notoriously sound sleeper and appeared to be unaware the dwarves knew of its existence. Set five hundred years ago, the dwarves had discovered that the alarm knew the sound of marching dwarves quite well. Had it been disturbed by the dwarves leaving the mountains in numbers great enough to form an army, it would have awoken and alerted its masters.

Two burly dwarves cautiously raised their heads over the rim of the plateau at the top of the mountain, then hunched back down. They signed to their comrades that there was indeed one hazard, and it appeared still to be asleep. They motioned in unison for the crossbowmen to ready their bolts, and for the sappers to head out first.

Even before leaving on their mission, the dwarves loaded their crossbows. Travelling with heavy, loaded weaponry involved risk, but they had no choice: crossbows being loaded are a noisy business and they did not want to set off the alarm prematurely.

Four dwarves in light leather armour crept silently up the path to the plateau's four compass points, thus surrounding their sleeping target. Two crossbows were raised, still concealed from below, just in case misfortune required them to shoot quickly.

The two dwarves who had peered over the edge remained where they were. Their heavy armour meant that they could not creep silently into position like the sappers. Their muscles were tight and ready for the fight. Beside them was a Rager, who was even less quiet than the defenders. His spiked shoulders moved up and down as he breathed deeply, mentally preparing himself for the bloodbath to come. The dwarves had been surprised when Thurzin suggested taking a Rager into battle against the alarm. Sure, Ragers could pummel just about anything to death and feel no pain in the throes of battle, but they were anything but subtle.

The soldiers prayed that he could subdue his noisy breathing as he fell more and more into his rage.

The last member of the group was a cleric of the First Dwarf Mother, Tium, sent along to keep the rest alive. Even with the element of surprise it would be a difficult fight, but a well-trained holy dwarf with magical healing powers could easily turn the tide of battle. Clerics rarely left the mountain halls, for those who could commune with Tium were highly valued and protected in dwarven society. The fact that a cleric had been assigned to this mission reminded each and every dwarf present that this was an undertaking of utmost importance.

The trap was ready. The sappers did not have long to wait.

The signal, they had all agreed, would be the Rager's sudden and wild appearance. There was no missing his approach when he rushed up the mountain path like a beast possessed. His battle cry was a prolonged, deafening scream as he rounded the corner. The sappers immediately lunged, their light hammers raining down surprisingly heavy blows on the silvery, drowsing dragon.

The drake, having been asleep for a very long time, screeched with shock at the sudden rain of pain all over its body. The hammers had been aimed to hit the tender flesh exposed by the scales that had risen up during slumber. Staggering to its feet, the wyrm smashed a sapper down the side of the mountain. The cumbersome beast deftly sidestepped more attacks, even as the Rager jumped onto the dragon's rump.

Two crossbow bolts flew at the dragon's left wing when it began its ascent, but neither bolt found its mark. The crossbowmen reloaded quickly, even knowing that the dragon would be far too fast for them to stop it.

More nimbly than anyone might expect, the Rager dodged a

swiping clawed fist and scrambled up onto the drake's back. He pounded his spiked fists into the scales, and his ebon armour allowed him to find a good hold on the dragon's otherwise smooth hide. Before the wyrm could fly in any direction, the Rager had advanced up the neck and began punching its skull.

The dragon shook its head violently from side to side to try to rid itself of the stubborn dwarf and, in doing so, lost altitude and fell to the ground. The impact shook the plateau and jarred the Rager loose. He slammed down to the earth with a heavy grunt.

The beast was again under attack from the sappers' stinging hammers. The defenders were there now, too, their heavy battle axes chipping into the monster's chest while they stood before it hurling insults. One bellowed, "Yer mother was a wee snake!" The other shouted, "The dwarves were the first, ye overgrown lizard, an' we'll be the last!" Meanwhile, the crossbowmen had reloaded, and let fly their piercing bolts. One found its mark in the dragon's shoulder, grounding it.

The silvery beast screamed angrily, and unleashed a blast of frigid moisture. This froze one of the dwarven defenders in place, coating him in ice. Knowing it was too late for the defender, the cleric rushed to the stunned Rager, muttering prayers of healing. The stubborn warrior rose to his feet and charged in for the wyrm's belly.

Claws, tail, wings, and teeth flew in all directions and battered the dwarven attackers. The dwarves knew it needed time to recover its breath before freezing more dwarves, and the stout warriors were agile and clever enough to know when to get out of the way of a flying clawed appendage.

The sappers were following the Rager's example and had clambered up on the drake's back, pounding constantly. The defender's axe cut into the side of the dragon's head when it turned to bite, and blood coursed over the beast's eyes. The Rager was prying scales from the wyrm's belly and driving his spiked fists into its flesh. The gore rained down, throwing the Rager even further into his element of fury.

With a final shudder, the dragon fell, smothering the Rager under it, and shattering the frozen defender to pieces when its head fell upon him. The remaining dwarves hollered with pride, for even though there had certainly been casualties, they had succeeded in their mission. The alarm had been eliminated and soon the dwarves would march.

They rolled the wyrm over, and found that the Rager had suffocated under the beast. None of them could think of an end better suited to an out-of-control warrior. With a great collective heave, they sent the corpse of the dragon over the mountain, and watched it plunge far below. As they carried the body of their fallen Rager along with the axe of the fallen defender, they sang a song of afterlife. The hymn's theme told of the ale to be drunk with all the dwarves who had fallen in combat before them.

Chapter 15: Final Preparations

There was a light rap at the door, but it opened before Ramar could answer. A tall, fair man with perfectly straight blond hair strode briskly into the wizard's chamber. His robes were golden with glints of shining silver trim, and his posture was erect. He folded his hands into his sleeves and his eyes turned with disdain to the cluttered room. Wizard Wettias firmly believed that a truly intelligent mind could work as well in chaos as in an organized room, so he did not bother to tidy his laboratory.

Ramar turned, and the newcomer's elegant eyebrow lifted slightly, a sign of curiosity at the wizard's emerald glasses. "Ah, excuse me," Ramar said, lifting the glasses from his eyes and blinking rapidly. "A gift from a dwarven friend of mine."

"Filthy creatures," the visitor said, starting slightly when the door closed behind him. "I come for your daily report to the king."

"I have been at work on these glasses all day," Ramar answered. "Come, try them on, Horus."

Horus stood still for a moment, obviously not wanting to enter any further. But Ramar waited patiently until Horus' interest won out and he approached. He gingerly took the glasses from the old wizard, and held them up to his eyes.

"What am I supposed to be seeing? Everything just looks green." Horus said.

"Put them on," Ramar said, turning away from Horus and washing his hands in a nearby basin of crystal-clear water. "They do not work unless you put them on."

Horus' lips pursed and his eyes narrowed, but he put the glasses on. "I still do not see anything."

"Look in the mirror," Wettias said.

Horus turned to the mirror and gasped. He tore the glasses from his head, and his slender fingers sent them flying across the room. They floated there with a word from Ramar, and made their way back to his waiting hand.

The two men shared a long moment, staring at each other knowingly. Ramar's steely grey eyes matched the intensity of Horus' green eyes, and neither blinked.

"You know why I cannot let you leave this tower, or even this room," Ramar stated firmly.

"You think you can stop me?" Horus puffed up his chest, trying to look intimidating.

"Easily," Ramar answered. It was not a bluff. In his own chamber, in his own tower, his powers were immense. Magic coursed through him in an unending stream. A wizard's home was not a place outsiders entered lightly. "This belongs to you," Ramar said, holding up a small gold ring. The band was plain, except for a few arcane runes etched into it.

"I thought it misplaced, but I see you for the thief you are. Give it back," Horus commanded.

Ramar's eyes narrowed. "Try to take it."

Magic blasted forth violently from Horus' hands, coming to the call of the powerful wizard, but its power simply ceased to be, as though hitting a wall before Ramar. Flames and fury were not enough to break the spell Ramar had cast upon the ring.

Ramar smiled. "My turn."

Wordlessly, Ramar held up the ring between his forefinger

and thumb. Horus, for the first time, showed fear. His eyes widened when Ramar wound magical cords around Horas' throat. The magic that had heeded Horas' call a moment before was surrounding and strangling him.

"My, what power you had," Ramar said with a hint of longing in his voice. "But it is mine now. You see, I discovered a fascinating text describing how to ensnare an enemy's magic. It is tricky to conjure, but the results, as you can see, are amazing. With your personal possession – this ring – properly enchanted and finished with your own magic cast into it, you cannot harm me. In point of fact, *I* can harm *you*. And when I tell you that you will not leave this tower alive, I mean it with the utmost sincerity."

Horus could not respond. His hands were weaving quickly through arcane motions, but every spell he summoned failed. Every attempt he made to strike down Ramar Wettias ended the same, with not even a spark of power leaving his fingers. His eyes bulged, and he bared his teeth in anger. With all strength leaving his body, Horus fell to his knees, his hands going to his throat in an attempt to tear the invisible cord from his neck.

Suddenly it was released, and Horus gasped for air greedily, filling his lungs as he sputtered curses at the man who had stolen his supremacy. "My kind will have your head for this, wizard!"

"On the contrary," Ramar said, turning the ring in his fingers, "I doubt they will have time to miss you at all."

"Time–?" Horus' response was cut off. The cord of magical energy cut deep into his neck once more. He shook his head in defiance, trying to invoke magical powers to his aid, but to no avail. Moments passed, as the golden-robed wizard struggled, flailing uselessly on the floor. Horus' powers failed utterly, and his body was forever stilled.

Ramar watched the dead man on his laboratory floor for some time. Turning his gaze out the single window, he looked toward the castle. Horus had come to see Ramar every day, at the King's behest. For years Ramar had obediently answered endless questions about his comings and goings. How many magical trinkets had he created for the King? And how many had he created for his own, private use?

Ramar looked at the glasses with the green lenses. It was a fine trinket. Crafted from large dwarven emeralds and wrapped in lightweight mithril frames, they were far more elegant and sturdy than the simple wire-wrapped glasses the goblin shaman had worn. How a mere goblin had ever come across something so wonderful was beyond his knowledge. The ability to see the truth otherwise magically concealed was a powerful tool.

How many wolves in sheep's clothing walked among them? Ramar would soon know.

His allies would arrive, and the truth would be laid bare.

* * * * *

The Winston compound was in turmoil as men and horses milled about. Eliza observed from the shadows as her uncle's men moved forth with purpose. Sarentha pointed to silent sentries from neighbouring compounds who were also watching the hubbub with great interest.

A man coughed lightly behind them, and Eliza jumped and turned to see Richard Winston, dressed in his light chain-mail shirt and leather greaves. Richard whispered, "Sorry for intruding. Father wanted to send Lyle or Denton, since they are both much stealthier than I am, but I thought with all this commotion in the courtyard, even a giant could stumble through the woods unnoticed."

Eliza smiled and hugged her cousin, relieved to see a friendly face. After their two encounters with Tamorran soldiers, she felt vulnerable.

Richard broke off the embrace and asked, "Where is your father? I was told he is meant to ride with us to the gates of Tamor."

"Change of plans," she answered. "He and the elves will be meeting us there."

"Excellent," he said. "We've received news that the dwarves are on the march."

"*What* is this all about?" Eliza asked, unable to take the suspense any longer.

Richard shrugged. "I haven't the faintest idea. Father is a man who overly enjoys theatrics. He keeps whistling tunelessly, refusing to tell anyone what is going on, and urging patience. Whatever he has in store, it will be grand, I'm sure."

"Does anyone know we're alive?" Sarentha asked. He continued to scan for anyone else who might be on the lookout.

"No," Richard answered. "But father said that the ruse is no longer needed. He wants me to take you into the compound through the front gates to showcase a rousing public victory when his treasured niece returns home, alive and well. He keeps saying we need to keep up morale in these final hours."

Eliza exchanged a curious look with Thomas and Sarentha, not liking the sound of those last words. It seemed bizarre that her uncle would make such a fuss about falsifying their deaths, and then turn around and proclaim they were alive. Whatever his game was, Eliza did not comprehend the rules.

Thomas stood up and brushed himself off. "How do I look?"

Eliza looked him over and laughed.

"Like a man who's been married to his horse for far too long," Sarentha quipped, running his fingers through his own greasy hair. "It will be nice to have a bath."

Spirits buoyed by the idea of being back in civilization, Eliza followed Richard. Sentries from other noble compounds pointed at the newcomers. People who had been watching the fury of activity were now distracted by the group heading toward the gate of the Winston compound.

When they arrived, the nearby activities ceased. Soon others stopped to see what was happening. They all looked as though they were seeing a ghost.

"Eliza Winston lives!" Richard called triumphantly.

Cheers erupted. Upon hearing the joyful news, the people in the manor's courtyard massed around her, reaching out to touch and confirm that it was she.

"My dear niece!" Lord Winston's voice cried from the front doors of the manor. The crowd parted as Lord Winston came forth with arms outstretched.

His commander, Ben, followed in his wake, beaming at the sight of Eliza. Their eyes momentarily locked, and she returned the smile, eager to speak with him.

Lord Winston yelled, "You are alive! Oh glorious day, to think you've come home!" He hugged Eliza in a crushing embrace, lifting her from her feet. The people nearby wept tears of joy and another cheer went up.

Lord Winston asked, "And who are these heroes at your side, my dear?"

Eliza turned her attention to Thomas and Sarentha. Her mind raced. "These two men, born as peasants, rose to the challenge of freeing me from the dreaded grasp of wretched forest goblins! After many weeks of planning, they broke through my prison. Together we felled the monsters and are returned home!"

As the people cheered, able-bodied men hoisted Thomas and Sarentha into the air. Erwin gestured the men toward the streets, so that they could celebrate with the citizens of Whampello, for many had mourned Eliza's loss. The mob flooded into the town, spreading the news. Nobles and peasants alike rallied around Eliza's miraculous return. Cheers broke out for the great heroes who had aided her escape from the goblins. The day wore on into night, and the tale became larger than life, with Thomas single-handedly killing three orcs, and Sarentha bypassing devious traps and riddles to unlock Eliza's magical cell. Drink flowed freely, and at some point early in the night it was decided to take the celebration into the broad streets and large inns of Tamor the following day.

The people bade their goodnights, and headed home for some sleep before the trek to the capital. Sarentha grinned from ear to ear, and even Thomas wore an easy smile while they made their way back to the Winston estate. Lord Winston himself showed them to guest quarters fit indeed for heroes. The canopy bed was wide enough for three grown men, and the sheets were silken and smooth. The down-filled pillows and mattress were like clouds beneath them as they sat on the edge of the bed, removing their road-weary clothing.

Thomas' smile faltered slightly when he saw Lord Winston's serious expression. "Tomorrow morning we ride to Tamor. It is as important for the peasants to see the truth as it is for us who are involved in this quest. There will be many innocent people who join us, and we must try to keep them at the column's rear. Soldiers will be riding up front, as will the two of you. At the break of dawn I expect you both up and dressed. I believe you will find fresh armour to your liking in the armoire, along with some well-crafted weapons. You two will be on display, and it would not do to have you dressed like peasants in badly worn equipment."

Thomas looked down at his trusty axe, and thought it did not really look so bad. It certainly was not the same quality as the kind Lord Winston's soldiers carried, but he felt it had more than proved its worth. He was about to argue, but stopped when he saw Lord Winston's serious stare.

Sarentha jumped off the bed and rushed to open the armoire. He let out a low whistle and took out a heavy leather breastplate with the customary Winston arrow symbol etched into its front. Two daggers with gleaming blades hung in a belt, and Sarentha hefted them, admiring their balance and keenness. There were words engraved on the blades, but when he showed them to his friend, Thomas found the flowing script was alien to him.

"The leather breastplate was crafted by my own people, but the daggers are from a previous age," Lord Winston said, watching Sarentha spin them deftly. "They belonged to a hero named Hendricus Wyrmstriker, who I have learned was an ancestor of yours, Sarentha. The full set of eight daggers was lost, but these two were entrusted to the elves before his death. The elves of the northern jungle held them in safe-keeping until we learned of your lineage."

Sarentha thought back to his favourite book growing up, *Clifford and the Ogre*. Clifford had been an ordinary man who had fabricated his own heroism. Would the story have had a different tone if Clifford had been the descendant of an actual hero? Certainly Sarentha had performed tasks that Clifford would never have dreamed of doing, but could Sarentha ever truly see heroism as his destiny? Lord Winston insisted on them looking the part, and maybe that would make it authentic. It was Lord Winston's deception, not his own. Perhaps one day he would live up to his heritage.

Thomas understood what Erwin meant about looking the part of a hero when he unsheathed the long sword that had been left for him. The work was exceptional. He could see the razor-sharp edge and the mirror finish. He had no idea what such a weapon would cost, or how talented the craftsman must have been, but he did know he would cherish the weapon for as long as he held it. On one side, etched runes flared to life in the room's brilliant candlelight. On the other side, the word "Strongblade" was legible.

Lord Winston spoke reverently. "I received a full history of the Strongblade in a letter from the elves. The blade was created for the hero Matthew Strongblade by the allied races in honour of his glory. This sword is crafted of the rarest of metals: adamantium. The dwarves forged it in their hottest fires in the depths of their mountain homes. While still molten hot, the dwarves hammered the runes into one side and the name of the blade on the other. Although Wizard Wettias no longer remembers this, he had a part in the sword's enchantment, with the aid of other wizards who died centuries ago. The combinations of spells woven into the adamantium prevent it ever from dulling, and give it immense power. Matthew Strongblade, the greatest hero of the human race, wielded the blade in his battles against oppression and injustice. Yet even with such an arm, he could not overcome the terrible odds in his final battle. Before he died, Matthew asked Hendricus to protect his sword, so that it would not be lost. In its day, the Strongblade was a shining beacon known to all. Matthew knew that to lose it forever would have been a travesty, for he believed the hope of his people rested with his weapon. The Strongblade, in the light of day once more and held in the hand of a hero, will inspire a new generation. The elves have rightly decided that the sword must go to Matthew's heir."

The news that he had descended from a hero who was the stuff of legends came as a shock. Thomas did not feel worthy of such a weapon. He did not feel like a hero. It was Sarentha who unlocked the sarcophagus with the amethyst, Sarentha who climbed the tree, and Eliza who brokered the deal with the jungle elves. What had he done to deserve all the acclaim? He did not even like to fight. How ashamed would this Matthew Strongblade, this true hero, be of him?

Lord Winston mistook Thomas' hesitation for awe, and clapped him on the back. "You will do the sword proud, Thomas. When the people of Whampello see you with such a weapon, they will not doubt your heroism. Until the morning."

And with that, Lord Winston left the room, leaving Thomas and Sarentha with their new gear.

Still inside the armoire was a metal breastplate for Thomas, and two fine sets of boots and reinforced leather greaves for them both. There was a dark brown cloak, which Sarentha took immediately, and a deep-red one which Thomas gratefully accepted. Decked out in all their gear they truly did look like heroes from olden times.

In the back of the armoire was a shield with an arrow painted on the front. Thomas had never owned a shield before. He was not even sure how to wield one. But when he hefted it, the solid grip felt like a natural extension of his arm.

"Do you suppose there will be fighting in Tamor?" Thomas asked, as he reverently set down his shield. "Is that why Erwin is outfitting us so well?"

"I don't see how there could be," Sarentha said, buckling up his leather armour. "You saw Tamor. It's huge and well-defended. All of Winston's men would only make up a tiny portion of the armies stationed in Tamor. No, I think he just wants us to look good so we fit the story Eliza told."

"Eliza just told the story today," Thomas said doubtfully, "and this equipment feels like it was made for us."

Sarentha sighed in exasperation as he picked up the brown cloak, wrapped it around himself and looked in the mirror with approval. "You just never rest that questioning mind of yours, do you Thomas? Do you honestly think Lord Winston would risk his own life, or the lives of those who serve him? I don't think he'd be that foolish. Just relax. Tomorrow we ride to Tamor, find out what Winston thinks is the truth, and then we can do whatever we want. I would like to see some of those ruins on Foodle's map."

Thomas nodded, thinking about the logic behind Sarentha's argument. Could he imagine Lord Winston, the careful, meticulous planner, suddenly being overcome by suicidal tendencies? He had to admit it did not sound likely.

"Ruins," Thomas muttered, lying back on the bed. "Well, I guess I don't have any plans after Tamor. If you're curious, we might as well go back and see those old ruins. Speaking of which, I must remember to give that old coin to Ramar tomorrow when we go to Tamor. That elf boy wouldn't want me to forget."

Sarentha positioned his daggers and struck a heroic pose for the mirror. "Sarentha, saviour of Lady Eliza!" He flourished his cloak, sheathed the daggers, and rolled across a thick fur carpet before springing back to his feet. "Of course, if we're off poking around some ruins, no one will see how heroic we look!"

Thomas smiled through his yawn, a twinkle in his eye. "But there could be more big gold coins in the ruins."

"Sold," Sarentha said with a huge grin, and he put away his new equipment. He continued to prattle on about riches and imagined dangers in the ruins of legends, but it all faded away as Thomas closed his eyes and drifted off to sleep.

Chapter 16: Party

A loud knock at the door startled Thomas from a sound sleep. Sarentha groaned, rolled over, and pulled the soft pillow over his head. An unfamiliar voice from outside said, "Time to get up! The party is starting!"

The events of the previous night came flooding back to Thomas in an instant, and he found himself alert and ready. He shook Sarentha, and nearly sprinted to the armoire. Without hesitation he began suiting up.

"You're not even going to bathe?" Sarentha said groggily from the bed as he rubbed his eyes. "Granted, I don't notice the smell because I probably smell terrible too, but heroes should be clean for a party in their honour."

Thomas nodded, and moved to the tub. It was already filled. The water was hot and lightly scented. Had someone come in while they were sleeping? He mused that after all the celebrating of the previous night, a band of goblins could have come thundering through and he would have slept through it.

After his bath, he pulled on the fresh clothing that had been laid out for him and shook Sarentha awake, again. Thomas knew mornings were always difficult for Sarentha, and the comfortable bed made rising even more challenging.

"Thanks for changing the water," Sarentha muttered. He crawled into the tub and let out a huge contented sigh. "The bath is almost as comfortable as the bed."

"I didn't fill the tub again," Thomas said, pulling a padded shirt over his head. "I left it dirty to punish you for sleeping in."

"But how could that be? You were filthy!" He looked down at the water with wide eyes. "So was I! And this water is sparkling!"

"I guess heroes get magical baths," Thomas said with a chuckle. "I could get used to this."

Sarentha lounged back in the sublime, warm water. "Me too. We probably shouldn't, though. If you think about it, this charade will probably be over by the day's end. Lord Winston will reveal his mysterious truth, and then he'll have no more use for us peasants."

"What do you think the truth will be?" Thomas asked. They had avoided the question for weeks but at this point Thomas found it hard to contain his curiosity.

Sarentha shrugged. "I don't know. I've been trying to work it out in my head, but nothing seems to make sense. First, we have the beheading of Lord Winston's father. So, a revenge plot? And the elves have been involved in the whole mess from the start, so they would want to get in on the action. But then why are other races involved? Igatiolus and Thurzin don't fit the revenge idea. So far as I know, they had nothing to do with Lord Winston's father's death."

After a pause, Sarentha continued, "And what about the memory loss? In the jungle, Finwe said the elves had suffered the most, so once again they fit the plot. Thurzin is connected with Wizard Wettias, who we know lost some of his memory. Maybe somehow Thurzin, who is highly influential with the dwarves, convinced his comrades to go along. But from everything I've pieced together, humans and gnomes haven't been affected by memory loss."

Thomas and Sarentha shared a long look before Sarentha shrugged. "I just don't know what to make of it. We obviously don't have all the information yet, so we'll just have to go along with the ride and be surprised like almost everyone else."

Strapping arm guards to his forearms, Thomas nodded his agreement. "Well, I look forward to finding out this big secret, and then we can get back to our normal lives."

"Maybe," Sarentha said, before he dunked himself underwater. When he emerged, he was clean from head to toe. "However, I have to say it has been fun going on adventures. The danger and intrigue..." he smiled wistfully, "it will be difficult going back to a mundane life. You don't suppose we'll sit around the tavern talking about our glory days and wishing we hadn't quit, do you?"

"Perhaps," Thomas answered, checking himself in the mirror. A hero from a bard's story, he thought, his breastplate gleaming in the dimly lit room. He touched the sword handle at his hip, and turned slightly from side to side, admiring himself. "Not many people have a story like this to tell."

"You know what I mean," Sarentha said. He reluctantly pulled himself from the water and towelled off.

Thomas knew. How could they go from hero status back to general labourers? Was it possible? He kept pictures in his mind of the things they had seen. Thoughts of the golden tree, the tall buildings of Tamor, the northern jungle, and all the different races spun through his head. They had not been adventurers for long, but he thought that if Lord Winston still had need of them after the truth was revealed, then he would have a hard time resisting this new life.

Sarentha, naked, leaped under the covers when a light knock

on the door sounded. Eliza stepped inside without waiting for an invitation. Dressed in a flowing light blue dress with a modest neck line, Eliza looked the part of a noble. She smiled at the string of curses emerging from under the covers. "Please," she said when he finished. "After all we have been through, seeing each other at our worst, you are still shy? Do you not trust me? I promise I will not make any remarks unbecoming of a noblewoman."

When Sarentha grumbled something unintelligible, Eliza examined Thomas in his new armour. "You look very handsome, Thomas. I trust that your new gear is more than adequate payment for obtaining the branch, and travelling to the jungle?"

"We get to keep it?" Sarentha's excitement could not be contained from beneath the bed covers.

"Of course," Eliza said. "You two are heroes. Uncle will not allow me to wear my armour today. He says that I must look the part of a lady, because appearing otherwise might draw suspicion."

Thomas nodded. "You look very fine, although I must admit I hardly recognize you without your armour and the crossbow slung across your back."

Sarentha hissed, "Can we talk about how wonderful we all look *later*? I would like to get dressed, so I don't miss our party!"

With a laugh, Eliza turned her back. "I will not peek," she offered. "I want to tell you of the day's happenings. Although Uncle Erwin filled me in on some of the plans, he remains silent about the truth. I have never seen him so excited in all my life. He has always been so reserved and watchful... suspicious even, of what I know not. But today it is as though a great weight has been lifted off his shoulders. This is the culmination of his life's work.

He says nothing can go wrong now."

"Famous last words," Sarentha warned. He put on his suit of leather armour and draped his cloak over his shoulders, before taking one last glance at himself in the mirror.

Eliza ignored his comment and continued. "In a few minutes, everyone is to gather at the town square. The party will not begin until we arrive, but we do not want to keep the people waiting. We are to recount the story about how I was captured by goblins, and how you two helped rescue me. Embellish on that as little as possible. After an hour or so of shaking people's hands and kissing babies, our party will move to Tamor. By the day's end we will make camp not far from Tamor's gates. During the night, Uncle Erwin's soldiers will gradually filter to the column's front."

There was a long, puzzled silence. "About those soldiers," Sarentha said hesitantly, "what's Lord Winston up to? Why would he want the soldiers in the front? Certainly he doesn't plan to attack Tamor. Their armies must be so much greater than his manor guard. And what would be the purpose?"

Eliza shrugged. "I do not know. All he said was that the revellers must not ruin the surprise; therefore the soldiers will keep them away from Tamor. May I turn around now? I am tired of speaking to a door."

"Sure," Sarentha said.

When she turned, she let out a low whistle. Sarentha's polished metal buckles were as bright as Thomas' breastplate, and the fine dark leather suited Sarentha's black hair. "You could use a haircut and a shave, both of you, but otherwise you certainly look the part of heroes. If I did not know better, you might even fool me!"

Thomas smiled at that, and slapped Sarentha's back. "I feel

rather heroic today," he said, standing straight in front of the mirror, straightening his cloak so it was even on both shoulders.

"Travelling the world is going to your head," Sarentha said.

"It is time, you two." Eliza opened the door and headed out. Through the windows Thomas could already hear the gathering crowd. His stomach tied in knots with worry. Hopefully everything would go according to plan and he would not make a fool of himself.

* * * * *

If Thomas' armour appeared to shine indoors, it was almost blinding in the morning sun. People shielded their eyes while watching the three heroes emerge from the manor. Raucous applause and cheering exploded from the group, thereby announcing their arrival at the town's centre. All manner of people were gathered to celebrate, from the simple labourers who had worked alongside Sarentha and Thomas when they were lumberjacks, to the nobles who were so fond of Eliza.

"Good to see you back, my lady," said a soft, excessively flattering male voice. Eliza turned to see the Duke of Whampello keeping pace as the onlookers parted the way. He was dressed in a bronze breastplate, but the rest of him looked decidedly gaudy. He wore puffy white sleeves, black pantaloons, and frills on his knee-high boots.

Eliza said, "Greetings, Your Grace. I hope all is well."

"As do I," the Duke said in syrupy tones. "Enjoy the spectacle in your honour."

Many others were calling their names and reaching out to touch the two heroic men. After all, it was not every day lumberjacks thwarted the plans of an entire goblin camp to save a fair lady.

Lord Winston stood upon a stage. White banners, embroidered with the symbol of the black arrow, hung from the four corner posts. Ben stood at his side, also dressed in full battle garb, though it was not polished to the same degree as Thomas'. Thomas supposed this was intentional, and that no one was to appear more heroic than he.

Lord Winston wore a dark purple tabard over his white dress shirt. The Winston arrow emblem shone gold on his chest, and his smile beamed. He held his arms wide and embraced Eliza when she stepped up for all to see. After a long moment he let her go and vigorously shook the hands of the men seen by the crowd as heroes.

Lord Winston held his hands in the air to hush the crowd. The morning was warm, and birds chirped merrily while the people stood quietly gazing up at the five figures before them.

Lord Winston asked, "Today is the perfect day for a celebration, is it not?"

The crowd roared their agreement.

"There is food and drink for all! I am so grateful that my niece has been returned safe and unharmed, and I invite you to partake in my joy!" Lord Winston slapped Thomas and Sarentha on their backs, and gave them a gentle push toward the appreciative throng. The musicians took their cue and began playing. The melody of the flute and lute floated softly through the air, punctuated by the beat of drums. Altogether, the music gave the gathering a sense of intimacy and warmth. Thomas took one last look back at Eliza and Lord Winston before being swept away to shake hands and recite the tale of their heroic quest.

Thomas was overwhelmed by the crowd's support and admiration. Such a short time ago, hardly anyone had known who he was, although he had lived in Whampello his entire life. Now there was not a person in the town who did not know him.

But some remembered.

"Woulda been better off staying gone," a man's deep voice spoke. The crowd opened in front of Thomas, and he saw his old boss Frank Grimbling flanked by his two remaining sons Adam and Buck. They appeared as angry as the day Thomas and Sarentha fled.

"Yeah, maybe you should have kidnapped the girl from the goblins and left well enough alone," Adam chimed in. Buck and Frank gave him quizzical looks, and Adam blinked stupidly a few times before realizing that kidnapping the niece of a lord was a pretty ridiculous idea, and probably not better than returning to the town of his brother's murder. Some townsfolk chuckled at the man's idiotic remark, only fueling the Grimblings' anger.

"I don't have any reason to fight you," Thomas said, speaking slowly and calmly to diffuse the situation.

"But you had reason to kill my son?" Frank's face was red, much as it had been whenever Thomas and Sarentha had been late for work.

"I'm sorry," Thomas said, holding his hands up defensively. "Your sons attacked my friend, and things got carried away. I did not intend to kill Hank."

"Well, dead is dead!" Frank roared angrily, advancing toward Thomas, fists balled and ready for a fight. He had only moved a few steps before Ben's large frame came between them. Ben looked down upon Frank Grimbling.

Ben's dark face had lost its usual big smile and was now deadly serious. His hand rested easily on the haft of an axe at his belt, and his muscles rippled with the promise of unbridled aggression. "Is there a problem here?"

Frank's eyes narrowed and he looked around Ben at Thomas, "What? The big hero like you can't fight your own battles? You need to hide behind a soldier? Pfah!" Frank's spit went wide of Thomas, but Ben's closed fist did not miss the mark. Frank went tumbling down before scrambling back up to his feet.

"This is a celebration," Ben said menacingly. "If you're not here to celebrate, you'd best not be here at all."

Adam and Buck had come to their father's side, but after eyeing up Ben and Thomas, they decided to leave well enough alone. The young men led their father away.

Ben turned to Thomas and clapped his shoulder, the two men standing eye to eye. Ben spoke quietly, "Thank you for returning her to us, Thomas. I owe you my gratitude."

"She did as much to keep us safe as we did for her," Thomas spoke humbly.

Ben burst out laughing, and clapped Thomas' shoulder once more. "I'm sure she did! Eliza is quite the spirited lady! Either way, I'm glad to see you all safely home. Enjoy the party."

With the mention of the party, people again began to mill about, the unpleasantness of the Grimblings soon forgotten. Thomas watched Ben make his way through the crowd to stand by Eliza. The two shared a tender gaze, before Eliza's attention was arrested by the excited crowd once more. The connection between Ben and Eliza suddenly became clear in Thomas' mind. How difficult it must have been for them to be apart. Eliza, Thomas, and Sarentha had been away for nearly a month and a half. Why had Eliza not told them? Thomas did not have long to think about this before being surrounded by admirers once more.

A half hour later, Thomas almost believed it: he had told the story of Eliza's rescue so many times that he did not even need to think about it anymore. The role of hero was feeling more and more real to him. But the truth came back to him when the time came for the party to be moved to Tamor. Lord Winston offered to pay all labourers their lost wages, and the people eagerly scattered to gather travel supplies.

Thomas was left alone again in the empty town square. His ears hummed in the sudden quiet and he felt relieved that his part of the charade was over for the time being.

"So," Sarentha started, his voice sounding hoarse. "I'm sort of glad that's over with."

Both men turned when they heard Ben and Erwin approaching.

"Well done, men," Erwin offered, shaking their hands. "You were perfect! The march to Tamor will begin shortly. If we have no delays, we should be close to the gates by nightfall. In the morning, we will enter the city to see the grand sights."

"What is expected of us?" Thomas asked.

Erwin's smile did not falter. "I have already filled Ben in. He will share the plan with you on the morrow. It is vital that we do not slip, and though I have faith in you both, there will undoubtedly be alcohol on today's trek. I cannot risk a slip of the tongue. I do not trust everyone who will be accompanying us."

Thomas understood the feeling. He looked over his shoulder to make sure the Grimblings were nowhere in sight. He would not have put it past them to use this moment of quiet to set upon him. Were there others in the town who did not believe their story? Although Thomas vowed to be vigilant and not drink along the way, he knew Sarentha would not refuse free ale.

At that moment Eliza approached, appearing very happy. She

was flanked by the gnome Igatiolus and the Duke. "It is good to be back in civilized lands!"

Erwin turned and hugged his niece. "It is good to have you home, my dear. But you need not keep up the ruse in our present company. Igatiolus and His Grace the Duke are both aware of our plans."

"Of course," Eliza said, offering them both a nod and smile. "It was, after all, Iggy who found the map. And the Duke made it clear that he knew there was more going on than a simple party."

"Yes, Erwin and I hatched this plan quite some time ago," the Duke said, with just a touch of chill in his voice.

Lord Winston smiled and winked knowingly at the Duke before turning to Igatiolus. "The gnomes?"

"Ready," Igatiolus replied.

"Excellent!" Erwin clapped his hands excitedly. "The gnomes and elves are accounted for. We will have more joining our party in Tamor."

If Thomas hoped for more information, he was to be disappointed. The group turned toward the manor and prepared for the trip.

Upon entering the stable, Thomas was surprised to see his horse. The animal had been groomed and tacked in a fine harness, with leather barding. Indeed, it looked the part of a heroic steed. Thomas looked at the boy who handed over the reins and imagined him as a young squire, training to become a great hero like himself.

Sarentha took the reins from the other stable boy, patted his horse's cheek, and whispered in her ear. She whinnied a bit before nuzzling at the apple in his other hand.

When Sarentha saw Thomas' amused stare, he explained, "I

was just promising to take better care of her. Seeing her all dressed up and fancy looking made me feel bad for not having brushed out her mane more often on the road."

Thomas laughed. "You can kill a man with your daggers, but the thought of your horse not being properly groomed upsets you? You are a wonder, Sarentha."

The Duke stalked into the stables and said in a furious hiss, "Do you have any idea how hard it is to find good stable boys?" Thomas instantly realized his mistake. The Duke grabbed the gawking lads by their ears, and spoke viciously, "You killed *goblins* with your daggers, you fools! Not men! *Goblins!* Do *not* make that mistake again." Without another word, he dragged the two confused-looking boys from the stables.

Thomas stood in awkward shame for a moment. Even the horses seemed on edge. Their tails whipped from side to side, and their ears flicked. Thomas laid a calming hand gently on his horse's neck.

Sarentha whispered, "You don't suppose–"

Thomas shook his head, "He wouldn't–"

Sarentha swallowed loudly. "He's just going to restrain them until later. That has to be it."

"They take this sort of thing seriously," Thomas said doubtfully. "I'm going to feel pretty guilty if those boys come to harm."

Sarentha nodded slowly, still staring after where the boys had disappeared with the Duke. "Let's mount up and get out of here. I just want to get this over with."

The incident had Thomas longing for calm. With the disappearance of two innocent boys, he now had second thoughts about staying on with Lord Winston.

Shaken, Thomas rode out of the manor complex to find hundreds of people preparing for the trip to the capital. Although merchants and craftsmen often travelled to Tamor for trade, most of the other townsfolk never had the chance to see the big city. The regular tasks of survival kept people both busy and poor, and travel was simply out of the question. Lord Winston's gracious generosity had given the people of Whampello even more reason to celebrate.

Several carts were already assembled with barrels of drink and boxes of foodstuffs. Thomas, still on edge, wondered if this instant readiness might alert people to the fact that this was not just an impromptu visit to Tamor. But nobody seemed suspicious.

Thomas felt a hand clasp his shoulder. He turned to see Lord Winston riding beside him, waving to the crowd. Out of the corner of his mouth, Erwin mumbled, "Act normal and wave to the people. Smile. What is wrong?"

Thomas forced a small smile and waved to the crowd, which seemed to appease them for the moment. Thomas leaned in and whispered, "What did the Duke do with the stable hands?"

Erwin appeared puzzled and asked, "Stable hands? Why would Calarin lower himself to deal with stable hands?"

"I was not careful in my speech," Thomas replied cryptically, and Erwin nodded his understanding.

"They were probably put down in the wine cellar until our party has left town." Erwin spoke in soothing tones, the same way Eliza did to calm his nerves. "Just remember the story and try not to say much else."

Thomas nodded. He still was uncomfortable with the situation, but managed to grasp the hands of a few folks when he rode by. At least those poor boys would not be killed because of his loose tongue.

Before long the assembled party became mobile. The happy travellers sang and skipped along, filled with energy and joy. As the trip wore on people conserved their energy and settled for talking and walking. Alcohol flowed freely, helping to keep the mood buoyant.

Thomas was unsurprised that Sarentha was deep in the drink by the time the column of celebrants had halted. The man was not used to being the centre of attention, and the liquid courage was helping him soak up as much as he could. The goblins became larger and more numerous with each telling, and his crowd grew more and more eager to hear the tale repeated again and again.

As Erwin had predicted, the group was near the city by the time they stopped for rest. Night had come, and the path was dark. Soldiers took out torches, and campfires were set along the road for warmth as the temperature dropped. Thomas pulled Sarentha away and helped him settle by their fire closer to the front of the column. Sarentha's head barely touched the ground and he was sound asleep.

Looking around in the firelight, Thomas saw that the plan was going smoothly so far. The majority of Erwin's soldiers had moved to the front without alerting anyone, while the celebrants remained at the rear. With everything set for the morning, Thomas yawned and hunkered down to rest. It had been a busy day and he felt exhausted. Tomorrow he would learn the truth, whatever it was, and all of this would be behind him.

When he closed his eyes, his mind wandered back to Whampello. He hoped that the stable boys were all right.

Chapter 17: The Truth

Thomas' eyes opened slightly to a hazy scene. Sounds of shouts and warnings filled his ears, but he was almost too tired to notice. A dark, blurred object came down towards his head, and his eyes snapped open.

The boot that had been poised to stomp on his face suddenly disappeared with an angry shout. He sat up, his hand moving for his sword. To one side a man was being wrestled down by a handful of Erwin's soldiers. To the other, a flashing black-clad figure was entwined with his attacker, trading blows and blood. In front of him, Thomas saw another man – Frank Grimbling – coming straight for him. Frank gripped his large wood-cutter's axe with both hands, his face contorted in fury. Guards yelled and pointed, but none were near enough to intercept the enemy.

Thomas bellowed in rage, feeling his adrenaline pump and his muscles tighten as he rose to his knees. It was all he had time for, but it allowed him to get his sheathed sword ready to intercept Frank's downward chopping axe. The two weapons clashed and rang, and the axe bounced harmlessly to the side. Thomas stood up, and Frank readied another mighty swing.

"This is for Hank!" Frank hollered angrily, his axe coming down in an arc.

But the axe blade buried itself in the dirt where Thomas had been standing. Thomas' gleaming blade protruded from the man's back. "So be it," Thomas breathed softly with a hint of sorrow. He pushed the dying man aside. The sword slid with a sickening sound from Frank's stomach and, coughing and gasping, he tried to hold in his intestines.

"Nice work, lad!" Thomas turned to the familiar voice of Thurzin, who was disentangling himself from another Grimbling corpse. The guards were pinning down Adam, the last living Grimbling son, whose eyes bored hatefully into Thomas. He cursed the loss of his father and brothers, and swore he would avenge them.

Thurzin said, "I'd 'ave taken 'em both out, but I figured why steal all the fun? Figured I'd give ye a sportin' chance by takin' the lead runner an' give ye an opportunity t' wake up enough t' fight the other one."

"Thank you," Thomas said quietly, looking down at the man he had just put to death. "Funny how I don't feel as bad about killing him as I have felt about killing in the past."

"Eh, ye get used to it is all, lad," Thurzin said with a smile. He flicked a bit of something off one of his long armour spikes. "Filthy cowards who'd attack a sleepin' man don' be deservin' any remorse. Ye did what ye had to, tha's all. If it be makin' ye feel any better, one o' our greatest clerics back home be a pacifist. His thoughts on it be, usin' the mantle o' pacifism t' avoid trainin' t' defend what ye love an' cherish is the stuff o' cowards. A true pacifist still be needin' t' know how t' fight, an' he'll choose it as his last option. But if the fight be comin', the pacifist be ready t' end it quick, fer he takes no pleasure in drawin' the battle out."

Thomas looked into the dwarf's bright eyes with newfound respect and admiration. His own feelings had never been summarized quite so well. He thought back to those who had died by his hand, and of the man squirming in agony on the ground before him, and realized he had never instigated any violence. He had responded as he should by saving those dear to him, and defending himself. Frank's movements slowed, and his grimace faded. All Thomas felt was disgust at this man who could not stop feeling hatred, and who dishonourably sought revenge against an unprepared opponent.

"Thomas!" He turned to see Erwin running over, his purple cloak whipping in the wind. "My men just alerted me! Are you injured?"

"No," Thomas said, looking down at himself, "thanks to Thurzin. I'm afraid my clothes have a bit of blood on them, though."

Thomas noticed people were looking at him in awe. The action had taken place over scant seconds, but a few had seen the speed and sureness of Thomas' blade. Witnessing such agility and prowess only helped to strengthen Thomas' image as a hero. The onlookers quickly told others of the attempt on Thomas' life, saying he had awoken from a deep sleep to thwart the attack with the help of a very scary looking dwarf. Word spread like wildfire.

Thomas was cleaning himself up as best he could when Sarentha approached. His friend wiped ale from his mouth before saying, "I was just getting to know some folks near the party's rear. So, I hear you took out five very large men single-handedly with a knife? Doesn't sound much like you. I'm sorry I wasn't here to help."

"It was the Grimblings," Thomas said, not smiling at Sarentha's jovial tone. "They came to kill me in my sleep. Thurzin took out one of them, the guards subdued another, and I killed Frank. It all happened so fast I had no choice."

"Never mind, they got what was coming to them," Sarentha said, clapping his friend on the back. "We're finally done with their kind. Adam won't see the light of day for a long time, from what I hear. Winston's fuming mad, and swore he'd lock him up in shackles for the rest of his days as penance for his family's crimes. Winston's not the only one who's angry, of course. Adam is swearing to avenge their deaths by killing you. But he can threaten all he wants. Winston's resolved to lock him away."

Thomas took in this information and hung his head, his brow furrowed in thought. Sarentha gave him a shake. "Don't let this ruin the party. Today's the day we learn the truth! Don't let the Grimblings steal our thunder."

"It's not that," Thomas said slowly. He turned to Sarentha. "When the moment came, I didn't think twice. I saw Frank coming, and I ran him through."

Sarentha nodded. "You're afraid you've gotten used to death. I don't think you can go through everything we have without becoming harder. I remember how I felt when you killed Hank with your lumberjack axe. That seems like a lifetime ago, and I feel like a different person now."

Thomas turned away again, looking down the road toward Tamor. "I'm worried we're not done yet. This truth is going to be colossal, I just know it. What if it's so big none of us can ever go back to the way we were? I'm not even sure I want to know the truth."

"Live a lie?" Sarentha balked. "That's absurd! No matter what happens, I think that knowing the facts can only help us."

"What you say has the ring of truth," Thomas said. He smiled then. "The Rogue of Truth. I think that will be my new nickname for you."

Sarentha grinned back. "There's the Thomas I know. Let's go see Winston. It's time."

Thomas returned to the camp fire, now spent. He brushed the dirt from his clothes and donned his armour. Once dressed, he headed to the front of the column.

The soldiers were ready, their eyes set straight ahead for their goal in the unseen distance. Thomas knew that they were aware of the plan. Everyone seemed to know the plan except the two of them.

Ben approached, concerned. "Everything all right, Thomas? Thurzin looked atrocious. Of course, he said that's because he made a mess of the other guy. Was it those louts I turned around yesterday?"

Thomas nodded. Ben frowned. "Well, it sounds like they got what they deserved. Good job. You seem a lot handier with a weapon than when we first met. Using arms in the field is better than any training regimen. I bet you'd make a fine soldier in our ranks."

"I'm honoured you would think so," Thomas said. He left it there. At that moment, he was not at all sure he would choose a life of soldiering. He may have been the largest, most intimidating man around, with the exception of Ben, but his heart was not in it.

"Today our eyes will be opened," Ben said, leading them toward the front of the group. Their horses had already been brought to stand directly behind Erwin Winston's mount. Beside Erwin rode Eliza, who smiled with relief to see them. Ben took up position between Thomas and Sarentha. The rest of the troops followed, out of earshot.

Ben spoke softly, "We're riding into Tamor. The guards at the gate are good men, and will let us in without question. The gnomes and humans of Tamor have taken up key positions, and the scheduling of the guard has made sure that sympathetic forces are strategically placed. According to Thurzin, the dwarves will soon be ready."

"Aye, just about," Thurzin announced, riding up on his horse in spiked black plates. When they looked back in welcome, Thurzin pointed down the road. Approaching at high speed was Wizard Ramar Wettias, his robe billowing.

He came to an abrupt stop and bowed low. "Lord Winston, a pleasure as always." He handed a small velvet bag to Erwin, and a long, linen-wrapped package. "And for you, Thurzin." said the wizard, giving Thurzin a similar velvet bag. Then he opened a sack. It was immediately clear that the sack was magical, for Wizard Wettias drew from it a shield far larger than the bag. The shield was wrought in silvery metal with a conical face in the shape of a great dragon's visage. There was a hole in the shield's middle, where the drake's mouth revealed fierce teeth. The shield had no handle.

"*Now* the dwarves be ready," Thurzin said with a long-drawn sigh of contentment. "It be a thing o' beauty, Ramar. Thank ye!"

"You're welcome, old friend," Ramar said, his eyes twinkling.

Thomas rode over to Wizard Wettias before he could turn to leave. "Excuse me, Sir. I have something for you."

Ramar looked at him authoritatively and said, "Do not call me sir, lad. It makes me feel old!"

Thomas looked down awkwardly and stammered an apology. Wizard Wettias guffawed, and extended his hand for the gift. "I jest, Thomas. I am very old, and have to find my fun where I can."

Thomas gave the wizard the large gold coin he had safeguarded since the jungle. "An elven boy from the northern forest gave me this, and told me to tell you that it is the key to unlimited magical power. He said I should tell you the name Arus Borneam of Cephae, and that you, or he, or both of you would help us become legendary. He was cryptic on that last part."

Wizard Wettias inspected the coin carefully, muttering incantations under his breath. Eventually, he slid the gold piece into a pouch on his belt. "Well, it has no magic of its own. I will need to investigate this further another time." He continued, "I will meet you all in the city. Make haste! The morning sun rises on a new age!" With a flick of his hand and another arcane utterance, he disappeared.

The Duke of Whampello rode up and looked skeptically at Thurzin. "What exactly does the word 'subtle' mean to a dwarf? Was I not inconvenienced enough to have to restrain two stable boys in Winston's wine cellar for the loose tongues of our peasant helpers? How do you expect to not draw attention holding that thing?"

Thurzin's glower settled squarely on the Duke. He pulled out a long metal tube from a bag at his belt, pushed it in behind the shield's hole, and snapped it into place with a click. "An' I suppose ye think a column o' soldiers ridin' inta town will be plenty subtle, ye daft foppish dolt?"

The Duke, incensed, straightened in his saddle, ready to lash out with the fine slender blade at his belt. Lord Winston quickly motioned for them to pay attention. Thomas saw he was wearing fine glasses with green lenses, similar to the shoddily-made ones Lord Winston had taken from the goblins.

"Put aside your quarrels, friends. We cannot very well fight amongst ourselves right now."

"Aye," Thurzin agreed, drawing another set of green glasses out of the velvet bag Wizard Wettias had given him. He pulled them over his eyes and blinked a few times. "Fer now."

The threat hung briefly in the air until Lord Winston signalled his horse forward, motioning to the others to fall into formation behind him. At the back of the column, observant celebrants began to note the new configuration of soldiers at the front. Their questions about this curious change received no answers.

Figures materialized out of the trees along the path when the gates came into view. Eliza found herself staring at an elf whose shoulders were stooped. His gaze was focused on something off in the distance. Finwe, the elf they had met in the jungle, prodded the other elf. When he looked up, his eyes grew wide.

"Katharine? Is it really you?"

"Father?" Eliza's eyes grew misted with vague recognition of the figure before her.

Lorrie'nar was visibly shaken, and Finwe held him so he would not fall. A single tear trickled down his cheek. "I am sorry, you look so like her."

Eliza dismounted to stand before her father. He was more slender than the other elves, and slightly shorter than she. Not having fought or travelled for years, he had become weak and thin. She noticed Finwe smiling at their reunion, and she felt a flood of relief and happiness. After his disappearance, she had always wondered how she would react when she saw him again. Now joyous tears streamed down her cheeks.

Eliza held her father tight, not wanting to let him go. "I am glad you have come."

Lorrie'nar looked around, as though unaware that he had travelled a great distance. "Where have I come to? What is this place?"

"You are outside Tamor," Eliza said.

Lorrie'nar appeared stricken, his eyes whipping about frantically. "I am not prepared! I cannot go in there!"

"Perhaps this will help," Lord Winston said. He pulled a long, shining sword from the linen wrap Ramar had given him. The arcing blade gleamed majestically in the morning light. Leaves of distant jungle trees were etched into the base of the blade, and the basket hilt appeared to have been woven from golden vines.

"Tallia," Lorrie'nar said, holding the blade reverently in his hands. As he caressed the shining steel, it hummed with his touch. Blue light sparked as the morning sun danced along the blade's surface. "How is this possible?"

"I know you did not mean to shatter it, those years ago. You were driven by grief," Finwe said. "I sent it to the dwarves to be reforged, and Wizard Wettias breathed life into it once more. Let your blade sing, Lorrie'nar, Raja Bladesinger of Amaroh, and let your enemies know fear at your return!"

With each word, Eliza's father gained strength. His jaw clenched, and he tightened his grasp around the blade's grip. He looked around, his eyes now filled with purpose and determination. "We are not enough," he said. "I survived that city by a hair's breadth. We cannot take Tamor with only a few hundred soldiers."

Thurzin grunted, "*Obviously* we've got a plan, ye daft elf. Now hurry it up. We got some truth t' be revealin'!"

* * * * *

The guard opened the gates of Tamor without a word, and the file of riders passed through with little fanfare. Thomas felt a nervous energy when people in the streets turned curious gazes to the column of armed men entering the city from the east. Though the circled arrow blazed on each soldier's tabard, Thomas figured the Winston symbol was largely unknown in the huge central city of the Tamorran Empire.

Lord Winston led the procession to the city centre, where the markets had already opened. Even that place went silent as the soldiers filed in. The foot soldiers created a semi-circle formation around Lord Winston and his mounted companions. The implacable stone walls of the castle stood before them, impenetrable and heavily guarded as more of the king's soldiers took up their positions. In all the years of the Tamorran Empire, Thomas never heard of any who had dared align soldiers against the capital city.

A tall spire pointed high into the sky, a sort of stone arm reaching toward the heavens. Word of the troops' arrival had apparently already reached the occupants. King Dalmethias appeared on a balcony, and looked down upon his subjects.

Thomas had never seen the king before, and the tall, handsome man was imposing from on high. A gleaming gold circlet topped his head, and he raised his hand from the confines of his rich purple cloak to point at them.

"Calarin!" The King called from his lofty perch. "Such a pathetic gathering of troops! I might have known one of such lowly birth and foolish ambition might dare try to overthrow me."

Not waiting for the Duke's rebuttal, Lord Winston interrupted. In his hand he held a small grey stone he had taken from Ramar's velvet bag. He put it against his throat, and his voice boomed across the city for all to hear.

"King Dalmethias, King of Tamor, Deceiver of his people, I assure you that Calarin had little to do with this. He has been my pawn, and little more," said Erwin. "We come of our own accord, and act in our own best interest. In this kingdom, there is as little room for him as there is for you!"

The King and the Duke stared at Erwin. The King was disgusted, and the Duke, stunned. The Duke hissed, "I will crush you like the insect you are if you think you can turn on me, Winston!"

"You honestly thought I would replace the King with you?" Erwin laughed dryly. "One slaver for another?"

The sound of metal on metal rang in the air, and Thomas turned after Thurzin affectionately punched Khrakhoom on the side of her head. "Ye think I be wearin' these stupid goggles because they be pretty? We know what ye be!"

The Duke faced Thurzin atop his squat, broad mare, the dwarf brandishing his new shield. "Dwarf!" Calarin spat the word like a curse.

"Have at ye, Duke Fluffy-pants!" Thurzin charged, barrelling across the ground. Thomas were stunned to see a lance of pure white light erupt loudly from the shield's draconic mouth. Ben pushed him and the others aside, away from the Duke as the dwarf closed the gap with increasing speed.

The Duke froze, and a look of fear gave way to one of understanding. With a mingled howl of rage and pain, the Duke and Thurzin collided. The lance of light penetrated the Duke, whose form appeared to shudder, sprawl, and grow. Thurzin recalled the lance of light, which disappeared as quickly as it had come forth. The immense form of a copper-scaled dragon lay dead on the stones of Tamor.

Silence fell upon the city. Shock, as Thomas stared at Calarin's crumpled true form. He turned and saw Erwin Winston's triumphant smile.

"Your lance of light cannot reach me here, fools," King Dalmethias called down. "I would thank you for destroying this treacherous monster," the King continued, "but your treason warrants death, not reward. Did you think you might fight your way through? My castle is filled with my loyal subjects. You cannot hope to reach me with any life left in your soft little bodies!"

From the long, linen-wrapped package, Erwin drew forth a second object. The violet, rune-covered stone throbbed with an unnatural light, filling the market place with faint purple illumination. Thomas recognized the pieces. The stone he had recovered from the tomb was set in the six-foot long, twisted and gnarled golden branch.

Lord Winston shouted, "King Dalmethias, Deceiver of the people, I seek not to enter your castle! *Morire Drago!*"

A collective gasp sounded when a radiant bolt of lavender light forked up toward the King on the balcony. The King uttered a scream of other-worldly outrage and he underwent a metamorphosis. Golden scales appeared and his body twisted and elongated. He bored his draconic claws into the tower in an effort to hold on, despite the wicked magic that coursed over his body.

The royal scream of shock was joined by others around the great city: Thomas saw drake heads emerge from nearby manors and houses. The dragons watched helplessly as the King writhed in agony from searing pain. The staff's crackle and thunder resonated around the city, more loudly than the dragon King's gasping breaths. With one final shudder, the golden wyrm plummeted to the ground.

The truth hit like a hammer, and Thomas was stunned by the blow. The Tamorran Empire had been ruled by dragons.

Thomas gazed up at the many dragon heads peering out warily from all around. An uneasy moment of silence passed before Sarentha whispered, "I told you that we'd want to know the truth."

Chapter 18: Vengeful Alliance

Chaos.

That was the only word to describe what happened next.

The dragons, seemingly as one, took flight, shrieking in defiance and anger. Some screams were cut short when dense volleys of crossbow bolts came whistling forth from the southwestern dwarven district. Hails of arrows fell from the rooftops, as the elves of the northern jungle took careful aim. Magic erupted from the city's southeast: the gnomes joined the fray with their spells.

The dwarves of Trahllen were not fazed by the prospect of death. They had marched through lethal mountains and evil marshes to get to Tamor, and they were not about to leave without a fight. A few clerics had accompanied them to support King Rhell Stonearm himself, who was battling alongside his warriors. The Archcleric held aloft The First Book of Throkden, uttering incantations that cast the blessing of Tium, the first dwarf mother, over them.

The first volley of crossbow bolts had given the dragons pause, and the beasts were reluctant to take to the air knowing that dwarven sharpshooters were waiting for them below. The dwarves knew all too well, when the wyrms took control over five centuries before, that they wiped the memories of those lesser races they had captured with a powerful spell. The actual mechanics of the spell were unknown to the dwarves, but the survivors had fled to Trahllen. Many dwarves had died in their flight from the drakes, and the dwarves had long memories. They were not forgiving.

But there was another even deeper meaning for the dwarves. As they marched down the streets of Tamor looking for battle, the Archcleric read from the Holy Book. "Dawn, Chapter 3, verses 4 and 5: And the serpent said unto the dwarm, ye shall not surely die: For the titan doth know that in the day ye speak thereof, then your eyes shall be opened, and ye shall be as gods, knowing good and evil."

The dwarven host growled, and the rumbling of their ire vibrated through the city. The serpent had lied to Tium, and that lie had led to the eviction from paradise of Tium and the first dwarf, Adaman. The Archcleric read on. "Dawn, chapter 4, versus 1 to 4: Now the serpent and the first dwarves lived on the land, but Air, who did *not* help create the dwarves took note of the serpent. She said, Serpent, ye told the dwarves of good and evil, yet kept them from the giant of life. *Thus* they are *not* as gods, and the punishment you endure *is* too harsh: I have dominion of the sky, and ye *shall* join me here above the beauty of the land. The serpent was raised up and given wings to fly through the sky, and Air saw that *it was* good."

"'TWAS *NOT* GOOD!" the dwarves shouted in unison, smashing their hammers and axes on their shields. The raucous sound reverberated for all in Tamor to hear, including a nearby dragon.

"I seen it first," King Stonearm growled when a monstrous bronze-coloured drake circled around a corner, tearing at a low-lying dwarven building and collapsing it. The royal guardsmen and clerics protested, but there was no dissuading the stubborn King. "'Tis me right! I called it, an' I'll take it!"

The wyrm roared, belching fire almost far enough down the road to incinerate the front line of the dwarven brigade. The King frowned, his braided beard singed. "Ye'll pay fer that one, stupid beastie!"

Crossbowmen stood at the ready, clerics held incantations of healing on their lips, and hundreds of warriors prepared to rush to the aid of their King. But King Rhell was no slouch in combat, as every dwarf knew. He had killed a most fearsome foe of the depths to become King, and the odds were not in the dragon's favour.

The Axe of Dwarven Lords caught the morning light, its rubies and emeralds casting dizzying prisms. The King's voice bellowed through the city, a rage of generations bursting forth as dwarf and dragon clashed. The drake's huge claws tore at the King, but his deep-forged armour did not bend. The axe whipped side to side, cleaving scales and wyrm flesh. After a long minute of trading blows, the dragon reared its head and breathed a blast of electric air at where the King had been an instant before. The battle-hardened dwarf knew what was coming as soon as the beast lifted its head, and he had scrambled for protection beneath its foreleg and given a mighty upward chop to the dragon's middle, cutting short the breath attack.

The King lifted his axe again, but with a mighty flap of its wing, the drake knocked him aside. End over end he tumbled down the road, then came to a stop at the feet of his troops. He looked at his expectant soldiers. They were primed for action, but he would not satisfy their need. He stood, straightened his helmet, and growled at the drake. "Now ye've just gone an' made me angry!"

The Axe of Dwarven Lords was lost, but that was not going

to stop the King. He sprinted back up the road. The wyrm was bleeding profusely from the King's deep gashes and could not fly. It attempted to flap its wings, but the chop to its middle had severed the muscles necessary for flight. The great beast bared its teeth and snapped at its enemy, but the King ducked to the side and punched the dragon in the eye. Outraged, the drake reared up and came down with all its weight to crush the persistent dwarf. But King Rhell, having spotted his trusty weapon off to the side, was no longer there.

With a triumphant holler, the dwarf king charged in again. The dragon's tail swept in overhead, missed its mark, and hit the cobblestone street with a thud. King Rhell stopped, turned, and chopped down on the threatening appendage, taking it clean off. The wyrm reeled in pain. It half-turned to run, but everywhere it moved, the angry little dwarf appeared, and gouged again.

Summoning the last of its strength, the drake reared back, closed its eyes, and inhaled to breathe out fire. The King's heavy axe swung in again, instantly severing the huge neck. The head and long neck fell, and the rest of the body collapsed.

A mighty cheer rose up from the dwarves. None had ever seen such a grand feat of strength, and the entire army was inspired by their King's heroism. Even the most battle-hardened dwarves were moved at the sight of their blood-soaked ruler.

But the fight was far from over. More dragons appeared overhead, and the King turned to his army with a big grin. "All right lads and lasses," he yelled for all to hear. "I've had me fun! Now ye can have yers! Let's teach these damnable abominations just what kind o' damage an angry mob o' dwarves can do! Fer Adaman! Fer Tium!"

* * * * *

In the castle courtyard, roots of ancient trees rose from the earth and followed the will of Finwe, who stood just outside the castle's great iron gates. The hybrid humanoid-dragon guards were startled at the sudden animation. Normally the dragon kin were disguised as humans. However, with the inevitable battle, they had reverted to their reptilian forms in an effort to intimidate the intruders. Too late, the draconic captain called his soldiers to hack down the trees. The roots twined themselves around the bars of the gates and, with tremendous strength, they heaved. With each pull, the surrounding stones groaned and shuddered. The dragon kin chopped into the trunks, but if the trees felt pain, they did not show it. Again and again the roots pulled. More and more roots joined the struggle. Finally, with one mighty heave, the stones paving the portal yielded and the iron gates flew free, spinning through the air and mowing down an entire rank of draconic soldiers.

Elves appeared atop the walls, raining arrows down on the dragon kin. At the front of the assault was Lorrie'nar, his sword Fallia singing with anticipation. Its high humming note filled the courtyard. Lorrie'nar moved directly for the draconic captain. More elves and dwarves poured in, engaging the other soldiers.

When the trees had ceased their movements, the dragon soldiers turned their axes toward the oncoming enemies. But the dragon forces were not prepared for the Forest Born. As if materializing from nothing, the druids stepped forth from the mighty trees and called down terrible blasts of lightning from the clear blue sky. The leader of the wrathful druids turned to his tree, laying his hands upon its torn bark. With closed eyes, he whispered to the tree's spirit, asking for one last gift. The tree agreed, the spirit left, and the great mass fell, pinning down the rear ranks of dragon men. Whenever allies fell, Finwe called their spirits back. From the remains sprang wolves, badgers, wolverines and bears that attacked the dragon forces with renewed bestial fury.

Amidst the chaos, Finwe calmly walked to the other standing tree. With soft words and a plea to the mighty tree's spirit, the druid laid his hands on its bark. Other druids, of the mending type, channelled their healing powers into the tree, which awoke to the call of the druidic leader. The pith of the tree groaned, its roots once again stirred; it lifted itself up from the ground, freed its roots, and moved to attack.

Despite its size, its strikes were sure and swift, plucking draconic soldiers out of combat and tossing them like rag dolls to their death against solid stone walls. One dragon dared to fly close enough and exhaled its fiery breath. The tree ignited and its bark exploded with the heat. But so long as it lived, the tree continued its single-minded attacks on the half-dragon soldiers below. The wyrm was forced to retreat in a hail of elven arrows.

Along with many others, the draconic captain fell quickly to the fierce song and bite of Fallia. Lorrie'nar made haste; every time he saw another enemy soldier issue commands, he charged. His blade danced and flashed in a dizzying display, his nimble feet allowed him to dodge multiple attacks. Wherever he went, Fallia sang with the glory of the elves, and Lorrie'nar's allies knew where to find him. The allied forces took heart that they were once again led by a hero.

Before its charred remains fell to the earth, the great oak's final action was to use its roots to rip open the main door to the castle. Half-dragon soldiers shot bolts down into the courtyard from above, until Wizard Wettias flew in and cast a spell creating a wall of stone over the entire area. The bolts bit harmlessly into the rock, and the invaders poured through the open doorway to attack the castle's guards.

The loyal dragon-men fought to the end, giving their lives for their drake rulers. Blood from both sides ran in the halls, but at last the allied races defeated the castle's draconic forces entirely.

* * * * *

From their tower windows gnomish councillors in the southeast city district watched the flag of Tamor being taken down. Igatiolus smiled, the others whooped and hollered. Freedom had finally come to Tamor, but he knew it had cost many lives. And not all of the dragons were gone from the city. He looked back to the smooth, seamless walls of the sterile white room. Another gnome sat alone at the large marble table in the room's centre, unable to pretend delight at the conquest.

"It's an amazing accomplishment," Igatiolus said, sitting down across from the other councillor. Dark green eyes glared at him. Igatiolus continued, as though unaware of the menacing gaze. "How pompous the drakes were, thinking they would know when a rebellion was happening in their own Empire. Their sense of invincibility and omniscience was their downfall. We knew, Chuphacious. You strutted around as if you owned us all, which is why we excluded you from our dealings."

Igatiolus held up a tiny purple button. Chuphacious' heated scowl did not relent.

"You actually sent your 'secret meeting' robes out to be laundered? Did you think no one would notice?" Igatiolus asked incredulously. "It's remarkable what technology and magic can accomplish. Tinzibelle created this wonderful device at ten times this size. We used shrinking magic so you would not notice this one new button sewn onto your outfit. Its microphone and spying lens allowed us to eavesdrop and observe that 'secret meeting' you and the other dragons had in that cave."

Yet another wyrm was torn asunder by gnomish ingenuity but Igatiolus ignored the fanfare below. While the great beast had been swooping down to torch a group of gnomes, strategically-placed claws running on steel wire shot out from the surrounding buildings to clamp onto the dragon. Faced with unnatural mechanical strength, the drake could not withstand the quartering.

Igatiolus continued, "On top of that, there were small magical transmitters inside the button which leaped unnoticed to attach to the other dragons at the meeting. After that, it was child's play for Theodonious Winkle to put together a map indicating where all of you slavers lived. Denton Marks took the map and spent weeks watching you all, monitoring your movements with goggles that enabled him to see your true forms. There were indeed many more drakes in the Empire than we had ever imagined. There *were*."

Chuphacious stood slowly, and rested her hands on the table's cool marble surface. Wild applause broke out on the streets when the roof of a nearby building slid open to reveal a gnome sitting in a gunner's seat. With joyful abandon, the diminutive figure released shell after shell from the cannon into the flying dragons. The explosive rounds battered the wyrms from their flight paths, forcing them to fall. They were easily finished off by packs of murderous automatons.

When the din died down, Chuphacious spoke. "Well played, Igatiolus. You have bought yourselves a temporary reprieve from our power. But in the grand scheme, your plot is insignificant. The time will come when our survivors will once again infiltrate your societies, or raze them to the ground."

"Which is why it is important none of you survive, don't you think?"

Igatiolus and Chuphacious locked gazes for a long moment. The crowd outside now craned their necks to see whether any more dragons would be coming to meet their doom. The streets below had grown quiet.

"Bolide!" Magical, deadly flames erupted from Chuphacious' outstretched hands. As the fires died, it was evident that only the area directly around Chuphacious had been affected. The white floor and ceiling were blackened in a neat circle directly below and above her.

"The security and well-being of councillors has always been top priority," Igatiolus said, nonchalantly. Chuphacious lunged forward, but was held back by an invisible magical barrier. She screamed and transformed into a dazzling brass dragon, but the confinement spell grew to hold her entire form. Holes appeared in the ceiling, and green gas began to fill the cylinder.

Without fanfare, Igatiolus murmured, "Goodbye, Chuphacious," before returning to the window to check on the activities outside.

* * * * *

A large silver form turned toward Erwin, and he raised his staff to blast it from the sky. Arcs of purple power danced along the wyrm's body, forcing mad convulsions as it hit the ground hard. It was utterly powerless under the cruel, killing grasp of the golden staff.

"The manors!" Ben shouted, and charged toward the noble houses near the castle. Thomas and Sarentha followed, wanting to get out of the open. Thurzin's horse thundered forward, and the lance of light sparked once more, piercing the writhing silver drake's head in one clean thrust. Lord Erwin immediately turned to face another dragon that was coming at him.

Thomas reached the gate to a manor and turned back to check on Lord Winston and Eliza. Another monster unceremoniously crashed to the ground, causing debris to fly everywhere. Lord Winston turned and let loose a crackling blast of death at yet another drake swooping in for the kill. He no longer had time to unleash the staff's full power as the wyrms were too many and too fast. But with each spin and turn, another fell from the sky. Eliza stood by her uncle's side, firing her crossbow where she could, though Thomas noted most of the bolts bounced harmlessly off the hard scales. Even so, she acted as a second pair of eyes for her uncle by pointing out any drakes coming for them. If the dragons killed Winston and stole the staff they would all be doomed. Her place was with him.

Dwarves charged through the streets, bringing axes and hammers down on the already felled beasts. Arrows rained down from above, which prevented the dragons from rising again. Human soldiers ringed Lord Winston in protection, moving out to dispatch any stunned wyrms that landed too close for comfort.

A battle cry of, "I see ye runnin', ye o'ergrown snake!" turned Thomas' attention back to Thurzin, who chased down a group of three people. Thomas surmised that they were dragons disguised in human forms and that, thanks to his magic glasses, Thurzin could see their true nature.

Another copper-coloured drake landed behind the dwarf where Thurzin could not see it. Thomas opened his mouth to yell, but his voice was drowned out by a thunderous explosion. The air appeared to ripple around the copper dragon's head, which shook mightily before the beast slumped to the ground. Wizard Wettias flew above them all, looking for another wyrm in need of killing. Thomas had no idea what kind of magic the wizard employed, but it was extremely effective at liquefying the insides of the dragons and bypassing their scaly defences altogether.

A group of soldiers had already entered the manor in front of Thomas, and Ben was waving for him to join them. "Safer in here! Even if there is a dragon inside, at least it's only one. We're going to go house to house to rout out any dragons hiding. Our ally Theodonious Winkle mapped out the manors for Denton showing where dragons are known to live. We're going to hit the entire list!"

As Thomas entered, he passed some soldiers with ashen faces running for their lives back out the way they had come.

"Report!" Ben shouted after a roar shook the house.

"D..d..dragon!" one stuttered, barrelling past.

Ben held up his hands and barred the others, who reluctantly came to a halt. "This is what we came for! This is for our freedom! We have no freedom unless we vanquish the enemy!"

The soldiers straightened, their colour returning. As one, they nodded and turned. Inside, the foyer was lined with soldiers in various states of fear. Seeing Ben leading in more troops, they screwed up their courage and stood ready.

"Where is the beast?" Ben asked.

All pointed to a large set of double oak doors, engraved with the image of a cloudy sky. Ben hauled open the doors and then Thomas saw why the soldiers had fled. A handful of humans stood frozen in place, coated in ice. Behind them glared an angry silvery wyrm with an open maw. Thomas and the others dove out of the way and the room was plunged into frigid cold with the breath of the monster.

The cloud of freezing moisture dissipated, and Ben arose and ordered, "Charge! Kill the dragon!"

Thomas could not be certain, but the dragon appeared surprised to see the humans rally so soon. Thankfully it did not rear back to let another blast of arctic air.

The grand room was small for the drake. It tried to back up, but its tail smashed into the stone wall behind. It roared and smacked two humans aside with ease. Their crumpled forms lay still on either side, but the dragon had no time to gloat – the rest of the allied forces came in hard and fast.

Thomas noticed the wyrm's eyes locked on Ben, charging with his battle axe and gleaming breastplate. Thomas was too late to call out a warning and the dragon lunged forward.

Ben narrowly dodged the dragon's teeth, which smashed shut with enough force to have bitten him in two. As he rolled and prepared to stand, Thomas cried out and plunged his blade into the dragon's exposed gums. The silvery drake jolted back, blood spraying from its mouth. The humans closed in and their sharp little swords, axes, and spears bit at the massive body. One individual would hardly have fazed the dragon, but with the humans united and unrelenting, the dragon was beginning to show its pain.

The drake extended its great claws, swatting men aside. But for every one it injured, another came to take his place. The beast swiped at Ben, disarming him and tossing him back through the doors.

Thomas cried out, thinking Ben would surely be killed by such a forceful blow. But Ben was resilient. He stood once more and called out for them to press their advantage. Drawing his swords from his belt, Ben charged back in to the fray.

The dragon growled and reared up its head, preparing to unleash another frozen blast and kill all the humans in one exhalation. But as the monstrous head rose, Thomas leaned down to grab Ben's axe. Without thinking, he raised the weapon over his head, and with all his strength he heaved it at the drake just as its open mouth came down. The axe buried itself in the roof of its mouth. Instead of freezing chill, the dragon could only let loose a cry of agony. Shaking its head to dislodge the foreign object, the wyrm smacked its skull against the stone wall, hard enough to shake the building. Its head lowered in pain, its eyes slightly crossed.

Thomas smiled, but his attention was drawn to Sarentha. In the melee he had positioned himself by the dragon's rear to avoid its claws and teeth. From the drake's leg, he jumped up onto its back and scrambled up. Thomas watched his friend sprint up the monster, and his memory flashed back to the jungle tree breaking under Sarentha's weight, but the drake's spine was solid and would not give. Up the wyrm's neck Sarentha went, and quick as a wink he was at the dragon's face, plunging his brilliant daggers into its open eyes.

Blinded and stunned now, the dragon went into spasms, throwing Sarentha to the back of the room where he disappeared from sight behind its great girth. Thomas watched his friend fly helplessly through the air as if in slow motion. Frantic, Thomas pushed soldiers aside to smash his sword against the hard dragon scales. His blade slashed cleanly through the scales and other soldiers paused, awed by the sword's capabilities. The Strongblade effortlessly penetrated scales, flesh, even bone. Ben rejoined the fight, and all of the men and women swarmed over the beast, driving their weapons against it while the dragon thrashed aimlessly.

It felt like an eternity to Thomas, but finally the dragon shuddered, and its head fell to the ground. The soldiers rejoiced, but Thomas scrambled over the monster's body looking for his friend. At the back, half buried by the tail, he found Sarentha lying unconscious.

"C'mon, Sarentha! You can't die now! We won! The dragon is dead!" He heaved mightily at the tail, grabbed Sarentha, and propped him against the wall. Seeing his friend slumped like a broken doll, Thomas fought back his tears. He knelt and lightly slapped Sarentha's face, hoping he would wake up as he had when Eliza hit him after falling from the tree.

Sarentha flinched slightly, and opened his eyes to slits. "Y' don't say." He coughed, and a spatter of blood came from his mouth. "That might make two of us."

"This better be one of your tricks!" Thomas said, watching his friend closely. Sarentha had feigned injury many times, but this time Thomas knew it was different. There was no simulating the force with which he had been thrown. There was no pretending blood. "You can't die now! There could be a treasure chest just waiting for a peasant like you to find it in this very estate!"

Sarentha did not respond, but slumped back against the wall.

Ben came, kneeling beside Thomas. "You fought well, Sarentha. If this was your last act, it was a noble one. You saved many lives by blinding it. Your sacrifice will not be forgotten."

Thomas and Ben shared a look. It was grave, indeed. With internal injuries and blood on Sarentha's lips, both men were helpless.

"Stand aside." Eliza, dishevelled and blood-stained, pushed

past. With her left hand she unstopped a bottle and with her right she forced it down Sarentha's throat. He swallowed and coughed painfully. More blood came up, and he breathed an apology.

"That should help," Eliza said. "You remember that gnome we thought we had killed on our way to the jungle? Well, his name was Zanderboot, and he lived. When he saw the truth revealed in the square, he rallied a group of gnomish priests. They found us and gave me a handful of healing potions. Zanderboot even went so far as to apologize for our misunderstanding, although we were the ones who left him for dead. He felt awful that he had been obeying orders from dragons pretending to be our benevolent leaders. Once I had the potions, Uncle Erwin thought you would probably need me here."

"He won't die?" Thomas asked, looking back at his friend. Already Sarentha's breathing was easier, but he had lost consciousness.

"I do not think so," Eliza said. "He will probably sleep for a while, but the magical elixir should stop the bleeding. I gave some to other injured soldiers on my way to find you. Let us hope not too many have fallen in the fight."

Thomas, overcome, caught Eliza in a crushing hug, repeating "thank you!" He could not have lived without his best friend.

Shouts sounded from the room's entrance, and they looked over the great wyrm corpse to see a young child entering. Tears streamed down the little boy's smooth cheeks as he stared at the fallen dragon. His fine clothes, trimmed with light blue, marked him as a noble child, and his reaction to the dead dragon brought Thomas to the same conclusion as the soldiers. This was no ordinary boy.

Blades were drawn once more and the soldiers prepared to

attack the motionless child. Though he obviously did not mean to fight, Thomas realized the child would be killed.

"Stop!" Thomas called out, scrambling over the dragon's body and pushing his way past the puzzled soldiers. "Don't attack! Can't you see he's unarmed?"

"Mother," the child whispered softly. "You killed Mother."

Thomas knelt before the little boy, who he gauged to be no older than six. "We had to," Thomas said, unsure of what else to say.

"You are killing my kind," the boy said, looking up at Thomas with icy blue eyes. "Why?"

"Dragons have enslaved us long enough. We have lived in poverty and filth while your kind has hoarded our wealth," Ben said, his axe held firmly in one hand. "Stand aside, Thomas. This beast does not deserve life!"

"You can't be serious," Thomas said, standing between Ben and the child. "He's just a boy. If he wanted to fight, he would have already."

Ben and Thomas, at a stalemate, stared defiantly at each other. Ben finally asked, "Well, what would you do with him?"

Thomas looked back at the boy. "I'm not sure, but it doesn't seem right to kill him. He's so young. It's not his fault the dragons secretly ruled the Empire."

"I'm not that young! I've seen six decades. But I could help end this peacefully," the boy said, looking up into Thomas' eyes. "I could talk to the older drakes and try to get them to stop, so you don't have to fight."

Ben clearly doubted this plan, but Thomas nodded at the boy. He had seen enough death for one lifetime. If there was even a remote possibility of peaceful resolution, he had to try. "That could save a lot of lives if it works."

A handful of gnomish clerics entered the manor and began tending to the wounded.

"Let's go," Ben said quickly, and turned toward the front doors. "There are more dragons in the city yet! We're not done here. Regroup outside, and we'll hit the next manor!"

The soldiers who could stand readied themselves. Thomas guided the young wyrm out and hoped he was not making a terrible mistake. If the dragon child led them into an ambush, they could all die, but Thomas had to trust that the child's grief was genuine, and that it wanted peace so that other young dragons would not be orphaned too.

Outside, it had become quieter, with monstrous corpses littering the area. Sounds of distant fighting carried over from other areas of the city.

Lord Winston approached, the staff clutched in his hands and the stone still glowing an eerie violet that washed over everything nearby. He was smiling and unhurt. Thomas was amazed the staff had kept him safe, despite the tremendous odds against them.

"All is going according to plan!" he announced. "The defenders have gone down, as predicted! How go the manor attacks? We cannot leave any in this city to strike–"

Erwin's eyes fell upon the drake child beside Thomas. His features hardened, and he levelled the golden staff at the boy. "Step aside! That is no normal child!"

"I know," Thomas said, standing between Erwin and the dragon. Erwin looked at Ben, confused, but the captain could only shrug. Thomas pressed on, "This child has offered to help us find peace, if it is still possible. We have killed his mother, and I think he wants to prevent any more needless deaths."

"Needless?" Erwin looked exasperated. For years, he had worked to bring down the deceptive draconic regime. Thomas understood that in Lord Winston's eyes every wyrm was deserving of death.

"How many of our own people are lost each time we kill one dragon?" Thomas asked, not backing down. "Sarentha almost died, and several men and women from your own house guard lie dead. That was just one dragon. If we do this with every manor we enter, there'll be no one left by the end. If this child can save even one life, then I say we give it a shot."

Erwin appeared skeptical, but nodded in agreement. He lowered his staff. "You are right, Thomas. I cannot protect all of my soldiers at once while the city is being cleared. Do what you must. I will continue to patrol the city and keep the rest safe." He paused for a moment, taking the measure of the common lumberjack he had hired in a graveyard. It seemed like a lifetime ago. He looked at this man in whose veins ran the blood of a wyrm-slayer, a man who would now protect a drake. "Good work, Thomas. I'm impressed."

Thomas did not know what to say. Flustered, he blushed and tried to reply but could not find the words. He was not used to praise, and had not expected Lord Winston to agree with him, much less compliment him.

But Lord Winston did not have time to wait for Thomas to find his words. A group of dwarves joined Ben and his men, and Lord Winston took his leave, joining his own soldiers in the hunt for lurking dragons. With the dwarves bolstering their numbers, they entered the next manor on their list. Thomas led the contingent with the drake child at his side, hoping that diplomacy would work.

This manor courtyard was filled with exotic flowers and trees the likes of which Thomas had never seen before. Vibrant purples and reds lined the walkway to the building's front. Tall trees bearing leaves broader than two spans of his hand reminded him of the northern jungle. He wondered where such vegetation came from, and how it survived in a climate so different from where it originated, as they proceeded to the grand entrance.

The file of soldiers watched the boy, alone, open the door and enter. Long minutes passed while the soldiers waited, alert and ready. No one dared stand in front of the doors, lest a dragon burst out to blast at them with deadly breath. The assembled warriors crouched, ready to leap into combat.

The boy came outside, walking between two adult male humans. Both men appeared to be in excellent physical shape, their muscles rippling under their fine white garments. Their eyes, arctic blue and calculating, swept over the humans and dwarves before them.

"So, what should we do?" the older man asked, holding his hands open and down in a gesture of peace.

"Let's talk," Ben said, moving forward. Thomas looked the men up and down, checking for weapons, but saw none. He surmised that the men had dispensed with arms since they could turn into drakes at any moment and easily obliterate their enemies. Ben said, "Thomas, you're with me."

Thomas strode forward, matching his pace with Ben's. They approached the dragons disguised as men. The boy watched.

"You were waiting until we let down our guard," Ben accused.

"Yes," the older man said with his face empty of emotion. "If there was to be a rebellion, it was deemed that some of us would remain hidden in order to stop the revolt and bring back order."

Ben spoke with confidence. "That's not going to happen. We know where all the dragons live, and we're going from house to house to make sure your plan never happens, one way or another."

The wyrm-man grimaced at the threat. "Shall we do this in a civilized manner? What plans do you have for us? You must know that you cannot contain so many of us."

Exactly. The allies had no plan for what to do with those who would surrender peacefully. There was not a prison in the Empire strong enough and great enough to hold even one drake, let alone a multitude of surrendering dragons.

"What would you suggest?" Thomas asked.

The wyrm raised an eyebrow curiously. "You would allow your prisoner of war to set the terms of his surrender?"

"Of course not," Ben amended, bringing the dragon's attention back to him. "But the idea of resolving this without killing all of your kind is new. I'm fine with Plan A, but if you want to live, we're interested in what you have to offer."

"Ah, of course," the drake said wryly. "The legendary dragon hoard. Well, despite what you robbers may think, you will not find any draconic treasures here. We cannot pay you for our freedom. All I can give you is my word that we will leave peacefully."

"And not come back," Thomas quickly added.

"Those who leave alive will not come back to attack you, I promise."

Ben and Thomas exchanged glances, each seeking guidance from the other. This interaction would have made Thomas laugh in any other situation. Here was the captain of Lord Erwin's forces looking to him, a peasant in hero's clothes, for guidance.

"It's a deal," Thomas said, turning back to the wyrms. "Get your kind out of Tamor."

The dragon bowed low before Ben and Thomas and said, "As you wish." With a wave of its arm, the beast motioned for the others to follow. The humans and dwarves made way for the drake child, who took the adults' hands and led them past.

"Isahk chapter 11, verse 6: 'An' a little child shall lead 'em,'" a dwarven warrior muttered reverently, bowing his head. Other dwarves in the contingent watched the dragons leaving before lowering their own heads and closing their eyes, reiterating the phrase quietly. The reference was utterly lost on Thomas.

"Ben," Thomas said quietly, "We should set up an escort to get them out of the city."

"Right, we don't want them to try any funny business," Ben agreed.

"I was more worried about Thurzin murdering dragons in the streets."

The two men grinned at each other for a moment. Ben ordered a handful of soldiers to follow the wyrms and another group to evict the remaining draconic residents from each house on the list. As they left, Thomas' muscles relaxed and he let out a deep sigh of relief. He had not been aware of his tension while in the presence of the drakes. Now, if things went according to the peace agreement, there would be no more death.

Chapter 19: Celebration

Thomas watched closely alongside Tamor's residents. A dozen dragons in human form were on their way out the city's gates. The dwarves grumbled that they should not have cut the drakes any slack and the elves kept their bows taut and ready. Thomas, however, watched them leave with contentment in his heart. There was no telling how much damage those dragons would have caused in open conflict. His plan had worked perfectly, and these wyrms were honouring the peace treaty. There would be no more bloodshed.

Once the dragon-men were out of the bowmen's range, the group transformed into their true shapes. As one, they leaped into the air and took flight in a tight V-formation, away to the north.

A chorus of cheers rose up from the city, as the drakes became smaller and smaller in the sky. Chants of freedom and life beginning anew spread through the crowds. Even the elves loosened the hold on their bows as the dragons became nothing more than specks on the distant horizon.

Thomas looked over at Sarentha, who was nearby but away from the rowdy crowds hoping to spare his battered body from their joyous jostling. The two shared a smile and Thomas walked over to his friend.

"Are you sure we wanted to know the truth?" Thomas asked with a rueful grin.

Sarentha nodded, and winced as he rubbed the back of his neck. "Yeah. I'm just glad we're alive to see it. So, what's next?"

"I don't know," Thomas said, looking toward the tall, looming castle. The sun's light was weakening, and soon it would be nightfall. The crowd was becoming increasingly raucous and he predicted a late night of revelry. "I haven't seen Lord Winston since the attacks stopped. I haven't really heard anyone talking about anything other than celebrating."

"He owes us danger pay," Sarentha said.

Thomas laughed, but stopped himself from slapping Sarentha on the shoulder for fear of adding to his friend's aches. "Well, I'm relieved to hear your adventuring spirit has finally been tamed. I wasn't really looking forward to travelling the lands again anytime soon."

"We've got the rest of our lives for that," Sarentha said, a twinkle in his eye. "I may not feel like it now, but maybe in a few years."

Eliza approached, dragging Ben by the hand. Thomas smiled at the pair when they advanced, holding up a defensive hand in front of Sarentha before she barrelled into him.

"We need to do this sort of thing more often!" Eliza said, her face aglow. Her beauty radiated enough to light the city in the setting sun. "Ben has finally asked to court me! I thought the day would never come, but he said being slammed across a room by a dragon helped him reassess his life goals."

Ben turned his eyes down sheepishly. "Had I realized Eliza would say yes so readily, I would've asked long ago."

"Congratulations," Thomas said. "The way you thanked me for bringing her back in Whampello, Ben, I assumed you were already betrothed."

"Well," Ben said, coughing lightly as he turned away, not looking at anything in particular. "You know how it is..."

"He can fight a dragon, but romance still makes him uncomfortable!" Eliza laughed. She stood on her tip-toes and gave Ben a big kiss on his cheek. If he had been flustered before, he was now speechless.

"Well, I'm very happy for you both. I guess you have a great many new experiences you'll look forward to sharing together," Thomas said.

"Don't think you're getting out of this that easily," Ben said, turning the conversation away from his own love life. "We will need a lot of good men in the army, and I've seen you in action. I have half a mind to recommend you for the elite guard!"

It was Thomas' turn to be speechless. Here he had been thinking about settling down, and now there was talk of him becoming a real soldier. He had no formal training, and only the goblin fable as any sort of reference. He supposed people might believe a man who had faced drakes to be more than he was, but his stomach tied in knots when he thought about becoming a soldier.

Eliza punched Ben playfully in the shoulder, and hugged him tight. "Now *sweetheart!*" She spoke loudly, making Ben visibly uncomfortable again. "Do not go giving Thomas ideas of grandeur. He is not used to this sort of thing, you know. Besides, do you think Thomas would join the guard without Sarentha?"

"No way," Sarentha said, shaking his head and wincing again. "I was never cut out for soldiering."

"I'm sure we could find something for you, Sarentha," said another voice. Richard Winston, Feng the orc wizard, Lyle the halfling, and Denton the rogue joined the circle of friends. "Not everything is toe-to-toe fighting, after all," Richard continued. He patted his sheathed sword, and pointed to Feng's staff. "You didn't see us out there, did you?

"Wizard Wettias had us busy enough, I'll tell you," said Richard. "Feng, Denton, Lyle and I were scouring the city, securing all manner of magical items and artefacts for the wizard's tower. We couldn't let the dragons leave town with their enchanted items to use against us later on. We even had a run-in with a drake."

"Just the four of you?" Thomas asked, shocked. Only four fighters facing off against a wyrm seemed suicidal.

Richard playfully put his arm around his younger cousin, holding her tight. "So, a Secret Guardian, an Air Wizard, a Ranger and a Combat Rogue walk into a manor. Seriously, though, we walk in, hear a noise, and I freeze. We thought that the dragon had already left. I turn around and there is *no one* in sight! Feng cast a spell of invisibility, and both Denton and Lyle hid in the shadows! So I take it upon myself to stay alive by casting some defensive spells. No sooner do I manage this than a beautiful human woman shows up. I think maybe she's a looter, but she says, 'You're a fool to break into my home alone!' and turns into a gold-scaled drake! Well, luckily I have the fire shield–"

"Wait. What?" Sarentha was looking at Richard's armour curiously. There was no shield in sight.

"Obviously it was a spell I had already cast," Richard said, quickly recasting it to show off his magical prowess. A shield materialized, glowing with white-hot flames, and Richard casually continued as if magic was second nature to him. "So anyway, I've got this fire shield just in time! The drake belches flame all over me, and I'm just hoping none of the other three are behind, because I know they'd be cooked. Well, it stops its fire breath to look at me curiously, because I'm still standing there quite alive, although a little singed around the edges."

"Standing? It looked more like you were cowering in the foetal position from where I was situated," Feng casually corrected.

Richard continued, ignoring Feng, "Thank goodness it didn't use petrification breath! I would have been doomed! Anyway, I'm standing there unhurt while the carpet around me is ablaze, and the dragon comes at me, all menacing. Well, it stops suddenly enough when an arrow comes flying out from the left; this here crazy rogue leaps at it with swords flashing, and a concussive blast of air smacks the drake in the face from Feng's outstretched, albeit invisible, hand! I'm not one to let my companions take all the glory, so I go in and start battering its face. It spins, flails, and kicks, but it is so utterly taken by surprise it simply can't recover. Denton keeps finding spots under the scales to drive in his swords, Lyle is peppering it with arrows – and I mean *lots* of arrows at once! Feng just keeps hammering away at it with the same damn spell–"

"That is untrue," Feng interrupted. "I used blades of air as well as the concussive blasts. And the blades gave it such sharp pains that the dragon was never sure of Denton's location."

"Whatever," Richard said, waving a hand dismissively at the nit-picking orc. "At any rate, the drake must have thought it was under assault by a dozen men with the pain we dished out in such a short time. It was dead before it could even recover its breath. It was a *spectacular* battle!"

Sarentha had apparently forgotten his pain, for he leaned far forward, drinking in every word. Recalling Sarentha's own encounter with the wyrm, Thomas could almost see Denton dancing over the dragon's body. Sarentha lacked skill and presence of mind in combat situations, but Thomas imagined that Denton was just as Sarentha wished to be.

Thomas poked Sarentha gently. "A few *years* before you're ready for adventure?"

Sarentha grunted and sat back in the shadows, nodding his head. This time, distracted by visions of incredible battles, Thomas noted that Sarentha did not wince. Thomas had a feeling it would not be so long before his friend was again talking about riches and exploring new places. It did his heart good to know that Sarentha's spirit was recovering.

"How do you perform magic spells?" Sarentha asked.

"Years of training," Feng said soberly. "I have been practising the arcane arts with Wizard Wettias for a decade, and still have much to learn. It is most difficult in the beginning, because the concentration required to summon magical forces from the ether does not come naturally. It is best if a wizard is taken in at a young age, for the unformed mind has an easier time learning to bend the forces of the universe to its will. Once you have the spark, the ability to use magic becomes as natural as handling a sword for a soldier. You can always practise, research, and push yourself to learn more, but once you have mastered a spell, it will come to you in a heartbeat."

Feng illustrated by slowly levitating from the ground. "There are many different types of magic, even among wizards. For instance, I specialize in forcing air to do my bidding, but Wizard Wettias dabbles in all four elements. There are some who blend their wizard powers with other professions entirely. For instance, take Richard here. He had humble beginnings as a Protector, using heavy armour to defend his comrades. But once he learned magic, he blended it to become something entirely different: a Secret

Guardian. When he did so, he swore an oath to defend me, as all Secret Guardians must pledge their protection of a wizard. When we are both present in combat situations, our magical bond gives him increased resilience to deal with threats. Alas, I do not receive any increase in power in his presence, but it is handy to have him in front of me."

"So do all of you who work for Wizard Wettias know magic?" Sarentha asked.

"Not I," Denton said, brandishing two short swords. He gracefully spun them several times before pounding them both back into their sheaths.

"I'm a ranger," Lyle said. "I started out as a simple hunter, but when I learned of the power of the gods to heal, I began to pray and perform ritual ceremonies with a group of halfling priests. Eventually the gods heard my prayers, and granted me the power to heal others. But don't think that makes me a sissy! I'm still a right good shot with my bow!"

"Lyle brings up a good point," Feng added. "Not all magic is offensive in nature. You can use magic for just about anything." Feng levitated over to Sarentha, and with another wave of his hand proffered a sample of the magical cake that Wizard Wettias had given them for their trip to the golden tree. Sarentha took a bite and mumbled something about tasting juicy pork sausage.

Thinking of his encounter with Zanderboot, Thomas said, "It's good to know that not all magic kicks like a horse. I was starting to think that magic was just another type of weapon."

"I love this stuff," Sarentha murmured with his mouth full. "If I could create this, I would never eat anything else ever again. What is it called?"

Feng replied, "You would grow tired of eating Mana after

some time. You begin to miss the texture of real food. If you eat it long enough, you come to dread the spongy feeling in your mouth, and the taste becomes irrelevant."

"Tired of magic," Sarentha mused before he swallowed the Mana. "I cannot imagine ever growing tired of being able to do such marvellous things."

Feng shrugged, "It is like anything else. As my people like to say, 'the deer's blood is always richer in the next forest.' It is our nature to think there is something better on the horizon, but truly wise people seek happiness with what they already have. Alas, I do not think there are many wise people in existence."

The group reflected in silence for a time, and Thomas absorbed Feng's words and thought about his own desires for the future. In that moment Thomas realized that he had everything he needed. The adventure was over. He and Sarentha could live comfortably on their earnings from Lord Winston. With the end of the quest, he felt peaceful and centred.

Eliza broke the silence when she pulled away from Richard and went back into Ben's waiting arms. She asked Richard, "So where is Uncle Erwin, anyway?"

"I don't know," Richard said, looking around as though he expected his father to materialize out of the air. "I'm sure we'll run into him soon. This celebration is more his than anyone else's. Speaking of which, I hear the taverns are offering free drinks to heroes. Care to come with me?"

Together, the eight of them joined the throng of people who celebrated their freedom.

* * * * *

But not everyone was joyful to learn of the dragon King's fall. To the west, the ramshackle town of Pothice was largely unaffected. The elves of the northern jungle had used the power of the Forest Born to take them to the town's centre, where a large tree acted as their gateway. Finwe came out first, and held the magical portal open for others to cross the threshold from Tamor.

Lorrie'nar, Kel'shorie, Pau'sien, Shah'lao, and a whole host of elves magically appeared. The last elf to step through was Sief, their aged leader. She had hoped that the fall of the drakes would restore the health of her people, but alas, nothing changed. The elderly sat about in a stupor that would not lift. Their eyes were fogged over, and they did not even recognize that strangers were among them.

Pothice's docks were on the town's western edge, where younger elves came in off the ships with nets full of fish. They hauled the food to the town's centre to feed the elderly, and their hardened stares showed little interest. They ignored the new elves in town, for the young had far too much work to do in order to keep the populace of Pothice alive. Sief could see that resentment ran deep among the young workforce: they toiled in the fields and at sea to provide for an elderly generation of elves who gave no sign of appreciation for the hard work and sacrifice of the younger ones. Yet a fundamental force kept them honouring their elders, refusing to let them die, even though the death of the elders would have liberated their care-takers. Sief took small comfort in that realization.

Some of the fishermen prepared small fires nearby, eyeing the strangers warily while they made simple meals for those who were no longer able. The crowd of newcomers parted for Sief, and she shuffled toward one of the fires.

A young elven man was filleting fish, while a young woman set up a heating rack over the cooking flames. Neither acknowledged Sief with greeting, but they kept an eye on her. Their glances were likely to make sure she did not get too close to the crackling fire. She had heard reports that it was common for senior elves to stumble unaware through the town and get into accidents.

"Young ones," Sief greeted. She knelt down and sat cross-legged with them on the cobblestone street. Still the two did not speak, but continued to attend to their work. They appeared surprised when she continued coherently. Had they expected gibberish from her? "I am sorry we have not been able to restore the minds of your people. It grieves me terribly that they remain lost to us."

The young elven woman asked skeptically, "Is this a trick?" Sief imagined all the youth had grown callous and distrustful. Hearing an elder speak without trailing off half way through a sentence must have been unusual.

"Feal'shah, be polite," the young man admonished.

"It is no trick, Feal'shah," Sief confirmed, and offered a gentle smile. That got the attention of both young elves. "There are some of us who remain safe from the vile magic that stole the elders' memories. We escaped far to the north, and have only now returned. The dark forces that kept us away have been vanquished. Our wish is to aid you in any way we can."

The two listeners were flabbergasted. Other young adults noticed the conversation and approached curiously. They all appeared shocked that there was an elder among them who was not mentally infirm.

Tears fell from Feal'shah's long, pale eyelashes. "Am I dreaming?"

"Not at all, my dear," Sief said comfortingly, reaching

A Noble's Quest

forward to gently touch her cheek. She felt her heart ache with Feal'shah's uncertainty. "You are just waking up. Too long have the young suffered under the dragons' cruel spell. It is time for you to see what life as an elf truly means."

Galvanized by her words, the elves of Pothice looked to their elders, who still sat mutely. For the first time in their long, young lives, they felt a sense of hope. The normally morose, quiet elven youths began chattering excitedly to each other.

Sief said, "If you allow it, we will take your elders with us to the forest, where they can live out the remainder of their lives more safely and easily. Our numbers may be diminished, but we are more plentiful in our jungle, and are better suited to care for these lost souls."

At first their bubbling words of relief and hope were tinged with guilt. The young had worked so hard for so long to keep their elders alive that they could not imagine a life where every waking moment was not spent caring for the needs of others.

Another youth asked, "Will they ever recover? Can they come back to us one day? Pothice will feel empty without them."

Sief forced herself to smile, and said, "It is to be hoped. Now that the drakes are gone, we wish to find the source of the malady and end it. But for now, we offer you help in caring for your elders, and we can bring trade goods to your city to aid in your growth. You will learn that some good things have emerged from your continued suffering. You have a powerful work ethic, and strong bonds with each other. I urge you to maintain these strengths and to make every moment count when this heavy burden is lifted from your shoulders. I will leave some of our youth here in Pothice with you to coordinate your efforts, and to maintain a link with our people. I promise we will never again be separated."

With new hope and reassurance that they were no longer alone, the young elves of Pothice were able to enjoy the fruits of their labours for the first time. They shared their fish, and learned traditional elven songs and dances from the northern elves. All night long they rejoiced at their change in fortune.

* * * * *

The sun lowered to the horizon, bathing Tamor in a peaceful pink glow. Scattered clouds shone like pink puffs, colouring the sky in celebration. The streets below were full of cheer while the victors danced, ate, and drank. Promises of renewing old, long-forgotten alliances sparked optimism. With the elves of the north, the dwarves of the southwest, and the Tamorran Empire in between all united once more, they felt confident, invincible. The dragons had been defeated, and they had no other known enemies.

Inside the castle's stone walls, Lord Erwin Winston paced the halls and rooms, slowly taking it all in. Although his manor in Whampello had seemed luxurious, it paled in comparison with the home of the dragon king he had bested. Rich carpets ran the entire length of hallways, with pedestals on which sculptures laden with gems and crystals were displayed at regular intervals. Magical torches lined the walls, illuminating great tapestries bordered with crests of the Empire's noble houses, and scenes of Tamor and the other cities. Erwin recognized familiar arcane runes emblazoned on some of the tapestries, and he knew they were akin to the ones hanging on the walls of his manor. The spells they wove guarded against prying magical eyes and ears.

"Home sweet home," Ramar Wettias said, coming up quietly behind Erwin. The two shared a smile. "Your dream has become reality, old friend. We are free of the rule of the wyrms. What will you do next?"

"Sleep," Erwin responded with a chuckle.

Ramar shared the laughter, but returned to the topic at hand. "You rid us of the dragon usurper, Erwin. The people, although happy for now, will soon realize how much stability the drakes offered. Their magic kept these lands safe and untroubled, giving the citizens no reason to leave."

"What do you mean?" Erwin had known of the wyrms' plot to rule, but had never thought there might be more.

Ramar held up a golden coin, dulled with age. "Young Thomas handed me this on the road. He said that a young elf lad from the jungle wanted me to have it."

Erwin took the coin in his hand and read the inscription. "Cephae? That is one of the marks on the Map of Foodle."

"Indeed. Apparently Cephae was once a human-populated town outside our own Empire," Ramar said, and the two continued walking for some length. The empty halls seemed to stretch on forever. Only their muffled footsteps broke the silence of the place.

"Nobody has known about these sorts of things for a very long time," Ramar said, as the two entered the lavish ballroom. Tiny magical lights sparkling on the giant crystal chandelier sent rainbow prisms spinning across the room. At the far end was a stage where the Empire's greatest artists had performed plays and music for the elite of society: the society of dragons.

Erwin gawked at the immense ballroom, but Ramar continued, uninterested in their immediate surroundings. "Nobody, other than Foodle, ever considered crossing the borders of the Empire. People were content to stay, because the dragons knew how to control our thinking. Their magical powers ensured that none of us would remember the past, nor would we want to discover it. Even with the dragon king overthrown, their magic still blocks *my* memories. I fear we will never understand the mechanisms behind the spell that cowed us into servitude by removing the past from our minds. The only reason you learned to doubt the masquerade is because Lorrie'nar gave your father the tablet with the words of the old human king."

"I know," Erwin said. "I had hoped to find the remains of that old human king still here, within this castle, but strangely I have not yet been able to locate the secret chamber foretold by the elves. But I fail to see what you are getting at, Ramar. After all, you are a wizard of considerable magic. If a gap has been left by the drakes' absence, can you not fill it?" Erwin asked, bending slightly to inspect the immaculate, polished wood floors.

"I cannot," Ramar admitted. "Dragons are timeless, and their magical ties are innate. It would be like asking a sparrow to fly to the moon simply because it has wings, or a rabbit to tunnel from Pothice to Whampello simply because it can burrow. The task is too great, and the creature is too ill equipped. Although I command considerable magic, it is small compared with that of the drakes. Even if I could, would you really want me to control the entire population of the Empire through enchantment? Would I not then be just as terrible as the wyrms we unseated?"

They left the ballroom and Erwin thoughtfully nodded his agreement. He knew the wizard was correct, but he was at a loss. "So have we undone the dragons for nothing, then? Will society collapse?"

"I think not," Ramar said, closing the doors of the great hall behind them with a wave of his hand. "But the people will need a strong leader. They will require a king who is wise and just. You gave them the truth, Erwin. They will naturally look to you for guidance in the days to come."

"King Erwin of the House of Winston," Erwin said, trying out the words. He had been so focused on ridding the Empire of drakes that he had not thought about the power vacuum that would result.

Ramar coughed lightly. "Of course, every king needs a trusted advisor. I happen to know a wise old wizard who might be of help."

"You need not ask, the job is yours," Erwin affirmed, to his old friend. "But there is much to think about. I had not considered the full scope. With dragons in all the major positions, we have vacancies for everything from military leadership to tax collection, and food to housing! My friend, I may have erred in my haste to vanquish the dragons."

"Plenty of people will be more than willing to grovel at your feet for such leadership positions. Most of them will even be somewhat qualified, I imagine," Ramar mused. "But these posts require people of integrity. And you had already surrounded yourself with these before arriving at this point, had you not?"

Erwin looked askance at Ramar and smiled archly. "Thomas? Sarentha? Can you imagine either of them holding a position of governance in the Empire? Do not forget, they were lumberjacks. They did well escorting my niece around the countryside gathering artefacts, but they are not leaders. And although they are from a line of heroes, I doubt they would be interested."

Ramar said, "You may be right, but I have a feeling, my friend. I am especially fond of Sarentha. I am glad Eliza was able to save his life."

"Sarentha? You cannot get more than a few words out of

him!" Erwin chuckled, the sound echoing through the hallways. "Thomas has a good heart, but the political arena would crush his spirit. I do not think either of them would do well, but I suppose for their efforts I could reward them with some land. They deserve at least that much for the part they played in the construction of the golden staff."

"Land comes with titles," Ramar reminded him. "Do you think they would be fitting nobles?"

Erwin thought, then said, "Perhaps not, but I will not deny them their rewards simply because they are simple."

Erwin reached a large set of oak doors trimmed in gold. Etched into the door was a golden tree, much like the one from Foodle's map. Ramar waved his hand, and the doors opened, revealing a long red carpet leading to a golden throne. Large rubies and emeralds adorned the throne, whose feet were carved to resemble claws resting on the stone beneath. Alongside the throne, tall slender pillars rose to the vaulted ceiling, drawing the eyes of all who entered to the figure who would be seated there.

"A wise decision, my liege," Ramar said with a hint of gentle mockery in his voice, and bowed. When he saw the faraway look in Erwin's eyes, Ramar rolled his own. "Shall we get it out of your system? You will have to get used to people offering you all manner of kingly titles."

Lord Winston smiled and shook his head. "I will let them surprise me, rather than have you list them all."

Erwin was taken aback by the vastness of the throne room. It was easily large enough to hold wyrms in their true forms. The wealth which the drakes had amassed on the backs of the people was truly impressive. Erwin was committed to redistributing all the riches to the rightful owners.

"Something bothers me still," Ramar said. Erwin circled the throne, his fingers tracing the gold and jewels, before turning his attention to the wizard. Again Ramar held up the gold coin from Cephae. "There once was a town that existed outside the Empire with its own currency. By the looks of the profile on the coin, the ruler may have been a human wizard."

Erwin tentatively lowered himself upon the gilded throne, and imagined dispensing justice from it. Images swam through his mind of families coming to thank him for the riddance of the evil dragons. Ramar's gentle "ahem" brought him back to reality, and he looked at his friend. "What about that bothers you?"

"If we didn't know about Cephae, might other markings on the map of Foodle represent more lost cities and towns?"

"You think there was once more to the Tamorran Empire than what we know now?"

"I am not sure," Ramar said slowly, his brow wrinkled in thought. "I hope to find answers in the library below the castle. The caretaker is an old drake, but he swears he holds no allegiance to the others. He just loves knowledge, and wishes to stay on to take care of the writings below."

An edge entered Lord Winston's voice. "And you trust him?"

"He was not lying," Ramar said confidently. "He told me outright that he was a dragon, before I had a chance to put on the magical lenses. If he'd wanted, he could have killed me before I realized who he was. Instead, he wanted to talk. Searching through the stacks of literature will certainly be faster and easier with the help of the old librarian. There may be notes on Cephae that will illuminate the past for us. If the tablet told us about the dragons, imagine what volumes of old writings might tell us about our own people."

Erwin frowned at the idea of a wyrm residing in the castle's keep. However, curiosity about the past was his one weakness. In the end, Erwin agreed.

"Imagine, a dragon is *our* servant, and we are free of draconic rule. It is a wonder for the Empire to behold," Erwin said, settling back into the throne with a smile. "Tonight the people celebrate, and a new era begins at dawn. It will be glorious!"

Epilogue: 450 AGW

"What news?" Hallo'mien barked at her general. Matthew Strongblade was only a man, after all. She had faced gods, and had thus expected a more spectacular battle given the reports from her half-dragon soldiers. The mortal hero now lay dead, his glassy eyes staring endlessly into the sky.

"My Queen," the lumbering general kneeled before Hallo'mien and spoke solemnly. "Your grace and power are beyond–"

"Enough prattling. Your incompetence has brought me away from the front lines."

"Apologies, my Queen," he said, lowering his serpentine head to the dirt. "Pellin and Marcus, two of their great wizards, have fallen. Ramar, the last, is more troublesome. By his cunning hand, Ezekiel has been slain."

Hallo'mien rested a cold hand on the commander's shoulder. With news like this, she longed to behead the messenger, but she knew the worth of her half-breed foot soldiers. Slaughtering them on a whim would not keep morale high. She still required their services.

Instead, she said, "This report is most unfortunate. It would seem that my dear mate Dalmethias again needs my assistance. A queen's work is never done. Before you move on to the human cities, you will create a shrine to this warrior. Matthew Strongblade was only human but he was remarkable for his kind. I gave him a warrior's death, and he shall have a hero's shrine."

The General raised his head and asked, "Might such a tribute prove an inspiration for the humans, should they ever find it?"

He had no chance to duck the swing of Hallo'mien's claymore, which neatly lopped off his head. Periodic failure was to be expected, but insolence was unacceptable.

Hallo'mien turned to the rest of her troops. "Sarsha-meshail's spell ensures that no human will ever locate the hero's final resting place. Men and the other lesser races will either die or have their memories erased. They will have no desire to wander from the spell's power base. They will have no reason to go to war, since the lesser races live in close proximity, yet segregated. Bound by trade and our King Dalmethias, the lesser races will be contained within the spell of those cities, and all will be calm. So you soldiers *will* honour this fallen hero, just as the soldiers who defeated Pellin, Marcus, and eventually Ramar will create shrines to honour the wizards' strength. If we do not pay respects to those who fall before us, we are no better than the lesser races. We are dragons and dragon kin, and we do not lower ourselves to thoughts of anger and aggression. If we allow the lesser races to move freely about this continent, so much more will be at stake. Never forget our true purpose here. We are jailers, and the prison must remain secure. The sons and daughters of Sharrow must never find him."

* * * * *

Calarin looked up from his seat in the cave to see Hendricus Wyrmstriker come in, the Strongblade slung across his shoulder. The dragon had remained hidden amongst the humans, biding his time. Humans harboured no suspicion that he had been working against them, for it was he who told the wizards how to craft the mythical artefact that would slaughter his own kind.

A Noble's Quest

In draconic culture, it was common for society's powerful to hold weapons that caused death in a heartbeat. Such weapons were symbols of the dragon's power and prestige, to fearlessly care for such dangerous devices within their treasure hoards. Though Calarin understood that the dragon forces would not be entirely defeated, he had hoped the humans would be able to strike down Dalmethias and Hallo'mien. In the resulting power vacuum, another dragon (himself, for example) could have taken control. Calarin had long envied the ruling dragons, and endlessly schemed to take their power. This time he had been thwarted, but he knew there would be other opportunities. He would remain watchful.

Wizard Ramar Wettias was there too, and he appeared troubled. He and Calarin understood why the Strongblade was here. Matthew was dead, humanity's fate was sealed.

"The blade must be given to the elves," Hendricus said, handing the sheathed sword to Ramar. "And let them take my daggers as well. These blades will be all that remains of our hope for our own homeland. It was Matthew's final request that the sword rest in safe-keeping until the time when it can be used again to forge freedom from our enemies."

The wizard looked upon the blade with a pained expression. "Sylvain," he whispered. An elf woman emerged from the shadows and came forward. She was accompanied by a young elven male, Kel'shorie, the squire to her previous guardian, Gel'niad, who had recently died.

Sylvain gently, reverently, took the sword. Power pulsed at her touch, but she did not unsheath the weapon. Tantalizing thoughts of destroying dragons by the dozen with such raw strength were hard to resist, but she understood Matthew

Strongblade's final wish. In the end, the blade must not fall into enemy hands.

She handed the Strongblade to Kel'shorie, along with Hendricus' wicked daggers. "We will leave immediately."

Ramar nodded his agreement. "The shield Jordak provided your people will not last indefinitely. You may be stranded outside the jungle for a time, and it is essential that you hide yourselves and these weapons. Convey Matthew's final words to the elders."

Sylvain slid silently from the cave, but Kel'shorie paused. He handed Hendricus his own slender knives. "It was nature's blessing to be able to fight alongside such a skilled warrior as yourself, Hendricus Wyrmstriker. Although I am commanded to leave the battle, I ask that you take my knives with you. May they spill the blood of a host of dragons."

Hendricus accepted the lightweight blades and offered his thanks. Kel'shorie left, carrying Hendricus' daggers and the Strongblade.

"There are other options," Calarin said. His mind worked quickly, trying to come up with a plan that would benefit him. He knew the arrangements for the humans. Six cities had been created in a precise formation. Once built, they were imbued with draconic magic. The lesser races would be spirited off to the cities used to create the spell form, and once the spell was activated, the memories of the lesser races would be removed. But he also understood the ways in which dragons honoured those who were exceptional among their own kind. "Ramar, you could surrender. You slew that dragon-kin wizard. You defeated their best magic-weaver! If you surrendered, they would honour you."

"I doubt that," Ramar said, peering out into the darkening

sky. "More likely they wish me to die for my crimes against them."

The dragon armies would soon be marching under cover of darkness. Calarin had to convince him quickly. "Well, then I will use my magic to fly invisibly over the field. I will take you with me. We may discover an opening."

Hendricus snorted. "I shall not fly. But I can create openings." He stalked out, clutching the slender elven knives in his fists.

"I suppose it would be poetic justice for me to die on the night of Matthew's death. He freed me, and our freedom ends together," Ramar reflected. Calarin rapidly cast spells that made Ramar and himself invisible, and caused them to fly through the air as swiftly as birds.

Calarin said, "Perhaps, but you have shown your powers to be immense and far-reaching. You could still turn the dragons back. You might even be able to kill their leaders." These words set off a cascade of schemes in Calarin's mind. He could have Dalmethias and Hallo'mien slain, and then destroy Ramar. He would be renowned as a powerful hero who avenged their leaders. None would doubt his ability to rule.

The two men flew over the dark masses of the dragon forces. Below, they discerned the faint shapes of three shrines that were nearly complete. Enhancing his vision with a quick spell, Ramar focused on the final resting places of Pellin Boltsmaster, Marcus Guardsman, and the dragon kin wizard he had slain, Ezekiel Half-Dragon.

"What are they doing down there? Why would they build shrines to *our* fallen?" asked Ramar

"Perchance I was right, and they honour your strength,"

Calarin stated. "You could surrender. Or *feign* surrender, and level their leadership! The dragons would scatter before your magical might."

But the look on Ramar's face told Calarin that the wizard's mind moved in a dangerous, more devious direction. In an instant, Ramar switched course and flew at high speed toward the dragons, landing before the largest golden form he could find. Breaking the invisibility spell, Ramar reappeared before Dragon King Dalmethias, sending shock through the ranks.

"I come in peace!" Ramar shouted, before the dragon could unleash its killing breath. "I am Ramar Wettias, First Wizard of New Home."

Blades were drawn all around, and spells waited on the tips of tongues. No human had ever come so close to the Dragon King, excepting for slaughter. But the tilt of Dalmethias' great head told his troops that the King was more curious than threatened by the presence of the small wizard. Killing a dragon kin was impressive, but the King saw no threat in the human wizard.

Calarin smiled viciously, conspiring anew while Ramar attempted to broker a peace deal. He knew Ramar's worth, and the presumptuous attitude of the King made Calarin anticipate novel ways of using this pawn. After taking his true form as a dragon, Calarin descended.

"This human has potential," Calarin growled, striding through the crowd of soldiers to stand by Dalmethias.

The King turned to look at the newcomer. "Ah, Count Calarin, I take it this is your doing."

"Calarin?" Ramar gasped. His shocked eyes showed that he was utterly surprised.

"No!" From behind them in the crowd, a cloaked figure

leaped forward. Hendricus Wyrmstriker's borrowed blades stabbed into Calarin's rump. They dug into the dragon's hard scales, Hendricus using them as pitons to ascend the dragon's great body like a mountain climber. Calarin screamed in pain and surprise, thrashing his massive form to try to dislodge the furious human.

Hendricus made it half-way up the dragon's body before Dalmethias' maw crashed down on his torso, instantly ending his life. As the corpse fell from his open mouth, Dalmethias chuckled. "I see not everyone approved of your plan."

Calarin winced, feeling the small stabbing pains through his lower body. He was grateful that Dalmethias had stopped Hendricus when he had. Even without his own daggers, the little human could have easily carved out his eyes with the elven knives.

Arcane words sounded before them, but Dalmethias swept a great paw forward and knocked Ramar down before he could complete his deadly spell. "Potential, you say, Count Calarin? Should we spare this one? He seems troublesome."

Without pause, Ramar prepared another spell. Calarin hit him this time, knocking the frail wizard unconscious. "We must be cautious in wiping his memory, of course," said Calarin. "He has a great many magical talents that could come in handy in the future. I do believe he could be worth saving."

King Dalmethias nodded his approval. "We will honour his strength. You will personally take him to Tamor for the ritual. However, if he gives you any more problems, kill him."

Calarin gently lifted Ramar in his large clawed paw, and offered a sincere, toothy smile. "So be it, Your Highness."

The pain in his body was fading. Calarin's magical

regenerative abilities healed his small puncture wounds, and his scales would bear the marks of the elven daggers until they were shed and replaced. But taking wing for the west, he realized his wounds were the least of his concerns. He held Ramar tightly to his chest. The wizard had potential. He had once helped in the crafting of the artefact. All Calarin needed was time to gather the components together, and possibly Dalmethias and Hallo'mien would not be so lucky next time.

###

A Noble's Quest

Sneak peak for *A Wizard's Gambit*, the sequel to *A Noble's Quest*:

Prologue: Old World, 252 AGW (252 years After Gods' War)

Matthew's smile fell. The demon lord's black cloven hooves smashed into the bow of the ship, causing it to rock wildly. Wood splintered around the demon's feet and his red eyes raked over the fleeing slaves. People clambered over each other in an attempt to escape his vicious fury.

Julian, Matthew's mentor, drew his sword. "Take up your arms! We are free, and this demon will no longer stand in our way! Fight!"

The demon lord focused his attention on the upstart leader. When their eyes locked, Julian's scruffy face grew vacant of any intelligence. The man sat with a thump, staring at the water running along the deck.

Matthew Strongblade trembled to see the now-mindless man who had taught him to fight. It was Julian who had trained Matthew to survive armed combat in the arena. Now a single look from the demon had stripped away Julian's essence.

Matthew wiped his hair from his face, set his muscular frame against the ship's constant heaving and prepared to fight. As he drew his weapon from its sheath, the Strongblade's glow flickered in and out. The sword's magic required complete concentration to activate, but Matthew could not focus on the fight that was to come with Glezxnodin, Demon Lord of Stone Island. Reminding himself that his fellow slaves needed him, Matthew pushed aside his fear and fixed his mind on his blade and his enemy.

Glezxnodin's maroon lip curled up in a sardonic grin. Striding forward, he unsheathed his own serrated blade, which ignited in Hells-flames. The Strongblade's subtle glow appeared weak and trivial compared to the fiery weapon.

But the Strongblade had been forged of the toughest metal known to man by a team of dwarves; it had been imbued by wizards. It may not have looked as terrifying as the demon's blade, but Matthew knew it would hold up in a fight.

If only Matthew could forget his fear and allow his muscles to remember their training.

Glezxnodin hacked at Matthew's neck, and he ducked it by a hair. Another slave, too close, received the tip of the sword across his nose, the flames singeing his hair. People were being pushed overboard by others frantic to escape. With thousands of humans attempting to flee the island to the sea, every ship in the fleet was filled past capacity from bow to stern. Matthew stood, holding his blade steady before him to keep the demon's attention away from the others.

Their swords met in a shower of sparks, and the heat of the demon's blade made Matthew wince. The crowd recoiled in fear.

Matthew summoned all his will to stand and face his opponent. Everyone knew someone who had been brutalized under the demon's evil reign. If Matthew could bring down the demon lord, his people would have nothing left to fear.

With two more ringing clashes, the Strongblade skittered across the deck, its light winking out as soon as it left Matthew's hands.

With a growl, Glezxnodin grabbed a fistful of Matthew's long hair and turned him toward the crowd of people. As he extended a

A Noble's Quest

black-clawed hand, a ball of fire flew directly into the midst of the group, exploded and flung passengers overboard. The deck shattered under the power of the spell, and screams from below told Matthew that the hull had been breached. While the vessel burned, the demon would single-handedly end their pathetic rebellion, and there was nothing Matthew could do to stop him.

Apprentice Ramar's voice shouted from above the deck, *"Forzare ballone!"*

Matthew staggered under the weight of a heavy magical blow. The spell surprised the demon as well, who lost hold of Matthew and turned to face Apprentice Ramar. Matthew realized his friends had witnessed the attack against his ship and come to his aid.

The welcome figure of Ramar floated in the air off the port side of the ship, his filthy, blood-stained robe whipped about, his hair hovered around his head like a halo. The wizard's smile made him look confident that he could face the demon. Beside him, Apprentice Pellin levelled a lance of flames at the demon lord.

Fire washed over Glezxnodin's body leaving his skin smoldering and blackened, but not melted as Matthew expected. The demon snarled. Stretching out his leathery crimson wings, he prepared to engage the two upstart wizards in aerial combat.

"Medio non morti!" Apprentice Arus called from the nearby bow.

Matthew watched a freshly killed slave rise from the dead and charge the demon, tackling him with inhuman strength. The demon lord's eyes widened with fear as he tried to break the zombie's iron grip. Matthew knew such a potent spell should have been beyond an apprentice's ability.

Glezxnodin turned to see Apprentice Arus and cursed the

pale, sickly looking youth. Taking flight, the demon lord headed back to land, flailing to free himself from the grip of the still-flaming zombie and sending it down into the water below.

Ramar and Pellin landed on the ship while Matthew stood and retrieved his sword. Matthew surveyed the ship and saw the sails had already burned away; the masts were flaming shafts reaching skyward. The inferno covered much of the ship's deck. Dozens of charred corpses littered the area. Matthew heard people below deck screaming, caught between water rushing in and flames above.

"The ship is doomed," Matthew pronounced, looking to the survivors with sorrow. "Our efforts have been in vain."

"But not entirely fruitless, Matthew. We managed to save you," Pellin said, grasping his arm. There was an urgency in her voice. The ship began to tilt.

Matthew pulled away, shaking his head. "You can't place more worth on my life than theirs. We were all slaves, equals. I won't place myself above them, and you'll not take me from my fate."

The flames moved ever closer and Ramar called out, "Don't be foolish! You helped engineer this whole escape. You're our beacon of hope. Anyone on this ship would tell you to flee to safety!"

Matthew's eyes filled with tears. People plunged into the icy water. Their shrieks filled his ears. He stared far off into the distance where the demon lord had fled. Cursing him, Matthew yelled, "My people will be avenged! You escaped today, but even you can't live forever!"

From behind, Arus struck Matthew on the head with his staff and the three apprentices hauled him up and rushed him off the sinking vessel. There was no time to lose, as flames swept over the deck.

The four friends rose into the air and streamed toward the next ship to the west. By the time their ship returned to the site of the battle, many had fallen victim to the icy water. Those who were lucky enough to grab on to floating wreckage were hauled aboard.

Matthew attempted to console himself with the realization that the dead were the first humans to die free of slavery.

* * * * *

Cold sun bathed the land and sea in gold, smudged only by a line of smoke hanging over the snow-covered port city of Pralus. Demon governor Glezxnodin looked on while a variety of creatures worked together to extinguish the blaze, but the flames resisted both water and earth.

From the overlooking hilltop, Glezxnodin watched the docks burn. His red eyes glared toward the horizon, where the last of the masts of the stolen fleet were about to disappear. He rubbed his burned flesh and his scowl deepened.

"My lord," a voice squeaked from behind. Glezxnodin turned to see a group of small, olive-green goblins. The demon's flaming sword cut across, neatly beheading the speaker. To address a demon lord before being spoken to was, in Glezxnodin's mind, a crime punishable by death. He nodded for another to speak.

"No ships survived. Our city guards were overwhelmed!"

The blade decapitated another goblin; his head bounced down the hill toward the shore. "Does anyone have anything to tell me that I do not already know?" The demon lord's voice thundered like an avalanche, causing the remaining goblins to shrink back. One broke into a full run, screaming in terror. Even this sight could not bring a hint of a smile to Glezxnodin, for he was preoccupied with dark thoughts.

"P-p-pardon me, my lord. There is more news."

"Speak," Glezxnodin said, turning back to the sea, his wings twitching in agitation.

The goblin knelt on one knee, and bowed his head humbly before speaking. "The emissary was slain as well."

Glezxnodin grunted, knowing the death of the Emperor's sixth son would not be well received. The demon lord would need to work many slaves to death to restore order and prevent others from contemplating escape.

"No doubt the Emperor will wish to see you, as you failed to protect his Son, and the fleet."

Another goblin head flew down the hill to join the first. Glezxnodin's fury raged near the surface, and he had to force himself not to slaughter them all. His glare flashed at one of the pitiful creatures, who suddenly found himself dumbfounded, babbling incoherently, and wandering off in a stupor. Although many of his subjects in Stone had witnessed his power, these rural goblins had only heard stories that the demon lord's angry gaze could enfeeble the mind of whomever he chose.

For good measure he cut down another goblin. Only one remained.

"Let me make this perfectly clear to you, worm," Glezxnodin said through gritted teeth. "This town was ill-defended, and I blame the mayor, who was far too lenient on the slaves. As a matter of fact, blame all the mayors of all towns everywhere. The slaves who escaped today were numerous. They obviously came to this place from many cities. Carry this message to the rest. You will convince the others of this truth. If I do not hear these words on the lips of your pathetic townspeople by nightfall, I'll add your head to the pile yonder."

The goblin was gone, flailing his little legs down the hill toward the port city. The demon lord's keen ears heard the green-skinned wretch crying out, "The slaves were treated too well, and today we have all paid for it!"

He knew he should not have killed the goblins. The Emperor would not be happy if he found out, but Glezxnodin would find a way to ensure the bodies were added to the official death toll of the human slaves.

Glezxnodin was yet displeased. He rubbed his shoulder again, picking off bits of charred skin. "Wizards," he grumbled. How in all the Hells had mere slaves learned magic? And how had slaves become strong enough to thwart his attempts to stop the ships? The humans in Stone's wizard tower were lowly apprentices and should not have been able to summon the powers he had witnessed. Had it not been for those meddlesome wizards he could have killed the "hero slave" who had stood before him with sword in hand, Matthew Strongblade. The leader's death would have discouraged any further resistance, crushing the hopes and dreams of the fleeing slaves.

Glezxnodin was certain he had the strength to destroy thousands of slaves without effort. He would have crushed any normal revolt easily by now. They must have used aids or tricks to enhance their powers. They could not possibly have learned such powerful spells right under their arch-wizards' noses.

Wizards. He could not be sure of their numbers. They had waited for his landing. Not only had they learned magic, but they understood tactics. Where had they learned such arts? Julian had been a trainer at the gladiator arena, but this seemed beyond his rudimentary knowledge. Try as he might, Glezxnodin could not put all the pieces together.

"They shall return, and in greater numbers," wheezed a faint voice. Glezxnodin turned to see an aged, hunched elf, panting and sweating after running to his master. Their magical link impelled the elf back to him whenever they were separated, a trick Glezxnodin often liked to use to torment the prophet.

He turned, gently picking up the frail elf by his shoulders. Their magical bond also forced the prophet to tell him the truth. "Is that so, slave? Tell me, how is it that you see their return, but could not *warn* me of their uprising?"

Dangling from the demon lord's grasp, Ellie'nothewe retained the ghost of a smile. "You never asked."

"Why would I have to ask?" Glezxnodin tightened his grasp but, remembering the slave's gift for prophesying, he paused. The old elf wanted to die. The demon lord would not allow it. Not yet.

Ellie'nothewe gasped reflexively when the hands around his shoulders loosened. "I would not betray my own son."

"Your son is with those human slaves?" Glezxnodin turned once more, unable to see the ships. "The pieces fit together. Does your son share your gift? Is this how they escaped?"

Ellie'nothewe smiled. "He does share my gift, but no, that is not how they escaped. The Strongblade is powerful, and his Lord is wise. They began scheming as soon as Strongblade was free from your gladiator pit of horrors. The Strongblade will bring about the undoing of your enemies and friends. The Lord's quest will be driven by his desire for justice and truth, two forces very dangerous to those who harbour deceit in their hearts. Even you will be undone by the Strongblade."

With the thought of his own demise before him, it took all his restraint to keep from killing Ellie'nothewe. If only the demon lord had been more cautious, and known the questions to ask earlier. This old elf was smarter than Glezxnodin had given him credit for. "You have foreseen my death and only now speak of it? The human was lucky this time, and protected by wizards. I do not fear him."

"As it should be, for you will never see him again," Ellie'nothewe answered cryptically. "However, their escape on this day is Sharrow's will. His children go to rescue him."

Shock at hearing the name spoken aloud hit Glezxnodin like a physical blow. The demon forgot himself but an instant, yet it was long enough. He cursed loudly and threw the prophet's body to the ground, the neck and shoulders snapped and crushed. Ellie'nothewe had finally escaped, after centuries of servitude.

Sharrow! It was impossible! Surely the prophet had lied. But Glezxnodin shook his head, crushing the limp corpse under his cloven hoof. The elf was incapable of lying. Their shared magical bond had ensured this. But how could this be? Could it come to pass? Prophesying was tricky. The demon lord knew that although the elf had spoken the truth, all might not be as it seemed.

Still, the demon paced, his wings twitching. How much power could Sharrow still wield? He had been trapped and without contact from the outside world for two and a half centuries. Powerful magical forces guarded the prison. It seemed inconceivable that any slave could break through the guardians and the magical barriers. Glezxnodin straightened and laughed. "Tricky devil," he said, wiping sweat from his brow, noting how his head throbbed with the broken magical connection to his prophet. Kicking aside the elf's remains, he said, "Of course it would be his will to have the human dogs escape. That doesn't mean he directly had a hand in the matter."

The demon lord paced. His thoughts began to turn to a solution. He could not overpower the humans himself. Years ago he had sent a ship of slaves across the sea to enquire about Sharrow's prison. The jailers' answer was to return the slaves' heads. No, the prison must still be intact.

He had some knowledge of artefacts that he could hunt down or construct that would aid in the killing of his enemies, from elves to dwarves, from giants to dragons. But he was bothered by Ellie'nothewe's warning of Matthew Strongblade bringing about his demise, although they would never meet again. This did not allow for much hope of finding answers, wherever the humans wound up.

Another problem presented itself: could the demon trust anyone else with the knowledge he now possessed? Ellie'nothewe was dead, and would speak of it no further. It was possible that the whispered voice of the elf had not even made it to the gods' ears. Glezxnodin realized he might have a singular and unique knowledge of what was coming. And knowledge, he mused, is power.

With this he finally grinned, and stopped pacing. Even if the humans were somehow called by Sharrow, Dowreth would find a way to escape as well. Certainly Dowreth would be furious, but the two forces might cancel each other out, giving him time to escape their wrath. After all, the prophet had said his concern should be Strongblade, not the two brothers.

So humans, it was predicted, would return in greater numbers, and Glezxnodin had no doubt they would refine their magical powers. If he could thwart their magic, he could repel their armies.

A Noble's Quest

There were rumours of an artefact, long since lost to time and mortals, which could help him. According to legend, this relic had been created by the most potent and evil dragon ever to exist, and was powerful enough to shield the bearer from every form of magical attack, including those from elder wyrms and gods. If he possessed it, he would be invincible against the wizards' attacks, no matter how powerful they became.

The Emperor would be certain of Glezxnodin's prowess when, alone, he thwarted the slave's uprising. But how long before the slaves returned? Looking down at the corpse of his old elven slave, he realized his mistake. He should have kept Ellie'nothewe alive a little longer to get answers.

Glezxnodin unfurled his wings once more and took to the skies. He would find the key to the wizards' undoing and would rule over all the lands.

When he had succeeded in his mission, even the Emperor would bow to him.

#

Thank you for taking the time to read my book. The second book, *A Wizard's Gambit,* will be available in early 2014.

If you enjoyed this story, I hope you will return to your retailer's page and leave a positive review.

If you would like the cover art or map art in digital format for a background, let me know. Physical posters can also be created if there is enough interest.

-Ryan Toxopeus

About the author:

Born in Ontario in 1979, Ryan Toxopeus lives with his wife and two children. He developed a love of fantasy and science fiction early on, but obtained a Master's in experimental psychology. His love of storytelling was encouraged by his good friend Ian, and so came *A Noble's Quest*.

If you enjoyed this book, you can connect with me online:

Blog: http://ryantoxorants.blogspot.ca

Google Plus: https://plus.google.com/u/0/106706679803112357243

Facebook: https://www.facebook.com/RyanToxopeusWriting

Made in the USA
Charleston, SC
06 August 2014